please don't call me human

Also available in English by Wang Shuo:

Playing for Thrills

please don't call me human

Wang Shuo

Translated by HOWARD GOLDBLATT

NO EXIT PRESS

This edition published in 2000 by No Exit Press
18 Coleswood Road, Harpenden, Herts, AL5 1EQ

www.noexit.co.uk

A CIP catalogue record for this book is available from the British Library.

ISBN 1-901982-94-7 Please Don't Call Me Human

2 4 6 8 10 9 7 5 3

Printed by Omnia, Glasgow.

Translator's Note

Face. Sometimes rendered as "shame," it is more widely interpreted as "honor," "prestige," or "reputation." For Chinese, individually and collectively, a loss of face is to be avoided at all costs. And saving face is one of the engines that drive Chinese society. So what better topic than "face" could there be for China's "bad boy" novelist, Wang Shuo, whose sardonic view of contemporary culture and mockery of national traits have installed him as spokesman for China's urban underclass and whipping boy for the official guardians of contemporary morality?

In *Please Don't Call Me Human* (a loose translation of the original title) Wang Shuo calls up a national loss of face—the awarding of the 2000 Summer Olympics bid to Sydney over Beijing—as a springboard for a comical and devastatingly irreverent tour into the national quest for "respectability" and China's simultaneous harkening back to the "glories" of the past. The characters in this novel, at least those affiliated with MobCom, remind us of the slackers and slick operators in Wang's previous novels, especially *Playing for Thrills*: Young, alienated, and irrepressibly devious, they revel in their marginalized status in the cities of 1990s China, and are as in-your-face antisocial as they can possibly be. No wonder the publisher of his four-volume collected works—found lacking in accepted standards of "spiritual civilization"—was informed in 1996 that sales of the collection must cease; at the same time, two cinematic adaptations of Wang's novels were canned well into production. In an uncharacteristic sally into understatement, Wang has remarked: "The Propaganda Department has said my works are reactionary and that they ridicule politics. They say the taste and the language are vulgar. I do not deny this." And well he shouldn't.

In *Please Don't Call Me Human*, Wang merges fact and fiction, sometimes indiscriminately and always in the service of his artistic goal, which is never to write anything that he or others find necessary for society, particularly if it is uplifting. MobCom, of course, is a parody of government institutions; events, personalities, and popular phenomena (the Alvin Keller Circus, for instance) are, more often than not, figments of the author's rich imagination. The Boxers, on the other hand (including their leaders, Cao Futian and Liu Nineteen), were not only real, but continue to represent national pride in the face of Western imperialism, at least in some circles. The Boxers United in Righteousness, as they were called, came into being at the close of the nineteenth century in direct response to the activities of Western missionaries in North China. Consisting mainly of young peasants and members of the urban working class and supported by a female auxiliary called the Red Lanterns, the Boxer movement was known for its skilled practitioners of martial arts and its devotion to mysticism and a variety of folk religions. The Boxers believed themselves to be invulnerable to the weapons of their enemy, a joint force of Western powers, whom they fought in and around Beijing. Sadly, they were not. The movement was crushed in 1901 and led to significant territorial concessions to Western nations by the Manchu court.

Other references in the novel, familiar to most Chinese readers, come from historical sources, from novels, new and old, from TV advertising, the theater, headline stories, official editorials, and from a wide range of documents. Except in cases where an absence of familiarity would seriously impact the reading, I have chosen not to clutter the text with explanatory notes or other devices that would ultimately contribute little to an appreciation of the novel. Somewhat greater attention has been paid to Wang's use of language—from gutter slang to officialese (note the parodies of encomia in the final chapters) and beyond—in order to convey a sense of why so many Chinese readers find Wang outrageously funny and why official circles do not.

For help in this translation, my thanks go to the author, who cleared up some intriguing points, to Sylvia Lin, who read the entire manuscript and made a number of suggestions, and, especially, to Chu Chiyu, who helped steer me through some of the more opaque sections of the text. Like the author, I undertook this task in part because it likely has no redeeming social value, and what could be better than that?

—HOWARD GOLDBLATT

please don't call me human

"There are four items on today's agenda. First, the Secretary-General of the Chinese Competition Committee, Comrade Zhao Hangyu, will report to the stockholders on the progress of our work to date. The second item deals with stockholders' expressions of no confidence in certain members of the Secretariat. To ease stockholder concerns and prove the existence and necessity of these crucial games, we have obtained a videotape of the Sapporo Games, which we'll play for you during the break. The third item concerns name changes for the Chinese and Foreign Free-Style Elimination Wrestling Competition Organizing Committee and for the Secretariat. The fourth and final item is intended to facilitate the implementation of work associated with the games. I'm talking about a third round of fund-raising and pledges, so please, don't anyone leave early."

In a theater with over a thousand seats, all currently empty, the attendees sat shoulder to shoulder around a large circular table on the stage. A spotlight shone down on the face of the presiding officer, an unusually hand-some young fellow.

The spotlight shifted slightly, to fall on the disheveled, ashen-faced man sitting beside the presiding officer. The light reflected off his glasses, hiding his eyes from view. The staccato, almost violent way he spat out his words showed he was an excitable person. He was none other than the Secretary-General of the Chinese Competition Committee, Zhao Hangyu.

"Regarding the work of the Secretariat, there are four points I wish to make. You may ask questions after I've finished. Whether submitted verbally or in writing, I'll answer every one I can. Those I can't will be answered by other members of the Secretariat. First, I wish to report that a good group is in place in the Secretariat, and that our work has proceeded nicely. Second, I want everyone to know that this is demanding work. Let me read you some figures. Since the first day of the Secretariat's existence, not one of us has enjoyed a single peaceful meal or a decent night's sleep. If you added up the miles we've traveled, the line would stretch from Beijing, across the Pacific, all the way to San Francisco. Altogether we have consumed more than seven thousand packages of instant noodles, smoked over fourteen thousand cigarettes, and gone through more than a hundred kilos of tea. We've kept a meticulous account of all our expenses, and not a penny of public money has found its way into our pockets. Third, while it's possible that one or more of the comrades might have dumped a fried egg or two into his instant noodles, or taken a few sips of Royal Jelly tonic along with his tea during an all-night work session, we have dealt harshly with every case of unwarranted expenditure, and welcome information provided by whistle-blowers, that is, any of you here. Now I'll wrap up my presentation with a report on the status of recent Secretariat work. At our last stockhold-ers' meeting, we approved a resolution authorizing a search for a latter-day Big Dream Boxer. Well, as soon as the meeting ended, we dispatched nine missions to the four seas to carry out the search. As of last night, eight of the nine have returned, all empty-handed, despite going up to the mountains and down to the seas. Our last hope rests with the ninth mission, which, happily, is under the leadership of Bai Du, our esteemed lady general. Before she set out, we gave her strict orders: Find a latter-day Big Dream Boxer or don't come back! I have absolute faith in Comrade Bai Du's abilities. As long as such a person exists, she'll find him, if she has to travel to the ends of the earth to do so. That said, harsh realities force us to consider the possibility that such an individual no longer exists, that Big Dream Boxers are, in fact, extinct. The last sighting of one was over ninety years ago, captured in a photograph of warriors from the Boxer Rebellion being led to the execution ground, one of whom is easily recognizable as the supreme Big Dream Boxer."

Zhao Hangyu picked up a black leatherette satchel from the table, opened it, and removed an enlarged black-and-white pho-tograph of a ragtag line of Boxer prisoners being herded to the execution ground by gendarmes with swords at their hips. A tiny black arrow pointed to one of the condemned, a swarthy, heavy-set, bare-chested man whose queue, that pigtail all Chi-nese were forced to wear, was twisted around his neck.

"One of our intelligence agents took this photograph in the Louvre in Paris. The arrow points to the supreme Big Dream Boxer of the time. His name and place of origin are unknown."

Zhao Hangyu handed the photograph to the man beside him to pass around the table. Their curiosity piqued, their interest stirred, the stockholders carefully scrutinized the scruffy man in the photograph.

"Looks kind of like a hog butcher, doesn't he?" Zhao commented to the person now holding the photograph, a skinny man with neatly combed hair and a pair of gold-trimmed eyeglasses; dressed in a Western suit, he looked the part of a corporate manager. "What you must keep in mind," Zhao said, lighting a cigarette, "is that appearances can be deceiving."

"How do you know he was a Big Dream Boxer?" the skinny man asked.

"We based our conclusion on four sources," Zhao Hangyu replied unhurriedly as he flicked his ashes. "First, we did research in the Qing dynasty archives, then read up on Boxer activites in the Beijing-Tianjin area. After that we pored over unofficial histories and popular narratives of military action. All these sources recorded the fact that during the Boxer upheavals, Cao Futian had under his Tianjin-Jinghai command an able general who was a master Big Dream Boxer. His strength was unmatched, and he was impervious to everything from bullets to artillery shells. He cut a murderous swath wherever he went, including the Purple Bamboo Grove foreign concession and the church in the West Shiku district, killing countless enemy soldiers. After the Beijing-Tianjin region fell to the enemy, he was spotted among Liu Nineteen's troops in Gao Family Village. Eventually, this authentic hero was captured in Beijing along with Big Sword Wang Five, and dispatched in the marketplace. That was our first confirmation. Then, using this photograph, we located a descendant of the commander of the gendarme unit in the photograph; the commander had committed suicide during the Cultural Revolution. At the descendant's house we found a copy of *The Big Dream Boxer Manual*. According to the commander's descendant, Gui Leiqing, who lives at One Twenty-five Little Guo Village Avenue, in the Tailai neighborhood of Tianjin's East River District, his forebear had come across the manual when he was in charge of dispatching Boxer prisoners. Just who gave it to him is unknown. The condemned prisoners, who refused to disclose their names, all shouted the same thing: 'In twenty years I'll be back, mightier than ever!' One thing is certain: The man participated in only one Boxer liquidation operation, forced to do so by foreign powers, who then photographed it. Which proves that this manual must have belonged to someone else in his unit. We then located a descendant of the French man named Paul Pierre, a missionary who took the picture. Currently attached to the French Embassy in China, the younger Paul Pierre happily prepared a list of his grandfather's friends who had been in China. Finally, we located a man by the name of Ladou in Toulouse, in southern France, who is the European soldier standing at the end of the column in the photograph. Over a hundred now, the old geezer is still going strong and recalls every detail of his expedition in China at the end of the last century. Now, of course, he's a true friend of China. After we told Ladou what we were looking for, he pointed to the man in the photograph beneath the arrow and told us he was a marvel of a man who could cause a bullet to change course in mid-air. He even said he himself had once engaged in hand-to-hand combat with a Big Dream Boxer, and that an entire column of soldiers had fired at the man, but the bullets had reversed course and killed a whole slew of them. Panicked, he'd shot his weapon into the air, and that bullet, to his amazement, actually struck the Big Dream Boxing master, incapacitating him long enough for the remaining soldiers to rush up and subdue him with shackles."

"A crying shame," the men around the table sighed.

"A postscript: Monsieur Ladou still feels deep remorse over his actions in China as a young man, and asked us repeatedly to express his apologies to the Chinese people."

"I have four questions for Comrade Secretary-General," a shrewd-looking dark-skinned agricultural entrepreneur said to Zhao Hangyu. "First, since there's no way of knowing for sure that a latter-day Big Dream Boxer even exists, do we want to continue mobilizing people and spending money searching for one? With all the schools of martial arts in China, don't tell me there isn't anyone to rival the Big Dream Boxers. The way you're relentlessly pushing them, sir, has me wondering if you've got some personal agenda. Second, since the foreigners want to patch up their historical differences with us, in the name of world peace, is it a good idea for us to 'go to war' with them again? Third, the Secretariat is made up of no more than a dozen individuals, yet in the week you've been at work, you've already consumed more than seven thousand packages of instant noodles and finished off over a hundred kilos of tea. In my view, that's excessive. How do you expect us to foot the bill if you continue at this rate? Either lower your standards, or fire the big eaters and heavy smokers. It was never our intention to determine how much a few people can put away. And fourth, why did you take a select group of stockholders with you on your Parisian holiday?"

"I'll answer the representative's questions," Zhao Hangyu said somberly. "All four points. First, we have no intention of hanging ourselves on the Big Dream Boxer tree. At the same time we're searching for one of them, we're establishing contact with boxers from other schools, such as Big Vulture and Eagle-Claw Monkey. If the day comes when we're convinced that no more Big Dream Boxers are to be found, we'll turn our attention to others. As for my personal interest in Big Dream Boxers, I assure you it is purely a matter of seeking the best opportunity to defeat our rivals. I have no hidden agenda. The vanquishing power of the Big Dream Boxers is the consummate fruit of thousands of years of Chinese culture. When you watch the video in a few minutes, you'll see what I mean. In terms of strength and ferocity, we herbivores don't stand a chance of overpowering those carnivores. I, for one, come from a long line of scholars and literati. Second, the old foreigners may be congenial, but the young ones are aggressive as hell. One look at today's world is proof positive that we can't compete with people from other countries in anything at all. We might put up the good fight, but if we come away with less than a gold medal, the prestige of our ancestors—their face, if you like—will be destroyed by their no-account, unworthy descendants: us."

"It's no easy matter for a whole nation to rise up," the presiding officer volunteered, "but entirely possible for a country of a billion to nurture one sterling individual. Except for eating, the only talent bequeathed to us by our ancestors is that of fighting."

"I haven't finished," Zhao Hangyu said to the men around the table, casting an unhappy glare at the offending officer. "This is something we absolutely have to do. If we can't find someone to purge the poison that's been fed us for a hundred years or more, it'll remain with us forever. Which is why I'll stop at nothing. If necessary, I'll take out my heart and I'll hand it to anyone who comes to our aid. Haven't you ever heard the foreigners say, 'One Chinese is a writhing dragon, a group of them is a can of worms.' "

"That's high praise."

"What is it with you? I didn't interrupt when you were talking."

"Sorry. Go ahead." Lowering his head, the presiding officer smiled apologetically. "I'm just a little high-strung, that's all."

With growing excitement of his own, Zhao Hangyu said to the stockholders, "That proves that the foreigners understand how formidable we Chinese can be, which is why we must be extremely thoughtful about whom we select."

"We appreciate that. We understand exactly what you're saying," someone said. "Now, how do you respond to the next question?"

"Ah, the next question. Since this individual is so important, what difference does it make if we eat a few extra packages of instant noodles while trying to find him? And while we're on the subject of eating *your* instant noodles, let me tell you something you may not know. If I clued the world in on what I was up to, I could eat anywhere I wanted in town, and it wouldn't cost me a cent."

"I take it all back," the agricultural entrepreneur said, "every word. Eat away, as much as you want. If you can produce results, it won't bother me a bit."

"Aw, forget it, I was just letting off steam. I'd never do what you propose. If you were to spread the people's wealth out in front of me, I'd gag on it."

"We trust you," they said to reassure Zhao Hangyu. "Would we have handed you our hard-earned money without batting an eye if we didn't?"

"Now that's the sort of talk that upsets me, gnaws at my gut." Zhao's tearful gaze passed through the lenses of his eyeglasses and honed in with unvarnished sincerity on the agricultural entrepreneur. "Have I ever forgotten any of you when something good was to be had? Your complaint about not asking you along on the trip to France is a bum rap. Who went? Nobody, that's who. I have no idea what direction the great door of France faces. That's all stuff we learned from members of our French subcommittee."

"Just forget I said anything, okay?" the agricultural entrepreneur said earnestly as he grabbed Zhao Hangyu's hand. "I thought you knew me better than that. We go back, how many years is it? I'm just a crude country boy."

"I know you just fine," Zhao Hangyu said as he patted the back of the entrepreneur's hand. "I'm not angry, and nothing I said was directed at you. I'm angry at myself, disappointed that I screwed up something so easy."

"There's nothing to be angry about," the presiding officer said. "Now that everyone has said his piece, that's the end of it. Let's move on to the next item on the agenda, or we won't get a thing done before the concert begins."

That comment turned everyone's attention to the musicians, who were finding their seats on the stage behind the shareholders and tuning up their instruments. As disjointed toots and twangs filled the air, stagehands began setting the stage and lighting up the backdrop, which was transformed into a scene with grazing sheep one moment and a city skyline the next. The presiding officer had to clap his hands to draw everyone's attention back to the business at hand. "Come on, now, we have work to do. Anyone interested in the concert can stick around after the meeting and watch to your heart's content. Now the next item."

Leaning toward Zhao Hangyu, the presiding officer said, "Since we're running short on time, maybe we should forget about taking a break. We can watch your video while we're discussing the third item, dealing with the makeup of the Chinese Competition Committee and the Secretariat. What do you say?"

"Fine with me." Zhao called out to a stagehand standing by the curtain, "Set up the VCR, so we can watch the video I gave you."

While the stagehand was setting up the VCR, Zhao Hangyu said, "What we've learned from our work so far is that the names of our organizations, the Chinese Competition Committee and the Secretariat, have been the cause of some difficulties. We need to change them both."

"I thought it was okay to call ourselves the Chinese Competition Committee," a young entrepreneurial stockholder with permed hair said. "It's got a 'gangbuster' sound."

"And that's the problem," Zhao Hangyu said. "When we went to engraving shops to have an official seal carved, no one would take the job. They all said that the Chinese Central Committee had never brought them any business before, and that there was a law against outsiders carving national seals. Nothing we said made any difference, and without the written permission of some higher-up, they all told me I'd have to take my business elsewhere. So after mulling it over, we decided that the name has too official a ring to it, and could lead to misunderstandings. In other words, trouble. As I see it, it's crucial for our organization to be spontaneous and linked to the people, not the government. The members of the Secretariat tried out some new titles, but none of them took our fancy. Like 'Awakened Lion Lodge' and 'Fierce Dragon Hall,' which are catchy enough, but don't convey what it is we're trying to accomplish. Even worse, we could be outlawed as some kind of reactionary secret society. So let's put our heads together and come up with something that will appeal to both refined and popular tastes. That way the people will flock to us."

Silence.

"That's a tough one," the agricultural entrepreneur said to break the silence. "There's nothing harder than coming up with names."

"I've got an idea how we can start it," the corporate manager said. "Tell me what you think. The National People's Mobilization . . ."

"Salvation through Loyalty and Virtue?" the agricultural entrepreneur volunteered. "The National People's Mobilization for Salvation through Loyalty and Virtue."

"No good," Zhao Hangyu said somberly after a momentary reflection. "National Salvation? Which nation? Salvation from what? Our nation's doing just fine, thank you, and getting better. What you're proposing smacks of scare tactics. Don't ever forget that we're in the entertainment business. The nation's in fine shape, everyone has plenty to eat, and leisure is the logical result. That you've invested in our enterprise proves not only that you've got plenty to eat, but that you're in the lap of luxury, doesn't it?"

"Then how about Move toward the World?" a private businessman said. "The National Mobilization Committee to Move toward the World."

"That's no better, too vague," the presiding officer said, taking his cue from the look on Zhao Hangyu's face. "If I'm not mistaken, there's already a Twenty-First Century Committee, or something like that."

"Here's what I think we should do," Zhao Hangyu said expansively, a broad grin on his face. "Since we can't come up with a name that reflects what we're doing, why force the issue? We can call ourselves the National Mobilization Committee. No one has to know what we're mobilizing for. Keeping it ambiguous has two distinct advantages. First, it makes it hard for outsiders to figure out what we're up to. Second, it opens up all sorts of possibilities, since virtually anything we want will fall under the umbrella. That, in turn, will unify people from all classes and walks of life."

"Let others try to figure it out?" the presiding officer asked with a little giggle. "Old Zhao's got my vote."

Everyone agreed, and a resolution calling for a name change from Chinese and Foreign Free-style Elimination Wrestling Competition Organizing Committee to National Mobilization Committee, "MobCom" for short, along with a reconstitution of the leadership, was passed unanimously. The newly approved Directorate quickly settled upon the following appointments: a permanent chairman and thirty to fifty nonpermanent chairmen, selected by the permanent chairman on the basis of need. The Directorate was to be directly responsible to the stockholders. The first permanent chairman was to be Zhao Hangyu, General Secretary of the original CCC, chosen with the enthusiastic approval of all present.

"Thank you, everybody," Zhao said with a nod to the stockholders, who were congratulating him with their applause. "You can count on me to give a hundred and ten percent. Now let's watch the video."

He lit a cigarette and walked out with the presiding officer.

"Aren't you going to stick around to watch it?"

"I've seen it," Zhao said with a wave of his hand. "Once is enough."

The TV set alongside the table flickered on and speeding

race cars filled the screen, followed by horses running around a race track, jockeys hunched over their mounts, butts sticking up in the air; the picture broke off abruptly, snow filled the screen, and when the picture returned, the scene was a wrestling ring with thousands of rabid men and women screaming and waving their arms. Spotlights above the carpet of black heads lit up the center of the ring, where a four- or five-hundred-pound Caucasian combatant with a full golden beard, fists clenched, was stalking a wiry Asian combatant, who was jumping around, also with his fists clenched. With quickness and agility, the Asian circled his opponent, sparring with both hands, like a monkey bluffing and blustering to intimidate an approaching lion. He struck like lightning, leaping up and smacking his opponent's neck with a sweeping kick. The white combatant stood stock-still for a moment, as a smile spread across the red lips in the middle of his golden beard; then he continued pressing toward his yellow opponent, who kicked out over and over, sending the white man's large head snapping from side to side, like a pellet drum. But he just kept smiling and licking his lips, the spotlights dancing on his golden beard. The yellow man rained punches and kicks down on his opponent, creating waves of approving roars from the crowd below. All of a sudden the noise stopped, then was replaced by a much higher-pitched sound in response to the sight of the yellow wrestler lying unconscious in the middle of the ring, the victim of a single blow from one of the white wrestler's piledriver fists. The bearded man raised his meaty arms in a gesture of victory.

Another Asian combatant stepped into the ring. Roughly the same height and size of the white man, he lacked the agility, and was knocked around the ring mercilessly, until he could only cover his face with his hands and wobble, beaten senseless.

He stuck it out for a few rounds, but ultimately, inevitably, he crashed to the canvas like a felled log.

One after another, the white man dispatched his yellow opponents of various heights and heft: One of them grabbed his beefy opponent by the wrist and crouched to flip him over on his back, but the man turned the tables on him and sent him sprawling to the canvas, facedown.

Once more the white wrestler raised his arms in triumph. Then he shrank to the size of a dot of light just before the screen went black and the TV was turned off.

Zhao Hangyu and the presiding officer walked out from behind the curtain. The people sitting around the table watched them approach, grief and anger filling their eyes. The stage was deathly silent; even the musicians' instruments were stilled.

"Well, how does that make you feel?" a somber Zhao Hangyu asked.

"Mad as hell," the private businessman replied sadly.

The agricultural entrepreneur's face was the color of raw liver. "What times are we living in, when people can push us Chinese around like that?"

There wasn't a Chinese on the stage, including the musicians and stagehands, who wasn't mired in dejection.

"That tub of lard who creamed our compatriots is a strongman with the Alvin Keller Circus. We've used every channel available to us to invite him to China. Our strategy," Zhao said somberly, "is to grab him the minute he steps foot on Chinese soil and loose our own martial-arts masters on him, a whole team of fighters taking turns attacking him until he's beaten to the ground, a team prepared to sustain as many losses as it takes."

"We've got no choice," the presiding officer said. "You saw

what a formidable enemy he is. We must do whatever's necessary to ensure victory for our top contender."

"By 'top contender,' are you referring to a Big Dream Boxer?" the corporate manager asked.

"You got that right," Zhao Hangyu said. "It's our only hope."

"Sounds good to me," the corporate manager said earnestly, turning to his fellow stockholders. "We can't leave anything to chance with an enemy this powerful. We must surround him with forces outnumbering him ten to one, holding our most powerful weapon in reserve for when he's least capable of offering resistance."

"That's exactly what we have in mind," Zhao Hangyu said. "First, lead the dog into a trap, then slam the door and beat it to a pulp."

"Are you sure you can trick him into coming?" the private businessman asked. "It's been my experience that people aren't as gullible as they used to be."

"Why wouldn't he come?" Zhao Hangyu asked. "He won't know why he's received such a warm invitation. He'll just think we're very hospitable people. Leave it to me, there'll be no problem. The only possible snag is money."

Zhao Hangyu cast a warm glance around the table, which lowered the head of everyone it fell upon.

"I'm not singing the poverty blues," Zhao said. "But, just think, with a project of this size, and involving a foreign guest, well, we must extend every courtesy. Then there's the training of our own competitors, and don't forget that the Directorate has to eat and drink. All that costs money. The forty thousand we raised the first time around is gone, and as of yesterday, we don't have a pot to piss in."

"Don't get me wrong, it's not the money," the corporate manager said. "For affairs involving national sentiments, anyone who wouldn't reach into his pocket would be branded a traitor, wouldn't he? But here's the rub: We're doing this for China, so shouldn't the entire nation be ponying up the costs? You can't keep coming back to the few of us for money and provisions, not when you can tap into the whole population. Even if you wiped us out, big deal! The problem is, the few meals we can supply won't do the trick. As I see it, we're looking at a bottomless pit. You can chop us up, bones and all, but how many dumplings do you think you'll fill with what you get?"

"If you want the truth," the agricultural entrepreneur said, "I don't care how much of my money you use. At worst, I've put in a few years' work for nothing, that's all. If you think you can get a decent price for me, go ahead, sell me. I have one condition, and that is, accomplish what you set out to do."

"You have my word."

"Your word? You haven't found your Big Dream Boxer, have you? And if you don't find that fine fellow, even if you trick that alien tub of lard into coming here, what have you accomplished? Let's not get caught in a trap we set in our own doorway. That would be so humiliating, a billion compatriots couldn't show their face anywhere."

"He's our only hope," the private businessman said earnestly. "If we don't find him, as far as I'm concerned, we close up shop, stop wasting our time, and admit failure."

"I said you have my word. By the day after tomorrow, at the latest, I'll present this individual in the flesh," Zhao Hangyu said. "There's absolutely no need to worry."

16

"Okay, show us the man, and we'll come up with the money," the private businessman said. "Since we're only talking about a day or two, you folks can eat at home till then."

"You really don't get it, do you?" Zhao's forehead was dotted with perspiration.

A modish young man walked gingerly up and whispered something to the presiding officer, who leaned over to Zhao Hangyu. "Let's wrap things up, Mr. Chairman. The manager of the People's Theater wants us out before the concert starts."

"We're almost done," Zhao said as he glanced at his wristwatch. "I can't believe we've been here this long. I have two more things to say, then we can adjourn. I'm still baffled that you can't see the big picture. I don't expect you to foot the bill for the competition itself. I'm just asking for help with what we call start-up funds. And it's not like trying to drive dogs away by throwing meat-stuffed buns at them. You're buying into an enterprise that will not only earn back your initial outlay, but will pay hefty dividends down the line. Think about it this way. No other major international sports competition is scheduled for the coming summer, and that will ensure the appeal of ours. It'll be the kind of event that makes the country sit up and take notice. Forget about money from the sale of admission tickets; that's peanuts. The big money will come from advertising. We've also got plans to sell corporate sponsorships and lottery tickets. When we get to that point, the returns on your modest investment will knock your eyes out. You have to take the long view. You can't trap the wolf if you won't use your kids as bait."

The opening concert bell rang, and a moment later, a handful of theatergoers began filing in, some with ice-cream cones.

Spotting the people on the stage, they quickly found their seats and sat down. A few ran back out to the lobby to tell their friends the show had begun.

"We have to wrap this up quickly. So, what do you say?"

"I say we don't release the hawk till we see the rabbit."

"Let's lower the figure for now, what do you say? A hundred apiece should get us through the day."

A young, ice-cream-nibbling fellow who was being dragged to his seat by his girlfriend complained loudly, "What's going on here? This is a play. I thought we bought tickets to a concert."

Backstage, Zhao Hangyu counted the few bills in his hand and grumbled loudly to the presiding officer, "That bunch of tight-wads bundled us off like a couple of bums."

"I think the problem was in the agenda for today's meeting," the presiding officer said with a respectful smile. "We should have shown the video first, then hit them up for money. Besides, you were too honest with them. Why didn't you just lie and tell them we found a latter-day Big Dream Boxer, and been done with it?"

"They got me so pissed off I wound up defending foreigners against us Chinese," Zhao complained angrily. "Come on, let's go see if Bai Du's back. It's all up to her now."

"I can't go with you," the presiding officer said. "The show starts in a few minutes, and I'm the emcee. If other people don't show, no problem, but I've got to be here."

"Tell me," Zhao Hangyu said, his eyes narrowed to slits, "how much do you make standing out there one show after another, day in and day out?"

"A guy's gotta do what he's gotta do," the presiding officer said. "Why go looking for Bai Du on a scorcher like today? What's wrong with the telephone? You'll get the same results."

"You might think I'm worried," Zhao grumbled as he and the presiding officer walked toward the backstage telephone. "I'm not. But if I don't follow through after all this hard work, just when success is within our grasp . . ."

In the undeveloped outskirts of Beijing, under the watery rays of the moon, a brightly lit train chugged slowly toward the radiant lights of the bustling metropolis.

2

A tall, elegant woman sat by the window of a sleeper in one of the middle cars; other passengers were busily taking bundles down from the overhead luggage rack, but she sat without moving, a frown on her face as she stared at the foldout table in front of her.

A stack of telegrams lay on the table, each with a progressively more terse message that gave witness to the anxiety and desperation of the sender.

MUST FIND A BIG DREAM BOXER AND BRING HIM BACK TO BEIJING AT ONCE.

BRING A BIG DREAM BOXER BACK TO BEIJING AT ONCE.

BRING A BIG DREAM BOXER AT ONCE!

BRING BACK A BIG DREAM!

HELP!

"Shouldn't we be getting our things together, Bai Du?" asked a brawny young man who stepped into her compartment. "We're almost there," he said, resting his arms on the middle bunk.

"Oh, sure, go ahead." Bai Du stood up, looked out the window, and said to a scrawny little guy who was sitting on the lower bunk, absorbed in a cheap strawboard booklet and striking a variety of boxing poses, "Liu Shunming, you're sitting on my purse."

Liu Shunming reached down, took out the purse, and handed it to her without so much as looking up.

"Shunming!" Sun Guoren, the brawny fellow, shouted at his scrawny companion. "Get your nose out of that stack of asswipe and help me here."

"What's your hurry?" Liu Shunming answered impatiently. "There'll be plenty of time when we reach the station. I want to finish this section."

"Stop with the bullshit and give me a hand." Sun pulled Liu to his feet. "Do you really think reading this crummy booklet is going to turn you into some kind of hotshot boxer?"

"It doesn't look all that hard to me," Liu said as he helped Sun lift a heavy, wheeled suitcase down from the luggage rack. "Isn't it just using four ounces of strength to overcome a thousand pounds? I've pretty much grasped the essentials."

"Is anyone from home meeting us?" Sun Guoren asked Bai Du. "The train's eight hours late, and there might not be any taxis at the station at this hour."

"Do you really think I've got the nerve to have someone from home meet us?" Bai Du replied. "What I'm wondering is if there's any need to go see Zhao Hangyu."

"What'll happen if we don't?" Liu Shunming asked blankly.

"We do what we have to do," Bai Du said with a meaning-ful look. "We've always done what we had to do."

"But I never got anything out of it," Liu said.

"Well, do what you want," Bai Du said. "If this all falls through, it's every man for himself. We'll just act like we never even met."

"I don't want it to fall through," Liu said. "Teaming up like this wasn't easy, and now that we get along so well, I don't want us to split up."

"We may not have a choice in the matter," Bai Du said. "You can't stage an opera without a diva."

The train pulled into the station and screeched to a halt. Passengers started heading toward the doors.

"How about this?" Liu Shunming blurted out as the three of them were stepping off the train. "Since the whole thing hinges on finding a Big Dream Boxer, why don't I take the part?" The muscles on his skinny arms were popping under the weight of the suitcase. "I've got all the moves down pat."

"I'd be afraid the foreigner would murder you," Bai Du said as she walked off.

Even though the square in front of the station was lit up by neon signs and an array of other lights, stillness reigned. Hardly anyone was out, except for travelers spending the night cocoo-ned in their sleeping bags, fast asleep. Well-lit streets spoking out from the square were virtually deserted, not a car in sight. From the station exit, the city looked like a theater stage just before the actors make their appearance.

The three companions headed toward a stand under a neon sign that announced "Taxi." The dispatcher's office was lit up, but deserted, as were all the taxis, their rooftops glinting under the bright lights, their interiors dark.

"I guess we'll have to hoof it," Sun Guoren said as he slung his backpack over his shoulder.

"Let's keep looking." Bai Du peeked into each of the parked cars. "We might be lucky and find a driver in one of these taxis."

"That woman's got a one-track mind," Sun said to Liu. "Stop looking," he shouted. "I'll take you home."

"That's okay," Bai Du said dejectedly as she returned from her futile search. "You go on, we live in different directions."

"I'll take her home," Liu said to Sun. "It's on my way."

"The same goes for you," Bai Du said to Liu. "It's out of your way. One's northwest, the other's southwest."

"That's okay, my grannie's house is northwest. I'll stay there tonight."

"Are you sure? I don't mind, as long as it's on the way."

"If you don't need me, then, I'll head home."

"Go on," Bai Du said to Sun. "We'll keep in touch by phone."

"If you run into any muggers on the way, don't forget your Big Dream Boxing," Sun said to Liu Shunming with a laugh as he took off off down the street, backpack over his shoulder and a satchel in his hand.

Just then a young man in a vest pedaled out of a dark corner on his pedicab, slammed on the brakes, and stopped in front of Bai Du and Liu Shunming. He smiled.

As Sun Guoren was forging ahead on the slippery, water-soaked sidewalk, a pedicab zoomed past. Liu Shunming, from his seat next to Bai Du, turned, grinned, and hollered, "Don't walk too fast, old buddy."

"Hey!" Weighted down by his luggage, Sun took off after them. "Wait for me."

"No room," Liu shouted back triumphantly. At the first intersection, the pedicab turned east.

Sun stopped running and stumbled on, breathing heavily.

"Bastards! How can anybody work with those assholes?"

The pedicab sped crazily onto the overpass on brightly lit Jianguomen Street, then coasted down the other side.

"This is the wrong way, driver," Liu shouted when he spotted the apartment buildings for foreign diplomats. "This'll take us to the suburbs, but we want to go to the Babaoshan Cemetery. Stop here."

"You should have said so earlier," the youngster said. "I can't hit the brakes now."

"How come?"

"They won't respond. This thing turns frisky once it gets started, and won't take a breather till it's run awhile." The youngster turned back to his passengers, an embarrassed look on his face. "This pedicab's possessed, and it won't stop till it's ready. But don't worry, I'll see if I can pull it over up ahead at the Beiyao overpass."

As soon as they reached the top of the Beiyao overpass, the youngster slammed on the brakes and pulled on the handlebars with all his might. "No good, it's not working. It's fighting me. I can turn it ninety degrees, that's about it. It'll spook it if I try anything more."

The pedicab sped relentlessly toward Third Ring Avenue.

"This pedicab of yours sure knows what it wants," Liu Shunming shouted with the wind whistling past his ears. "And goes wherever it wants."

"I'll try again, up there on Sanyuan overpass," the pedicab driver said. "I promise to get you home before sunup."

"No. If you can't handle it, get down and let me give it a try."

"Not on your life, old buddy. It's the middle of the night, and we'd better let it have its way. If it suddenly decides not to go at all, we're stuck. And where do you think the three of us will find another ride way out here?"

"This is new, getting pushed around by a pedicab," Liu Shunming griped. "Talk about bizarre!" He glanced over at Bai Du, who sat calmly in her seat, a smile on her face.

"We're getting a ride," she said, "so why get all worked up? It's not like we're working or anything. Let it go if it wants to; it sure won't hustle us out of Beijing."

"That's the sensible way to look at it," the driver said, turning to give Bai Du an approving look. "Our comrade Miss knows what's what. On a moonlit night like tonight, knock on any door and ask if they'd be willing to take you on a joyride around Beijing—at this hour."

"And at no added expense."

"Say what?" That got the young driver's attention. He spun around and looked right at Bai Du. "I never said that."

"You can ask for more if you want, but you'll be out of luck," Bai Du said with a smile. "We don't have more than ten yuan between us."

"Are you saying you expected to ride in my pedicab for ten yuan?" the incredulous youngster asked wide-eyed. "You've sure got guts."

"Which is why I said we'll leave the driving to you. It wouldn't be worth it to let you haul us around for nothing."

"Aiyo!" The youngster rubbed his chest and laughed. "Who do we have here?" he asked himself. "What the hell am I putting myself out for? I guess I'm too new at this business. I figured you would have pocketfuls of cash."

"If we'd known we were going to meet you, we wouldn't have spent all our money beforehand."

"So to hell with me, is that it?" He slammed on the brakes, bringing the pedicab to a screeching halt. He turned and gestured with his hand. "Here we are, you can get off now."

"We're where, exactly?" Liu Shunming asked, taking a quick look around. "None of the houses around here look familiar."

"I don't know where we are," the pedicab driver admitted. "All I know is, we're wherever ten yuan will take you."

"Come on, driver," Bai Du said in a gently persuasive tone. "You can't dump us out here in the sticks."

"Says who? Of course I can. Where did you plan to go without any cash in your pocket?" He jumped off the pedicab and began taking down Bai Du's luggage. "No need to worry; there are no wolves around here—the hunters got 'em all. We're still within the confines of Beijing."

"How about this," Bai Du said to the youngster. "If you think we're taking advantage of you, hop onto the passenger seat here and we'll drive you around."

"Cut the bullshit. Don't wait for me to drag you down from there." The youngster curled his lip, flaring one of his nostrils. "A grown woman out on a pedicab with some man in the middle of the night; what would people say? They'd call you a loose woman."

"Okay, let's put our cards on the table," Bai Du said, hugging her bundle to her chest as she stepped down. "If you dump us out here, you can forget about that ten yuan."

"Aiyo!" As if stabbed in the heart, the youngster spun

around, his face pinched into a pained scowl. "You're beginning to piss me off," he said. "I don't believe you."

"That's up to you. But you're not getting the money." Bai Du looked up at Liu Shunming, who was still sitting in the pedicab. "Come on down, Shunming. We'll see what he can do about it."

"Hold on, you two, just take it easy," Liu Shunming said as he climbed off the pedicab and stepped in front of Bai Du. "It's your fault for not telling him who we are. He wouldn't be acting this way if he knew."

"Who the hell cares who you are?"

"What's your problem?" Liu Shunming groused. "I'm trying to talk some sense into you."

"Save your breath," the youngster said, planting himself in front of Bai Du. "For the last time, are you going to pay me or not?"

"Not," Bai Du said bluntly.

"Okay, if that's the way you want it." He took a few steps backward, massaged his fists, and began limbering up. "I guess you want to spend the night on some rooftop."

"How dare you talk like that in broad nightlight!" Bai Du growled defiantly.

"Okay, then," the youngster said, pondering the situation. "Since it's wrong to hit a woman, I'll punch this scrawny monkey's lights out."

With that he strode menacingly up to Liu Shunming, throwing punches in the air, a fighting look on his face. "Come on," he hissed, "choose your rooftop."

"Help, mugger!" Bai Du screamed in the direction of a watermelon stand under a nearby streetlight.

As the scream hung in the air, a bare-chested young man lying down behind the melon stand sat up and said to his companion, also bare-chested, also lying down, "There's a mugging over there. Want to go see what's up?"

"Nah," his companion said. "A mugging—big deal. Besides, it could be a trick to steal our melons."

By this time, Liu Shunming and the pedicab driver were squaring off, crouching over, arms out, feet planted, taunts spewing from their mouths.

"We'll see who spends the night on a rooftop. I may be skinny, but a tiny scale can support heavy weights. It's all in how you use it."

"If you can't take a punch, bluffing won't help. Not unless you plan to rise from the dead. You'll spend the night on a rooftop, or I'll kiss your ass!"

"I can tell you've never met up with a master before. I pity your folks for all the wasted care in bringing you into this world."

"Knock off the bullshit, and let's get on with it—now!"

Fists flew back and forth, a spirited, colorful dance, and the chatter never let up.

"Hey, why aren't you up there yet? Now you're really pissing me off!"

"Keep your eyes open, and learn a thing or two from a little man for a change. Watch out, here comes a punch, and another! Stay clear of me, or you're toast."

They fought on, loving every minute of it, sweat soaking their bodies, as Bai Du stood off to the side engrossed in the scene. "Good punch!" she shouted encouragingly. "Good kick!" Her shouts for help long forgotten.

Before long, a pattern emerged. Each punch, every feint was

part of a strategy, with an occasional break in the pattern. On and on they fought, sweating and giving it their all, like a choreographed dance, with neither side gaining an advantage over the other. It was a real fight, all right, but anyone happening by might have thought it was a sparring match between a couple of martial-arts masters.

"I thought you were supposed to be learning from me. At this rate, it doesn't look like we're going to settle anything. You're not fighting fair."

"Who's learning from whom? You're doing all right, not backing down. Which means you're stealing my tricks."

Bai Du, confused at first, then amused, and finally astonished, yelled out, "Stop it, both of you!"

The youngster and Liu Shunming jumped back and relaxed their fighting stances. Still gasping for breath, they kept up the verbal sparring:

"Why'd you stop us? I was just about to flatten him."

"What kind of game are you playing, fight a little, talk a little?"

Bai Du walked up to the youngster and sized him up. "Who are you, anyway?"

"My name never changes, whether I'm walking or sitting . . . what makes you think I'm going to tell you? You'll just call the cops. My mother didn't raise no fool."

"Don't get me wrong, I don't want you arrested. I'm interested in your unusual fighting style. It's a style that hasn't been seen for years. Where'd you learn it? My God! Don't tell me you're the inheritor of Big Dream Boxing!"

"What if I am? And what if I'm not? Stop the gabbing. Give me my money, and we're square. But if I hear 'no' one more time, I'll knock you both into the next county!"

"Okay, okay, the money's yours," Bai Du said with a mixture of surprise and delight as she took out the money and handed it to the youngster. "Where does our young hero live? And what's your name?"

"I'm not going to tell you just because you gave me what you owed me," he said as he strutted over to his pedicab, money in hand.

Bai Du ran up and shouted, "But I must know." She clasped her hands in a show of respect. "I hereby salute you."

"I live at Yaochi, home of the Mother of the West, and you can just call me by my full name: Bas Tard!"

"An immortal?"

The next thing Bai Du knew, the driver was back on his pedicab and pedaling off.

"Go after him, damn it!" Bai Du shouted to Liu Shunming, who was straightening his clothes and fanning his sweaty face. "If you still want to live up to your reputation, that is."

3

It was still early morning, but the sun had already climbed high in the sky and was baking the street, the narrow lane, and the little courtyard. Pots and pans cluttering the yard soaked up the sun's rays; crickets in the old date tree in the middle of the yard were chirping loudly. It was a run-of-the-mill, old-style compound, with dilapidated buildings whose colors had faded beyond recognition and a crumbling brick wall; the roof tiles were covered with moss. What was once a spacious yard had been eroded by a motley assortment of brick-and-oilpaper kitchens thrown up by tenants, until all that remained was a tiny patch of weeds, nameless grasses, and undergrowth; ceramic pots and chipped basins filled with water offered no pretense of cultivation, but the greenery flourished and was pleasing to the eye, a sign of life.

Mrs. Tang, an off-white jacket with a slanted lapel covering her large, sagging breasts, weaved slowly through the yard with her eyes closed, arms thrust out in front. Not seeing the path didn't stop her from threading her way unerringly through the pots and pans, her tiny bound feet negotiating spaces too small even for a needle. The trick had a name: Prancing Stork.

Mrs. Tang's daughter, Yuanfeng, an eighteen- or nineteen-year-old with big eyes and dark, bushy eyebrows, stepped outside holding a mug and a toothbrush; foamy toothpaste filled the corners of her mouth. In the doorway, she cocked her head as she brushed her teeth, casting a sidelong glance at her mother.

"Be careful, Ma. Don't kick over any flowerpots," she shouted as she took her toothbrush out of her mouth and sprayed the ground with toothpaste.

"Don't worry," the old woman said with an expansive wave of her hands, like a bird flapping its wings. "My mind is like a mirror after all these years."

"One of these days you'll kick one over," Yuanfeng said, holding up one leg with her hands and bending at the waist. "It scares me just watching you." She straightened up, stuck her toothbrush back into her mouth, and scrubbed hard. "Yuanbao, aren't you up yet? I need to air out the bedding."

"What are you shouting about so early in the morning, raising hell before the birds are even up!" Tang Yuanbao, the young pedicab driver from the night before, strode energetically out the door; he was stripped to the waist, and wearing a pair of trousers tied at the ankles and cinched with a wide belt. He stood on the steps, clasping his hands and stretching at the waist. "You'll wake up the dead. One of these days I'm going to tie off your vocal chords." He stuck out one of his legs and rested it against the doorframe, his body forming the character 大 , for "big."

"Brush your teeth," Yuanfeng said as she deposited a mouthful of toothpaste and spit on the steps in front of him. "Your rotten breath has stunk up the whole house. I woke up in the middle of the night and thought I was in a gas attack."

"How else am I going to keep the mosquitos at bay? I can leave the doors and windows open, and still go all night without getting bitten." Yuanbao lowered his leg and stretched out its mate, bending it backward so that his taut tendons showed.

"Cut the crap." Yuanfeng rinsed her mouth, then sprayed the ground with water. "Hey, look, a rainbow!" she shouted, pointing at the water.

"Idiot!" Yuanbao lowered his leg and glared at his kid sister, then sucked in his breath and walked down the steps. Picking up two cactus pots, he ripped open the nylon straps covering them and tied one around each calf, then strutted over to the old date tree, legs spread, knees out.

"You're the idiot!" Yuanfeng bellowed from the steps behind him. "The way you lift your leg, you look like a dog taking a piss!"

When he reached the tree, Yuanbao squatted down into a riding position, straining until his face was red as he held his fists at waist level and began pounding the date tree, reaching out after each punch to steady the tree, as if afraid he might knock it over. Every third punch was followed by a foot kick, keeping his balance—remember, he had a cactus plant tied to each leg—with the skill of an acrobat.

"Hey, Yuanbao, what is it between you and that tree? First thing in the morning you're out there beating it black and blue!" their neighbor, Mrs. Li, hollered as she emerged from her tiny kitchen beneath the tree and quickly found herself wearing a bonnet of date leaves and twigs. "With you punishing it like that, instead of dates, the only thing it produces these days is aphids."

Yuanbao, mind focused, eyes riveted on the tree in front of him, didn't miss a beat—three punches and one kick—as if he hadn't heard a word.

"How about it, old friend, what say we compromise? You can climb around on our roof, but stop your son from pounding our tree."

A peal of queer laughter emerged from her roof. Yuanbao's father, a muscular man, bald and bare-chested, was hanging upside down from the eaves of Mrs. Li's veranda, arms and legs spread out like a giant lizard, but more at ease than any lizard could possibly be.

"One of you making our lives miserable is plenty," Mrs. Li pleaded, looking up above her.

The old man let go and landed with a nimble spring. More laughter. "Old auntie," he said, "I do these body-strengthening exercises to protect the neighborhood. And don't turn your nose up at my son. He has lofty aspirations."

"Old man, I haven't heard talk like that since the Republican era. It's out of fashion. Nowadays people keep a civil tongue, stressing courtesy and manners, hoping to be among the first to get rich. Practice all you want, but it won't do you any good. And don't think I don't know what I'm talking about. My grandfather organized a local militia group in the late Qing dynasty, but he never realized *his* lofty ambitions. I've never seen anyone as hard on himself as you or your son. Am I right or aren't I, Mrs. Tang?" she asked, seeking support from Yuanbao's mother.

"I've been saying that to these two for the past eight hundred years," Mrs. Tang said as she hobbled over on her bound feet, clapping her hands. "But I'm just wasting my breath. Do you think either one of them has ever heard a word I said?"

Just then the silence in the lane was broken by shouts and approaching footsteps. Mrs. Li's son, Blackie, who was about Yuanbao's age, ran into the yard, gasping for breath. "Bao," he stammered, "there's a gang of people in the lane asking about you. And they don't look friendly!"

"I wonder what this is all about." Yuanbao straightened up and, with his hands on his hips, said to Blackie, "I'll go take a look."

"Not so fast," Mrs. Tang said, blocking his way. "Don't you go out there."

Whoever was making all the racket had nearly arrived at the compound gate. Mrs. Tang planted herself squarely in their way. Liu Shunming, his face glistening with sweat, was pointing at the gate.

"It's this compound," he announced to his companions. "I saw that guy run into this compound." When he spotted the pedicab parked beside the wall, he looked it over carefully, then clapped his hands triumphantly. "This is the place, all right," he announced. "There's his pedicab."

"He's right." Bai Du turned to Zhao Hangyu. "He can't get away now. He has to be inside."

Zhao Hangyu sized up the run-down compound, looking right through Mrs. Tang, then pulled out a fan, snapped it open, and began fanning himself. "Some of you guys go call him out here," he said.

But when the bespectacled young men made a move toward the compound, they were stopped by Mrs. Tang.

"Not so fast. If you've got something to say, tell it to this old lady."

"Where'd she come from?" Zhao Hangyu asked Bai Du. "Have her step aside and let us carry out our duty."

"Old missus," Bai Du said congenially, "we're not looking for you; it's a young man we're here to see."

"Don't you be sweet-talking me! Who are you here to see? And why? Tell me, or you're not getting in. With your gleaming knives and savage Cultural Revolution looks, I hope you're not entertaining ideas of ransacking my house."

"Absolutely not. See there, the gleams are from their eyeglasses."

"Quit gabbing with her, you're wasting time. I want that young guy." With a wave of his hand, Zhao Hangyu signaled his henchmen to go on in. But first they had to peel Mrs. Tang's fingers from the gate.

"Ouch, that hurts! Help, murder!" Mrs. Tang cried out to the heavens.

"Let her go!" A shout rent the air, and Tang Yuanbao appeared beside the gate. Zhao Hangyu's henchmen backed off.

"That's him," Liu Shunming whispered in Zhao's ear.

"Are you the pedicab driver who was at Beijing Station last night?" Zhao asked.

"What if I am?" Yuanbao recognized Liu Shunming and Bai Du. "A real man accepts the consequences of his actions. Step back, all of you, and give me some room." He strode down off the steps and parted the crowd in the lane.

Watching the scene develop, Mrs. Tang turned to Blackie. "Go get some help."

Grunting an acknowledgment, and seeing that no one was paying attention to him, he slipped out of the yard, took a few slow steps, hugging the wall, then took off like a shot.

Meanwhile, Yuanbao was moving more and more purpose-fully as he circled the area, herding Zhao Hangyu, Bai Du, and the others up against the wall. The imposing figure of Yuan-bao's father appeared in the gateway. "Show them your spin-ning routine," he called out to his son. "That'll send them scurrying before a single punch is thrown."

Yuanbao responded by swirling his long arms in wide circles and beginning to gyrate, until he was little more than a blur, raising a dusty whirlwind in the air.

His sister, Yuanfeng, walked out holding a basin of water, which she handed to her father. "Watch this!" he shouted as he flung the water in the direction of Yuanbao. A wave of glistening drops soared through the air to form a neat liquid circle, perfect in every respect, then rained down evenly on the heads of everyone in the crowd. But not a single drop fell on Yuanbao, who stood perfectly still in the center, dry as a bone.

"Bravo!" everyone shouted.

"That water trick is all we need to see." Zhao Hangyu was all smiles as he walked up, clasped Yuanbao's hand in both of his, and shook it hard. "You're everything they said you were. You've opened our eyes. Glory to the country. Glory to the Chinese nation."

"What's that supposed to mean?" Yuanbao was baffled by the line of bespectacled young men walking up to shake his hand. "Didn't you come for a fight?"

"We came for a fight, all right," one of the bespectacled young men said. "But not between you and us."

"You know how to fight, that's for sure," Zhao Hangyu said. "We're completely satisfied. You're the one."

"The one for what?"

"He doesn't know what he's been chosen for," Zhao said with a laugh.

"For a great honor," a bespectacled young man said. "You should be very happy."

"Tell me this." Zhao smiled and said with the patience of a teacher, "If you saw someone being bullied, would you just stand by and watch?"

"Why not?" Yuanbao said. "I'm no cop."

"What if it was a relative?" Zhao was still smiling. "What if a friend or relative was getting beat up?"

"I'd have to know why. Did he deserve it? Stick your nose in where it doesn't belong, and you're just asking for trouble."

"I'm surprised you have such a keen sense of right and wrong." Zhao's smile now seemed a bit forced, but there it remained. "So no matter who's getting beat up, as long as it isn't you, it's none of your business. Is that right?"

"Why not? That's what the government and the police are for. Who am I to take matters into my own hands? And what could I accomplish?" With a snicker, Yuanbao swept the crowd with his eyes. "Ever since I was a kid, my dad told me to mind my own business."

"Now what if the one being bullied wasn't a person, but was our country?"

Yuanbao's eyes widened. "Someone's bullying our country? That's news to me. All I've heard is that we were whipped in the Olympics in South Korea."

"He'll never get the picture this way," Bai Du said in frustration. "Give it to him straight. It's like this . . . oh, right, I don't even know your name. What is it?"

"Tang Yuanbao, yuan as in *yuanshuai* [generalissimo], bao as in *baozi* [leopard]."

"It's like this, Comrade Tang Yuanbao. We represent the Directorate of the All-China People's Mobilization Committee, formerly the Secretariat of the Chinese Competition Committee."

"So?"

"Right, who we are isn't important. What *is* important is why we came looking for you. Our leader explained to you just now that the country has suffered recently. I guess you hadn't heard. It happened this spring—some foreigner beat up our people in Sapporo."

"Badly?"

"Very badly. Horribly, in fact."

"You'd have died of rage if you'd seen it," Liu Shunming said. "We wept when we saw it, and our only thought was to find a way to get revenge. Each one we crush is one less to worry about."

"Why didn't you?" Yuanbao asked.

"We weren't in Sapporo," Liu explained, "that's why."

"How come we never heard about it?" Yuanbao asked, looking up and down the lane. "Wasn't it on the radio?"

"Are you kidding?" Liu said. "It was too humiliating."

"And then?"

"And then me and my friends refused to accept that we Chinese had to submit to foreign bullies. Why can't we do the bullying for a change?"

"So we formed an organization to teach the foreigners a lesson." Bai Du flipped her thumb behind her. "These comrades are all dyed-in-the-wool nationalists."

"We plan to bring that foreigner over here," Zhao Hangyu said. "Then beat the shit out of him. Which is why we came looking for you. We've heard about the incredible skills of Big Dream Boxing, and we figure that's our only chance."

"Don't turn us down." Liu Shunming, his eyes filling with tears, fell to his knees in front of Tang Yuanbao, followed by a whole group of solemn, respectful delegates. "We Chinese have suffered for a century at least, but no more. The Chinese people look to you. If you refuse our request, we'll knock our heads on the ground and dash our brains out at your feet."

"Get up, get up." Yuanbao ran over and helped Liu Shunming to his feet. The others sprang to theirs. "I understand your feelings," he announced, "I really do. So no more of that. I can't stand seeing people kneel. I, Tang Yuanbao, am a descendant of the Yellow Emperor, and if the people are in peril, I cannot be happy. I understand the situation. Snapping the leg of a foreigner is no big deal. The question is whether or not the government has been notified. We can't turn this into some sort of mob activity. Matters like this require organization. I don't want to kick some foreigner's ass, then have the government on *my* ass."

"Not to worry," Zhao Hangyu said. "Just hone your skills and give it the fight of your life. Even if you kill the guy, I've got plenty of people willing to do the time for you."

"What do you think, Dad?" Yuanbao turned to his father. "Should I do it?"

"What are you hesitating for, boy? I thought you'd been looking for a way to make a name for yourself. I'd do it myself if there was a senior competition."

"Well, listen to the old warrior!" Zhao said, leaving the

crowd and clasping his hands in a show of respect. "Pardon us for our blindness. We didn't realize who we had in our midst."

Stunned, the others stared at Yuanbao's father. Liu Shunming was the first to regain his senses. "I thought they lopped off your head after the Boxer Rebellion."

"What kind of talk is that?" Yuanbao said, obviously displeased. "You started off talking like gentlemen, so why turn on my father all of a sudden?"

"If I'm lying, I'm an eggplant." Liu Shunming took out the photograph of the Boxer prisoners being led to the execution ground and, looking at Yuanbao's father, pointed to the dark, husky man in the photograph. "One and the same—how did you come back to life?"

Yuanbao took the photograph, looked over at his father, and froze. "You've hardly changed in all these years."

The old fellow snickered as he took the photograph and rubbed it with his finger. Caught up in a welter of emotions, he said to Zhao Hangyu, "I guess this means bringing the Boxers back."

"Yes, bring the Boxers back." Tears of joy glistened in many eyes.

"If you ask me," Bai Du said softly to Zhao, "since the old Boxer is in our midst, shouldn't we return the manual to its rightful owner?"

"Absolutely!" Zhao said, giving a sign to one of his henchmen. "Give the Boxer manual to our old warrior here."

Holding the strawboard book in his hands, and with aging tears streaming down his face, Yuanbao's father looked up and called to his son, "Come here, Yuanbao. If you don't tear that foreigner limb from limb, you're no son of mine."

"Careful, Dad," Yuanbao said with mounting passion. "While I'm at it, I'll settle scores with your old enemies."

"Break out the hard stuff," Zhao Hangyu shouted to the men behind him. "For the old warrior here."

A bespectacled young man came forward with a crock of liquor and some large drinking bowls, which he filled with the transparent liquid.

Handing a bowl each to father and son Tang, Zhao Hangyu said, "Don't you think this calls for a drink?"

"I do indeed," the old warrior said as he held out his bowl grandly. "Bottoms up!"

Everyone present held a bowl in both hands and drained it, broad grins on their faces.

Yuanbao, his face quickly turning red, mumbled to Bai Du, "The truth is, no one understands me like my father. I've wanted to give up this pedicab business for a long time, just itching to do something spectacular to show what I'm made of."

"This will be spectacular, all right," Bai Du said as she tossed away her empty bowl. "I guarantee it."

"Where's our fighter? Where is he?" Before the shouts had died out, a man at least six and a half feet tall, head bandaged, arm in a sling, elbowed his way into the circle and threw his good arm around Yuanbao. With tears streaming down his face, he said, "You must settle this score for me!"

"This is the fighter who was beaten so horribly by the foreigner in Sapporo," Zhao Hangyu said. "Just look at him, bruised and battered from head to toe."

"My god!" The crowd erupted.

Their gasps of alarm were quickly drowned out by angry shouts: "Where's the enemy? Where are they?" Blackie came into view, leading a gang of locals in wide belts and trousers tied at the ankles, brandishing swords and clubs like a martial-arts troupe as they came running down the lane.

"Out of my way," Blackie shouted as he tore into one of the bespectacled young men.

"Chinese shouldn't be fighting other Chinese." Liu Shun-ming courageously spread his arms to keep his leading cadres out of harm's way, like a mother hen protecting her chicks. One leg-sweep from a local tough deposited him on his back-side.

"Stop that!" Yuanbao's father bellowed. "These esteemed visitors have come on national business, so knock it off!" He turned to Zhao Hangyu. "Don't be frightened, Chairman Zhao."

"I'm not, don't worry," Zhao said as his eyes swept Blackie and his men. Forcing a smile, he turned to Yuanbao's father. "This lane of yours is a true dragon's lair," he said.

4

"A telegram from 008." Zhao Hangyu, Bai Du, and the others were seated at tables that had been pulled together in a large restaurant, food and drink arrayed around them. The secretary took a telegram she had just received from a folder and, with a blank expression, read it aloud to Zhao.

FATSO HAS TAKEN THE BAIT STOP ACCEPTS INVITATION WITH PLEASURE STOP WILL LEAVE FOR CHINA WITHIN DAYS STOP.

"Send a telegram," Zhao said with a frown as he chewed on a piece of half-cooked meat. He pushed his glasses up on his nose.

DRAG YOUR FEET. STALL. SIT ON FATSO AS LONG AS YOU CAN. MAKE UP AN EXCUSE. WE NEED TIME TO GET EVERYTHING READY.

"That 008 is an idiot," Sun Guoren grumbled after the secretary had left. He kept eating. "He doesn't have a clue about what we've got in mind. Who told him to bust his butt like that? If you ask me, we're going to have to dump one-track idiots like him."

"You said it," Liu Shunming concurred, also digging into his food. "Who asked him to send Fatso so soon? He comes here and, with three clicks of the abacus, the match is over; then what? He could have waited till our investment started paying off."

"That's not what I meant," Zhao Hangyu said. "My primary concern is with the image of Tang Yuanbao. He'll be representing the entire Chinese race, and just winning a match won't be enough. This must be a rout in every sense of the word. That way he takes glory with him wherever he goes, the subject of veneration every step of the way, a national hero. At the moment, he isn't up to the challenge. We need time to start a training program to hone his talents. Comrades, we must act prudently. Just beating up some foreigner won't do it. Our ultimate purpose is to establish a national model. Do not, under any circumstance, underestimate the importance of our work, for what we are engaged in now is an enterprise of historic proportions—the mere thought makes me shudder."

"Old Zhao is a man of vision. Why can't the rest of us think like him?" Exchanged glances, accompanied by sighs all around. "Old Zhao," Liu Shunming said with emotion, "a few words of inspiration, please. You must clear our muddled minds."

With a deprecating wave of his hands, Zhao said, "Don't mind me, I'm just blabbing. There's nothing wrong with what you guys were saying. We need money, we sure do, and we need to find ingenious but open-and-aboveboard ways of getting it, to keep people from talking. But finding money and training Tang Yuanbao are not mutually exclusive activities. Hype is the key. An aggressive, properly run publicity campaign will produce maximum results with a minimum of effort. Have we notified the media of our discovery of a latter-day Big Dream Boxer?" he asked Bai Du.

"Yes," she said. "It'll be in the evening papers and on the nightly news."

"Good. We need to strike while the iron's hot." Zhao picked up a longish fish with his chopsticks and stuffed it into his mouth, head, tail, and all. He swallowed the meat and spit out the bones. "What I'm talking about are the principles behind our work. The nuts and bolts I leave to all of you. You'll have to come up with the essentials, and don't worry if you stumble from time to time. If Yuanbao needs more teachers, hire them, even if they're a bit weird. The broader the base, the more he learns. Whatever works."

"In my view, old Zhao, we need you to assume command on this, since no one holds a candle to you in remolding people," Liu Shunming said to Zhao admiringly. "Knowing you're out in front is all we need to keep going."

"I don't agree that old Zhao has to be involved in every aspect of the enterprise," Sun Guoren said indignantly. "Do you think he's not pulling his weight, or something? Haven't you noticed how he's been wasting away these past few days? Poor old Zhao's heart is nearly in shreds over this. But instead of trying to lessen our leader's worries, we're actually making things harder on him."

"Do you really think I want to wear out our leader? What I mean is, have old Zhao give the orders, and we'll run around carrying them out."

"Point taken. You're looking out for old Zhao, but I've got a bone to pick with him," Sun said, turning to Zhao Hangyu. "I'm a straight shooter, I say what's on my mind, not just what people want to hear. And you bug me. I don't know what you're up to, and I'm not afraid to say it to your face. We know how you work, but don't you ever rest?"

Zhao replied with a belly laugh. "Okay, you two, that's enough wrangling. I get the message. How about this: I'll stay clear of Tang Yuanbao and leave it all up to Bai Du. What do you say, Bai Du, any problem?"

"Fine with me," she said with a smile, taking a break from daintily picking at her food.

"Put a team together, and you've got the Tang Yuanbao contract. The man is yours. So who do you want? It's your call."

"I'll stick with Sun Guoren and Liu Shunming," she said with a glance at the chosen two.

"Good eye," Zhao said with a smile. "You've just deprived me of my two best men."

"That wasn't my intention," Bai Du replied, smiling at Sun and Liu. "I'm just interested in a congenial working relationship."

"Not so fast, Bai Du. Since you've chosen us, there's something we want from you," Liu Shunming said. "Get everything out of us you can. Don't treat us as humans. If you go easy on us, it'll only make us angry."

"Lighten up, Shunming. There are long days ahead of us, and we'll take them one at a time," Bai Du said with a smile. "If you say everything now, what's there for me to listen to later on?"

"How's this?" Zhao said. "If you run into problems, bring them to me. Brothers, sister, put your shoulders to the wheel and give it your all."

"How do we stay in touch?" Bai Du asked him. "Where do you plan to set up your operation?"

"Don't ask. Old Zhao's a floater by nature," Liu said. "I know the score. If you need him, go out on the street and shout. He'll be there, guaranteed."

"No, no more floating for me. This time we've got our digs, haven't we? Starting today, this restaurant will be our headquarters. Twenty-four hours a day, this is where you'll find me."

"Leave it to old Zhao to find the perfect place."

"Waiter!" Zhao clapped his hands to get the waiter's attention, then pointed to the food on the table. "Another round of everything." He turned to his companions. "I'm in a great mood today."

"Extra, extra, read all about it!"

Newspaper vendors shouted the news beneath traffic signals at busy intersections all over town.

"Read all about it, miraculous powers of the Big Dream Boxer on display again."

"Read all about it, a treasure unearthed in Tanzi Lane."

"A Boxer warrior has come back to life, the lost Big Dream Boxer manual has reappeared."

"Wondrous news, the headless warrior was a comrade of Big Sword Wang Five. His son, a pedicab driver, the greatest fighter in the world."

Pedestrians and drivers stopped to gawk and fight over the newspapers, bringing traffic to a chaotic halt.

In the tiny Tang family yard, Yuanbao, Yuanfeng, and their mother, plus a score of neighbors, sat in front of a fourteen-inch black-and-white TV set, happily slurping up cold noodles from a motley assortment of bowls.

On the TV, Du Xian and Xue Feizheng were taking turns talking to people all over the country.

Du: "Late-breaking news: This morning, in Beijing's Tanzi Lane, representatives of MobCom, acting on leads from the masses, discovered the last surviving warrior from the Boxer Rebellion, an individual somewhere between one hundred twenty and one hundred thirty years of age. But to look at him, you'd think he was fifty or sixty."

A picture of old man Tang, surrounded by a crowd, appeared on the screen, a scene of drinking and revelry.

"See my dad! That's my dad!" Yuanfeng, lips beaded with perspiration, screamed.

Du: "The old guy's still got all his teeth. He loves meat and still likes a drink."

Laughter filled the yard. Blackie, neck thrust out, eyes staring, lips smacking, said appreciatively, "Old Master Tang can take it easy and start enjoying life now. The hard fact is, before Liberation, he was caught up in revolutionary work."

Xue: "The unearthing of the old-timer was accompanied by the discovery of his son, Tang Yuanbao."

The imposing image of Tang Yuanbao appeared on the screen.

That announcement produced an uproar in the yard. Blackie thumped Yuanbao so hard on the back, he nearly forced the noodles in Yuanbao's mouth to come shooting out of his nose. "Watch the TV, keep watching," Yuanbao said affably.

Xue: "There's nothing special about this Tang Yuanbao fellow, except he's the accomplished descendant of a martial-arts school that was thought to have disappeared altogether. In a word, except for his aged father, he is China's sole practitioner of Big Dream Boxing, a skill that, up till now, we had only read about."

Tang Yuanbao appeared on the screen, strutting around the yard shadow boxing. A basinful of water was flung into the air, drenching everyone in sight, everyone, that is, but Tang Yuanbao, who stayed dry as a bone.

Du: "According to experts, this recent discovery in Tanzi Lane holds enormous significance in the study of recent history, in particular of the Boxer movement."

A bespectacled scholar appeared on the screen. Adjusting his glasses, he said, "Up till now, our discoveries were limited to a few eunuchs. As for actual Boxer warriors, this is the first. This will fundamentally change the study of recent history, which has thus far been based on ancient texts, unofficial histories, and oral transmissions."

He was replaced by a fat, shaved-headed man who was rubbing his hands. "Comrades in our museums were thrilled by news of the Tanzi Lane discovery. While they have a rich supply of historical artifacts, this is the first flesh-and-blood addition to their display of martyrs of recent history, an unprecedented discovery . . ."

A skeletal man so old he could barely keep his eyes open was seated on a sofa facing the camera. In a tiny voice, he said, "The panda bear, our so-called living fossil, pales in comparison with old Mr. Tang. This counts as the greatest archaeological find since the discovery of the mummified woman in Mawang-dui . . ."

Tears welled up in the glazed-over eyes of old man Tang as he stared at the TV screen. "How can I measure up to such high praise?" he muttered. "Even in my wildest dreams I never believed that by surviving the better part of a century I could make a contribution to the nation."

In the smoke-filled central room of the Tang household, *The Big Dream Boxer Manual* lay proudly on the altar under a desk-clock cover, nestled among an offering of steamed buns, apples, and bananas. Burning incense stood in a censer beneath portraits of the God of War and Chairman Mao, both gazing kindly out on the world below.

Old man Tang led a delegation of his descendants and neighbors in paying their respects: First, they clasped their hands reverently, then bowed deeply, over and over again. Following that they kowtowed, first on one knee, then lying on the floor, arms and legs spread grandly.

"I entrust the care and upkeep of all this to you," old man Tang said to his wife. "From this day forward, place nothing else in this spot. Keep it clean and free of dust."

The blare of automobile horns and the screech of brakes echoed out in the lane, as cars pulled up in front of the Tang house. A delegation led by Bai Du streamed into the room, everyone's rank and status marked by his uniform. In a crisp, unemotional voice, she said to Tang Yuanbao, "The car's waiting."

The bald, fat man they'd seen on the TV screen, a magnifying glass in one hand, pointed to old man Tang. "You, too!"

Father and son embraced and looked into each other's eyes.

Their parting words: "Let us both gain glory where we're going."

Others stepped up and separated them, then led them away.

As their menfolk walked out the door, Yuanbao's mother and sister called out tearfully, "Let us send some warm clothes with them."

"Be brave, Mama!"

A caravan of bulldozers, cranes, and dump trucks rumbled into Tanzi Lane, accompanied by a mighty army of excavators armed with shovels and hoes. A hard-hatted, whistle-blowing foreman led the procession. His bosses stood in a nearby jeep with the top down, studying a blueprint with the aid of a flashlight, pointing from time to time up and down the lane and at the Tang compound, giving orders to underlings clustered around the jeep.

Workers, tools over their shoulders, ran in all directions to close off the area with wooden signs.

The rear gates of trucks were let down to offer up their loads of chain-link fencing.

A searchlight set up atop the house was turned on. Then a second, and a third, sending beams of light up and down Tanzi Lane from all directions, turning night into day.

No sooner were the lights in place than a column of motorcycles roared up the lane, bringing a company of armed men in black uniforms. Jumping off their motorcycles, rifles and bayonets in hand, they took up positions at each intersection and at key spots on high ground.

A motorized pedicab specially built for the disabled came tooting up the lane right behind the motorcycles. Liu Shunming, in a pressed black uniform, hard helmet, and high leather boots, looking for all the world like a Party security officer, stood holding a transistor bullhorn. He flipped on the switch, tested it out, and announced to the horde of excited spectators crushed against the walls of the lane, "I am Major Liu Shunming of the security detail. As of now, all activity in Tanzi Lane falls under my command."

"Excuse me, Comrade Major," the chief archaeologist said as he walked up to Liu Shunming with his staff of engineers, "but I'm supposed to be the highest authority at this site. Commander-in-Chief of the Tanzi Lane Project."

"All right, Comrade Commander-in-Chief," Liu replied breezily. "What say we institute a system of dual leadership here in Tanzi Lane?"

A cacophony of automobile horns and human shouts erupted at the entrance to the lane, where a mob of men and women waving a variety of credentials were angrily voicing their displeasure to the "black shirt" sentries.

"I'm from the Central Breeding Station, and have important business to discuss with Tang Yuanbao."

"I'm from an advertising company . . ."

"No admittance, period!" Liu Shunming announced officiously as he elbowed his way past the sentries, his hand resting on his holster. "I have orders to use deadly force, if necessary, to keep people from getting anywhere near the Tang house. Anyone—and I mean anyone—who wishes to see either old man Tang or his son must secure permission from MobCom. Requests will be considered in the order in which the proper fees have been paid."

"You can't monopolize Tang Yuanbao; he's a national treasure belonging to all the people."

"Everyone shares in this meal!"

The mob was growing ugly.

"Back off!" Liu drew his pistol. The troops behind him took aim.

"I'm going to count to three. One, two, two and a half . . . You're forcing me to do something I don't want to do," he said with a sigh. "Open fire!"

From his pistol first, then from all the other weapons, streams of water hit their targets.

"Do you know why we brought you here?"

"Yes, you want to learn about my participation in the Boxer movement."

5

In an otherwise empty, soundproof room, the bald, fat man sat behind a desk in the shadow of a desk lampshade. Light from the lamp shone directly into old man Tang's face, whose hands rested in his lap as he sat respectfully on a stool fastened to the floor.

"Your name?"

"Tang Guotao."

"Age?"

"One hundred and eleven."

"Where did you live before you were taken into custody?"

"Number thirty-five, Tanzi Lane."

"When did you join the troops?"

"In March 1899."

"What were your ranks?"

"Team leader, guard leader, Second Elder Apprentice, First Elder Apprentice, and First-rank Master."

"Decorations or punishments?"

"I was sentenced to death in 1900."

"Do you have corns?"

"No."

In a snowy white examining room Tang Yuanbao sat on the edge of an examining table, dressed only in a pair of bathing trunks, and answered questions from a female doctor, who recorded his responses on a chart.

"Body odor?"

"No."

"Hemorrhoids?"

"No."

"How come you don't have anything?"

"You can smell and look if you don't believe me."

"I'll take your word for it. You're not a bed wetter, I assume."

"I was, but I'm not anymore."

"Get on the scale," the doctor said, pointing to a freight scale in the corner.

A nurse moved the weight back and forth, then straightened up and reported to the doctor, "On the high side of a hundred and seventy-five pounds."

"Take off your shorts and go behind that screen," the doctor said as she laid down her pen and stood up, rubbing her hands.

"What for?" Yuanbao asked nervously.

"I want to see how well developed you are," the doctor replied unemotionally.

"Do as she says," Bai Du said cordially from where she stood nearby. "Don't worry; she's past menopause."

"But I've never let anyone look before," Yuanbao said shyly as he walked around behind the screen with the doctor.

In a matter of seconds the doctor came out from behind the screen and washed her hands at the sink.

"Average," she said to the nurse, who had assumed the duty of writing on the chart.

"On that night eighty-eight years ago, that is, the night the Allied forces entered the city, where were you?"

"I was home," old man Tang replied, looking perfectly calm in the lamplight.

"Why weren't you out fighting? Big Sword Wang Five was, as was the father of the novelist Lao She."

"I had a far more important duty."

"What was that?"

"I ran home and strangled my parents, my wife, and my son. It was as dark then as it is tonight, and as cold, and I had no sooner eliminated my family than I heard a knock at the door. 'Master's wife, open the door, hurry.' I opened the door, and the person rushed inside, carrying an infant in her left hand and a red lantern in the right . . ."

"Who was it?"

"My wife, the woman you saw at my house. At the time she was one of the Red Lanterns."

"And the child in her arms?"

"Huo Yuanjia, the future martial-arts master."

"My God, how come this is the first I've heard of that?"

"As soon as my wife saw me, she fell to her knees and mumbled, 'Master, Master, the master's wife, my sister-in-law, they're all dead.' And I said, 'Yes, I killed them.' And she said, still crying, 'From today on, I am yours, and this child . . .' I interrupted her, 'You take this child back where you found it.' "

"Then what?" the fat man said as he wiped his tears.

"Then gunfire erupted and a Japanese soldier rushed in shouting *bakayaro* [son of a bitch]! He asked me, 'What you do?' Everything happened faster than it takes to tell, but when he barged in, I'd already crawled into bed, and my new wife was still on her knees, facing the other way. She kowtowed to the Japanese. 'Your honor,' she said, 'he's a bean-curd maker, a common, law-abiding citizen.' The Japanese smirked—heh heh heh—and nudged her with his bayonet. 'Pretty lady' he shouted. That's when I threw back the covers and roared, 'Let her go! I'm one of those Boxer leaders you're looking for! This has nothing to do with the common folk!' "

"Elder Tang, you're spreading it a bit thick, I'm afraid," said the fat man with a frown. "To the best of my knowledge, the Boxers had no grassroots party organization."

"That's where you're wrong, young man. A hundred years ago, we were already laying down our lives for the Cause."

Tang Yuanbao was quick-marched down a long corridor by Sun Guoren, who had a tight grip on his arm. Sun led him into another examining room, where a cluster of men in white surgical gowns strapped him into a chair with suction cups and clips attached to his limbs and torso. An X-ray machine was wheeled up and aimed at him.

"Test the machine—energize," the attending physician said.

Yuanbao squirmed in his chair as the electrical charge hit him.

"Ow!" he protested.

A doctor quickly slapped an analgesic patch over his mouth to silence him.

The machine lit up like a pinball machine, green waves of light flashing on the oscilloscope. Weird noises.

"Now we begin the tests. All consoles report."

"Heart present."

"Liver present."

"Stomach present."

"Kidney present."

"Hold it—only one kidney?"

A technician's head popped out from behind the equipment. "Where's your other kidney?" he asked Yuanbao.

Sun Guoren ripped the patch from Yuanbao's mouth, turning it bright red. "Isn't one enough?" Yuanbao replied.

"No," the technician answered. "Everybody comes with two. Now, think hard. What happened to it?"

"Who knows? I was always losing things as a kid."

"Measure the size of the existing kidney," the attending physician said.

The technician's head slipped back behind the equipment. "About the size of a pineapple," came the report.

"Now you're talking. His is the size of two normal kidneys," the attending physician said. "Let's move on."

"Lungs, eight hundred millimeters."

"Enough fatty tissue to support a chopstick."

The electronic device chattered, spewing out data on a long strip of paper.

The attending physician and Bai Du studied the test results.

"Everything seems in order," the physician said to Bai Du, "short of doing biopsies."

"Remove the straps," Bai Du instructed the attendants. Then she turned to Yuanbao, who stood up and flexed his wrists to get the circulation going. "This way, please."

Yuanbao was quick-marched back down the long corridor. In another snowy white examining room, a row of doctors peered at Yuanbao, who was seated in a chair after being bundled in by the brawny Sun Guoren.

A middle-aged doctor in dark sunglasses held a sheaf of cards in his hand, rapping them softly on a table as he said affably, "We're going to perform a little test, sort of like questions your parents asked you as a child. Nothing to worry about; just answer the ones you know. I'm sure you'll do fine. They aren't hard questions, so don't be nervous."

"Fire away," Yuanbao said earnestly. "I'll do my best."

"Thank you," the doctor said. "Here we go. Look at this card, please. It's a picture of a monkey and a man. In your own words, describe in one sentence the basic difference between men and monkeys. Your answer, please!"

"Monkeys have hair all over their bodies. Men only have hair in certain places."

"Correct. One point."

Yuanbao laughed—heh heh—and, with a smug expression, glanced over at the doctor holding the chart to record his scores. But one look at Bai Du wiped the smile off his face. He turned back and sat up straight.

"Next question, based on the same picture. Which of the two is least afraid of losing face, the monkey, the man, or neither? Your answer, please."

"The man."

"Wrong. Deduct one point!"

"Wait a minute," Yuanbao said, anxious over seeing his gain

wiped out. "The man is least afraid, since he has the thickest skin. A monkey's face is always red, but a man's seldom is. Obviously, that makes his skin thicker."

"Wrong. You should have said that a monkey's *ass* is always red, and a man's seldom is, even if it's exposed to the sun. But this, of course, is not our concern, since I asked about faces, not asses. The correct answer to this question is, the monkey is most afraid of losing face, his is the thickest skin; since man has no face to lose, man is shameless."

"Then what is it you're showing me?"

"A face, the face," the doctor replied gloomily. "This is a speculative question, and you obviously missed the point."

"Let's go to the next question."

"Question three: In your view, which of the two, the monkey or the man, has the stronger sense of tradition? And why do you think so?"

"The monkey, because monkeys have stayed pretty much the way they've always been, but man keeps changing."

"Correct. One point. Now for my fourth question: In your view, which of the two, the monkey or the man, is happier? And why do you think so?"

"They're equally happy. Monkeys do not engage in study, men do, and both—studying and not studying—bring boundless pleasure."

"Wrong. Deduct one point! How can not studying bring pleasure? If men don't study, they'll become backward. Haven't you ever heard that?"

"But monkeys don't study, and they don't become backward."

"You don't think they're backward enough already?"

"They don't learn from anyone."

"Who do you emulate? Who have you set up as your model? Your sense of right and wrong is all backward, and you don't distinguish between man and demon. . . . Ready to give up? Where logic is concerned, you're no match for me, because studying is more important to me than to you. Now I have a different kind of question. The same picture, also four questions, all true or false. No thinking, just rapid responses. First question: The monkey in this picture feels inferior to the man, true or false?"

"True."

"One point! The man can kill the monkey if he wants to, true or false?"

"False."

"Deduct one point."

"Of course it's false. First, the man has no organization behind him; second, he has no gun. It's one on one, and he'd be lucky if the monkey didn't kill him."

"Third question: Since monkeys and men are related by blood, and you're a man, are you related by blood to the monkey in the picture? In other words, you and the monkey are kin, but if you were charged with raising the monkey, you would mistreat it, true or false?"

"True!"

"Deduct one point! Okay, let's see how you did." The doctor turned to look at the scorecard. "Too bad, you didn't score a single point."

"I'd like to know your criteria for scoring."

"Impressions," the doctor said. "We score on impressions alone. Do you think that's unfair?"

"No, I can't think of anything fairer. I'd have been surprised if you used anything *but* impressions."

"What do you say to this?" The doctor returned to Yuanbao after a whispered conversation with his colleagues. "One last question to settle things. The same picture, a monkey and a man . . ."

"Why don't you test me on some of those other cards in your hand—you've got a whole bunch of them."

"No deal! For questions about life, you'd be in great shape if you could answer the questions on this single card. The rest are for other people. Now then, the same picture. This monkey and this man, staring at each other, can you tell us what they're thinking?"

Yuanbao and the doctor stared at each other.

"They're both thinking, 'I'd hate to be him.' "

"How was that?" Bai Du asked the doctor.

The doctor looked at Bai Du, then at Yuanbao.

"I'm awfully sorry, but I can't give him a point. Naturally, there's no need to deduct a point either. I need time to ponder his answer."

"Then let's talk about impressions. You don't have to give me a scientific answer right away," Bai Du said.

"Impressions?" The doctor leaned back in his chair and stared at Yuanbao. "He's not very intelligent, that goes without saying. Great loyalty is like betrayal, he'll have a long life, two marriages, no children, some financial successes, will be troubled by petty people, but will benefit from guardian angels at critical moments. How's this? Maybe he'll understand what I'm getting at better from a couple of lines of poetry: 'Spring winds twist poplars around willows/A man walking down the street is enchanted by the sight.' That's the best I can do without subjecting his palm to careful study."

• • •

"That's not what the book says. Let's turn to page forty-four, fourth line from the bottom."

In the interrogation room, the bald, fat man read aloud, "On that night, the city was ablaze, the sound of gunfire like thunder. The foreign soldiers advanced like a tiger attacking a herd of sheep, torching and killing. The soldiers and the Boxers scattered like birds and beasts, and all the first-rank masters fell into the hands of the French soldiers at Hadamen, who trussed them up, despite their ferocious resistance. Shortly after dawn, I was beheaded by the French in the marketplace, along with over a hundred Boxer bandits, including leaders like Big Sword Wang Five and Little Sword Zhao Six . . ."

The bald, fat man looked up and said to old man Tang, who was wearing a pair of reading glasses as he followed along, his finger stopping at each word, "Naturally, if you believed everything in books, we'd be better off without them. This *Memoirs of the Green Tower* is nothing but a collection of ghost stories and fantastic tales, but there's no harm in keeping it around, since it represents one way of looking at things. We all understand that rumor is the twin sister of fact."

"Are you saying I'm wrong?" old man Tang asked blankly, looking up from the page. "I clearly recall being taken into a blockhouse by the Japanese and shot."

"You've read *The Little Soldier Zhang Sha*, haven't you?"

"Yes," old man Tang said with a nod.

"I'm not surprised. A few days ago, we interrogated the fat interpreter, and he couldn't remember if he stood with the Japanese or against them."

"Why couldn't I have been executed once by the Japanese and again by the French? It's already been settled that I came back from the dead."

"I didn't say you couldn't. The question is whether or not you had time to be executed by the Japanese and then rush over to be executed again by the French."

"Why not? There's nothing illogical about it. When the bullet hit me, I fell to the ground and closed my eyes, pretending to be dead. Then, after the Japanese left, I crawled out of the execution pit, stood up and cleaned the blood off, filled with hate and a taste for vengeance against the imperialists. I ran off and rejoined the battle."

Cocking his head, the bald, fat man pondered what old man Tang had told him. "I see nothing wrong so far."

"I went down East Fourth Avenue, killing the enemy along the way as I headed to wherever the sounds of battle were the loudest. When my guts began spilling out, I stuffed them back in. When one of my eyes fell out, I picked it up and swallowed it. I was possessed by a single thought: *Don't fall, keep going. If you fall, China is done for!*"

"Then what?"

"Eventually I did fall. I lay on the ground, seeing spots before my eyes. Then the world began to spin, and I blacked out. . . ."

"What do you recall about the beheadings at the marketplace?"

"That's where I was when I came to. People were lined up to be beheaded. Before I could say a word, it was my turn. As to methods, it wasn't much different than cutting up a rack of ribs—holding it down with one hand and chopping with the other."

"You must have said something, a farewell to your comrades or last words before the executioner's sword fell. That's common sense."

"I'm not sure, but I might have said. 'Long Live World Revolution.' "

"Hardly."

"Oh, now I remember. I shook hands with Wang Five, and we exchanged knowing looks. Then I turned and growled at the executioner, 'China will be destroyed by the likes of you!' "

"Now that sounds more like it. The executioner was Chinese?"

"No, he was French."

"Raise your left hand and make a fist. . . . No, your other left hand. Okay, it's time to swear an oath."

"Swear it to whom, who do I swear it to?"

"To me, watch me." Bai Du and Tang Yuanbao stood facing each other, each with left arm raised, fists clenched, eyes fixed solemnly on the other's face.

"I'll say a line, then you repeat it: Serve the organization, sacrifice oneself . . ."

"I'll say a line, then you repeat it: Serve the organization, sacrifice oneself . . ."

"From now on, the organization is my only family."

"From now on, the organization is my only family."

"My head can roll, my blood can flow."

"My head can roll, my blood can flow."

"I'll climb a mountain of knives and dive into a vat of boiling oil."

"I'll climb a mountain of knives and dive into a vat of boiling oil."

"A frown will never crease my brow."

"A frown will never crease my brow."

"I did not choose the day or time of my birth, but I can choose the day and time of my death."

"I did not choose the day or time of my birth, but I can choose the day and time of my death."

"Copyrighted material, no unauthorized reprinting."

"Copyrighted material, no unauthorized reprinting."

"Whoever violates this agreement must compensate the victim for all losses."

". . . must compensate the victim for all losses."

The oath completed, Bai Du gave Yuanbao a warm handshake. "As of now, we are comrades."

A broad smile creased Yuanbao's face. "That doesn't go far enough. What you should say is, As of now, we . . . we aren't human—not ordinary humans."

"What I really want to know is, how did you return from the dead? You must be aware that no one, no one but you, has ever been resurrected from the dead."

"Haven't you ever heard the comment, 'You can never kill the Chinese'?"

"Yes, I have heard that. You can never kill all the Chinese!"

Klong, klong, klong—*toot, toot, toot-ti toot—*

A band of drum-beating, horn-blowing middle-school girls marched in orderly fashion onto the busy street. Right behind them came several strapping young peasants with goatskin bandannas wrapped around their heads, pushing an enormous drum on a flatbed cart. *Dong, dong, dong.* They took turns beating the drum with a flourish.

A splendid variety of popular entertainers sailed paper boats up and down the street, danced with huge lions, and walked on stilts, bringing joy to everyone in sight.

A "Liberation" truck rumbled slowly down the street behind the entertainers. Tang Yuanbao stood in the bed, hands behind his back, a wooden placard sticking up behind his head, like a garden-variety condemned man. He was sandwiched between two armed, uniformed, and very menacing guards.

The sight of the truck and its contents baffled the spectators, who were unprepared for the sudden appearance of bespectacled intellectuals who raised their arms and shouted, "Celebrate the birth of China's superhero!"

The shouts were followed by enthusiastic applause. Then more shouts:

"Down with imperialism! Imperialism and all other reactionary movements are paper tigers!"

Some began distributing handbills.

The spectators blindly echoed the shouts from the spectacles and stormed the truck to applaud and shout hosannas to Yuanbao.

"Celebrate the birth of China's superhero!"

"As I said early on, the masses are a vast storehouse of enthusiasm."

As they sat in the cab of the truck, Sun Guoren said gleefully to Bai Du, "Do you believe me now?"

"I still think we shouldn't trot Tang Yuanbao out prematurely. Establishing a reputation too soon will hinder his remolding."

"But you have to take my situation into account. I have strict orders from old Zhao to reach his profit quota."

"You have your instructions, I know that."

The truck threaded its way through the colorful rice-sprout dancers and turned down another street, where Liu Shunming was running around madly, dispatching his black shirts all along Tanzi Lane to form a welcome party.

Men, women, boys, and girls were hustled out of their houses, lined up against the wall, and given little paper flags by Liu Shunming's troops. Liu himself stood at their head, waving his own paper flag to show the residents how it was done.

"As soon as the truck appears in the lane, wave your flags

like this and shout as loud as you can. Remember, shout with all the fervor of the Koreans, give it everything you've got, and if you feel like weeping, go ahead, don't be shy."

"Here it comes, it's coming!" a running black shirt screamed.

Snapping his head around, Liu saw Pigsy, right out of the novel *Monkey*, and Qin Xianglian, the fictional abandoned wife, who were standing nearby, wagging their heads at him. He spotted Sun Guoren and Bai Du in the truck's cab.

"Hooray—!" Thrusting out his arms, Liu Shunming began whooping it up.

"Hooray—!" His troops thrust out their arms.

Men removed their hats and waved them in enthusiastic welcome to Yuanbao. Women shook their paper flags, their bodies swaying rhythmically, a stream of guttural sounds emerging from their mouths.

"Hooray—!" Once again, Liu Shunming thrust out his arms; he was smiling and his eyes were closed.

"I seem to recall lining up like this once before, a long time ago," Mrs. Li whispered to Yuanbao's mother, who was standing beside her. Mrs. Li's jowls quivered, as if she'd stepped on a hot wire. "Waving little flags and mumbling things to someone passing by."

"It must have been 1949."

"No, earlier than that."

"Then it must have been 1937."

The truck turned another corner. People lining the street frowned at Yuanbao as he stood behind the cab. A few angry women even spat at him when he passed. "An evil man like that deserves nothing less than execution!"

"What's going on?" Bai Du asked Sun Guoren. "Where are our comrades?"

"Beijing's too big for us to position them everywhere. They're already dog-tired from running around bringing out crowds for us."

"Then you should have mapped out a route that took us only down the big streets. What must Comrade Tang Yuanbao think of this!"

Yuanbao, smiling the whole time, repaid welcoming and damning looks alike with a gentle gaze.

The Treasure Palate restaurant, decorated inside and out like a temple, was lit up like a pleasure palace.

Bai Du, Sun Guoren, and their friends escorted Yuanbao, his face covered with a rash and holding up his ankle-tie pant-legs, up the wide and very steep white marble steps.

They were met at the top by crisp applause from Zhao Hangyu and a delegation of large-headed, big-eared men. They all wore broad smiles.

Zhao stepped forward, clasped Yuanbao's hand, and said with a smile, "Elder Brother Yuanbao, did you have an enjoyable trip?"

"It was fine, except for the wind blowing in my face and the sun beating down on me."

"Don't you remember him?" Sun asked the obviously puzzled Yuanbao, who was staring at the oily-faced Zhao Hangyu. He made a hurried introduction. "This is Director Zhao Hangyu, the one who discovered you and your father."

"Oh, Director Zhao. And how are you? If not for you, sir, my father and I would never have seen this day."

"Good, wonderful, perfect," Zhao said as he led Yuanbao over to the delegation of large-headed, big-eared men.

"Let me introduce you to the managers of the Treasure Palate, each a true patriot. Don't mistake them for common businessmen, for they are firm believers in righteous causes. They've graciously offered to take responsibility for all your meals, promising to fatten you up with delicious food."

"Ah, our warrior has arrived." The head of the delegation, a portly man, took Yuanbao's hand and said, "My comrades and I have decided to spare no expense for you. We're putting it all on the line. We'd join you as beggars before we'd sell out like a bunch of traitors or compradors. Since our options are limited, we'll make the best of it, pretending we're back under the rule of the Japanese."

"That's the sort of talk I like to hear. I only wish I could have met you sooner."

"Let's go in," Sun Guoren said, urging them to enter the restaurant. "Who in his right mind would stand out here under a blazing sun chatting away?"

"Good idea. We can continue this inside," the restaurant manager agreed, wiping away his tears. "After all, it's a group of Chinese sitting down together for a good meal. I'll take comfort in knowing I'm not fattening up any foreigners."

Attendants dressed as Qing dynasty eunuchs pulled back the curtains and bent low at the waist. The party passed through a high doorway and entered a gloomy dining hall, laughing and talking as they approached a large round table covered by a cream-colored tablecloth and fine place settings and china.

"Did you put the posters up after the procession?" Zhao Hangyu whispered to Sun Guoren at the rear of the party.

"Yes, I sent the whole gang out to put them up as soon as the procession ended. There's nothing to worry about. I've planned everything down to the last detail."

When everyone had been seated around the table, Zhao picked up his napkin, which was folded in the shape of a crane, and tucked it into his shirtfront. Then he turned to Yuanbao and said excitedly, "The cuisine here is special. This is a meal I want you to truly enjoy."

"I'd like to say something," Bai Du announced as she stood up. "We had reasons for choosing the Treasure Palate for today's banquet. First, to celebrate. Second, Tang Yuanbao's training and transformation begin today. The Treasure Palate's cuisine is special, and training begins with food. Every dish on today's menu has profound ties to Chinese culture, and will cause us all to ponder our great nation. Why not call it 'cultural cuisine,' the partaking of which can be the equivalent of completing a spirited course in Chinese culture. In the history of the world, ours is the only civilization whose food has been passed down without change for generations, which is why for millennia China has stood tall among the nations of the world. We can cut off our queues, unbind our feet, even change into Western suits, but we cannot stop eating. That has formed a national characteristic, instilling pride in us as descendants of China's earliest rulers. Our ancestors took great pains to keep us from forgetting our roots. Now dig in."

Waitresses dressed as traditional serving girls entered in single file with an array of dishes as beautiful as potted flowers. The diners' eyes nearly popped out of their heads, as the fat manager stood up lethargically and described for the honored guests the name and unique qualities of each dish.

"The core of this dish is three walnuts and a meatball. It's called 'When three men walk along, one of them is my teacher.' The meatball is called a lion's head."

"Ahh—!"

"This one has potatoes cooked with thirty-six spices. Its name is 'Only books bring knowledge, all else is inferior.'"

"Ooo—!"

"The next dish is made of mushrooms stewed in a crock pot. It's called 'The nation cannot survive a single day without a ruler.'"

"Wow—!"

"This one is a thick soup consisting of a small hen, a large rooster, a small rooster, and a male crab. Its name is 'At home obey your father, after marriage obey your husband, after your husband dies, obey your son.'"

"Wa—!"

"Next comes a simple dish—boiled eggs. Since there's no way of telling whether they are male or female, we call it 'Seek not accomplishments, but avoid mistakes.'"

"Hey—!"

"The next dish is steamed bear's paw and fish. When it's done, the bear's paw is removed, leaving only the fish, and is called 'Bear's paw or fish, one or the other.'"

"Ohhh—!"

"This next one is stewed pork loin, with all the meat removed from the bone. Its name is 'The weak can travel the earth, the strong can hardly take a step.'"

"Ai—!"

"Here we have fried lizard and earthworms, which is called 'Face the strange with no fears, and its fearfulness disappears.'"

"Yow—!"

"This is a baked pigeon. We call it 'The bullet strikes the bird with its head up.' "

"This is a dessert made of agar-agar, cocoa, and five duck bills. Its name is, 'Don't pursue a desperate enemy.' "

"This is horsemeat with the hair left on. The meaning should be clear: 'When a man is poor, his aspirations are low. When a horse is scrawny, its hair is long.' "

"This is a whole roasted pig, prettied up by the chef to give it a determined, peaceful expression, and to carry the meaning, 'Dying in glory is worse than living in ignominy.' "

"Well, what do you think?" Bai Du asked Yuanbao.

"Quite an education," Yuanbao blurted out as he emerged from his astonishment.

"This is just the beginning. You must learn——much, much more."

"Where do I sleep?"

Following the banquet, Bai Du showed Yuanbao to his quarters. The room was completely empty, not a stick of furniture, except for a barracks bench.

"There," Bai Du said. "Starting today, you must place strict demands on yourself. Any problem with that?"

"No, no problem."

"Then get some sleep while you can. Good night."

"Good . . . night."

After seeing Bai Du out, Yuanbao looked the bench over carefully, trying to figure out the best way to sleep. Finally, he curled up on it as best he could, but he no sooner closed his eyes and began to relax than he fell to the floor.

• • •

In the next room, Bai Du and Sun Guoren were discussing their work.

"Some of the courses have been taken care of," Sun reported to Bai. "For instance, I was up all night talking to famous masters. I haven't been able to pin down the luminaries on your list, since they're too busy, or they only instruct women, not men. The sagely fellow I chose will do just fine, since he's brimming over with knowledge. Most important, he's a proponent of scientific management, and uses a coin-slot system. Friend or stranger, he'll talk as long as you feed him coins. No personal connections or back doors necessary. It's very convenient."

"How would you rate the quality of what he says?"

"Every word's a pearl, of course. He's a sage, after all. His teeth are pure ivory. He's high on everybody's list. I asked around, and what I learned was, anyone who's heard him 'expound' comes away feeling fabulous. People rave not only about the quality of what he says, but the quantity as well. You won't be disappointed. Every time he opens his mouth, words spew out like a fountain, and keep spewing till the time's up. In the past, he wouldn't open his mouth for any meeting of fewer than eight thousand people, and he could speak for four or five hours without batting an eye. Now he'll just be spreading leftover heat. Since he has time on his hands, and is afraid you'll be flitting around like a headless fly, he's going to set up a clinic at Jieyi Temple to illuminate the Way and cure the sick."

"I'm glad all these people have time on their hands," Bai Du said. "Otherwise, we'd be up a creek."

"As for the training class in politics, I've made a number of contacts," Sun said. "But so far they're all returnees from the U.S., not quite what we wanted. I've asked around town, run my legs off, in fact. We're looking for someone who's absolutely uncontaminated, aren't we? Well, there's only one place I can think of. I've contacted the people there, and they've given their OK for us to participate in their activities. But we have to keep this under our hat. We need to wear disguises when we go, and we can't get in without using a password. I've got it memorized."

"Good, we'll get on this right away." Then Bai Du asked, "Anything else?"

"Not at the moment. Everything else is moving along smoothly. Those are the only two that might present problems."

"Then that's it for today," Bai Du said, stretching lazily and yawning. "Go get some sleep; you've had a busy day."

"I can't," Sun said as he heated water over a hot plate and poured two cups of tea. "Just thinking about what we're doing gets me so excited, I can't sleep at all."

"I know what you mean," Bai Du said as she picked up her tea with both hands. "I'm as excited as you are. For the first time in my life, I'm doing something that makes me feel like a real person. We're lucky to be given the chance to get swept up in the mighty torrent of another human being's transformation."

Caught up in dreams of the future, they stood in the red glow of the hot plate. "There'll be plenty of time to sleep once the revolution is won."

Bai Du and Yuanbao walked incognito down the street. She was wearing shades; he had on a billed cap, pulled way down low.

7

Posters with Yuanbao's photograph decorated walls and utility poles along the way. Sun Guoren's name was printed over his signature and a red "X."

People with nothing better to do were examining the posters, some reading aloud:

"Tang Yuanbao, male, five feet eight inches tall, square face, no distinguishing marks. A powerful physique, loves literature, has a home to go to. Last seen wearing a cream-colored jacket, brown corduroys, and black plastic sandals. Wears a blue glove on his left hand."

Yuanbao followed Bai Du into a narrow lane, where she took off running and slipped into a women's toilet. Yuanbao followed her, but slammed on the brakes just short of the toilet.

Yuanbao and Bai Du swapped disguises. Now he

was wearing shades and she had put on the cap. Side by side they swaggered down the lane.

A bus heading their way came to a stop. Bai Du hopped aboard at the last minute, with Yuanbao right behind her. But just as the driver was about to drive off, she jumped out, leaving Yuanbao pinned in the closing door. Pleading with the ticket taker, and pelted by shouts and curses from the other passengers, he managed to free himself and jump to the sidewalk.

In a room with windows covered by blankets sat a group of men and women with blank expressions. There was a knock at the door. A burly young man opened it a crack and asked, "Who're you looking for?"

"Third Brother sent me with a message that Third Sister-in-law has returned from the countryside."

"How is Third Brother?"

"He's fine, except for a ringworm on his face."

"Come on in," the burly young man said as he opened the door.

An excited Bai Du led Yuanbao into the room, where a scrawny bespectacled fellow with a pompadour stood up and shook hands with Bai Du.

"No problems getting here?"

"We had a tail, but we lost him," Bai Du said as she took off her cap. "Mr. Liu," she said by way of introduction, "this is the fellow worker I told you about."

"A pleasure to meet you," Mr. Liu said, shaking hands with Yuanbao. "I've heard a lot about you, and have been looking forward to meeting you."

Bai Du nudged Yuanbao. "What did I tell you? Have you forgotten already?"

"I've been looking forward to meeting you, too. What this lantern in my heart has been needing is someone to light it."

"Same here." Mr. Liu's hand swept past the other faces in the room.

Bai Du and Yuanbao sat down beside a fat, dumb-looking fellow who stuck out his hand. Yuanbao shook it and smiled. No reaction by the man.

"The meeting will come to order," Mr. Liu announced, running his fingers through his hair. "The issue I want to discuss with you fellow workers today is: Why must China wage a campaign of class struggle?"

"Yeah, why?" a fat fellow asked softly.

"Because only by waging class struggle can we enjoy good times. Is there anyone here who doesn't want good times? If so, please raise your hand. . . . No one? Good. So now you all know why class struggle is necessary, right?"

The sound of whispering skittered around the room; voice boxes were in the silent mode.

"Back when I was a guerrilla in the Taihang Mountains, the locals all called us the 'bitter boys,' " the fat, dumb-looking fellow muttered.

"Which is why I was so resolute in chopping off the capitalists' tails," a pasty, middle-aged woman said. "If you don't have any food, there's nothing wrong with begging. But if you don't have a doctrine to follow, the food won't taste good."

"My sisters are always down in the dumps," a young woman said as she gazed up at the ceiling. As fantasies floated in her head, she added, "We try looking nice for people who cause us nothing but grief."

An ashen-faced Yuanbao walked out of the whitewashed mental hospital behind Bai Du, looking somber and self-assured.

"How do you feel?" Bai Du asked as they walked down the steps.

"Much better. Not so light-headed."

"You have to know more about society," Bai Du said thoughtfully. "When three men walk along, one of them is your teacher."

"Yes, yes, so I've discovered." Yuanbao rubbed his temples. "I hope you don't mind my asking, but are you a Party member?"

Bai Du stopped, spun around to face him, and erupted. "You're the Party member!"

The bulldozer moved ahead at full speed; with an earsplitting *crash*, part of the wall around the Tang compound toppled to the ground, leaving behind a pile of splintered bricks and a cloud of dust.

8

Yuanbao's mother ran up to the man in charge and screamed, "We've got a gate, you know!"

"Old lady," the man in charge explained patiently, "we have our methods. Have you ever seen an archaeological expedition enter through a gate? What's needed is digging and scraping."

"If there's no gate, dig away. But there is one, so what's the idea of knocking down the goddamned wall?"

"I'm sorry. We have fixed procedures, and I'm not authorized to change them. Besides, the workers are used to them."

Now that the wall was down, the bulldozer moved into the yard and headed for the house. *Crash*! A gaping hole opened up in the wall, the rubble blanketing the furniture on the other side. Sparks from electrical wiring started a fire that quickly spread to the rubble and began to crackle and pop, sending balls of flames into the air.

"What are you doing to me?" the old lady screeched, stomping her feet. "Not even the Japanese brought down my house during the war."

"Commander Liu," the man in charge called out to Liu Shunming, "would you please escort this old lady away from the work site? She's making a pest of herself."

"I'll fix you bastards! What's the worst you can do, kill me?"

"Let's go, old lady," Liu said to Yuanbao's mother. "Don't you know any better? This is what we call 'go for the old.' The old stuff is worth a lot more than anything new."

"That's something I won't understand till the day I die."

"Use your head. Do we have anything new that's better than what the foreigners have? The only reason we Chinese have any standing in the world at all is because we know how to take advantage of old stuff."

"Come on, Ma, let's go," Yuanfeng urged her mother, her rolled-up bedding tucked under her arm. "Remember what Yuanbao said when he was leaving—he told us to be strong."

"The house has been ransacked, the inhabitants gone, and I don't know if I'm dead or alive. I've lived for nothing." The old lady was weeping.

"It's not just us who are in trouble. The organization is in even greater trouble. We have to stick together through the hard times."

"Take them to the relocation center," Liu Shunming, teary-eyed, directed one of his men.

A team of laborers with hoes and brooms came up to clear away the rubble, using the former to break it into smaller pieces, the latter to sweep it up. They were followed by a team of archaeologists with brushes and magnifying glasses. They wasted no time digging through the broken bricks and roof tiles, unearthing a variety of cans and bottles, which they dusted and cleaned meticulously before subjecting them to detailed scrutiny under a magnifying glass.

"As agreed," Liu Shunming said to the man in charge, "whatever you find that belonged to the old guy is yours, but we get anything that belonged to his kids."

As Yuanfeng helped her mother leave the area, the two weepy women looked back longingly. They met Mrs. Li and her son, Blackie, at the entrance to the lane; they, too, were walking away, grief-stricken, loaded down with bundles of personal effects.

Mrs. Li broke into tears at the sight of Yuanbao's mother. "You lost your house, and gained a king. But what did we do to deserve this?"

"Where are you going?" Yuanfeng asked Blackie with a sob. "The relocation center's right here in the lane."

"Fleeing from disaster," Blackie barked angrily. "You won't get us into that concentration camp."

"What about your neighborhood brothers?" Yuanfeng's mother asked Blackie. "Most of the time they're raising hell and causing mischief, but when you really need them, they're nowhere in sight."

"They were rounded up by Commander Liu," Blackie said, hanging his head. "Some were thrown into a POW camp; the others went over to the enemy."

"What's this Commander Liu in command of?" Yuanbao's mother asked. "Does he work for the government?"

"Who dares ask?" Blackie said. "I just about pass out at the sight of a uniform."

"Any news from Yuanbao's dad?" Blackie's mother asked Yuanbao's mother. "How come we didn't see the two of them in the procession?"

"I don't think they've shot him. All I know is he's not in the enemy's hands."

"How come you joined the Boxers in the first place?"

"At first I didn't want to, especially when I thought about those soldiers in green uniforms. My mother was a wet nurse to Prince Chun, so I went to ask him for a job. He told me to go back to the countryside and work the land. His principle was, the better he liked someone, the less inclined he was to give that person special treatment. He had to set an example for others, so he could get strong backing when he spoke to the Emperor and the other princes. Then the Boxer movement got under way, and the countryside was no longer safe, so I went to see Prince Chun again, and volunteered to join his army. After I told him how things were out in the countryside, he thought for a minute, then said to me, 'Can you write that up so I can show it to the Emperor? He has no idea things are so bad in the provinces.' I told the prince I'd consider it an honor. He told me how to write it, then had me affix my thumbprint. He said not to let anyone know he was involved. I knew what a difficult position he was in, what with the Qing monarchy on its last legs, and all, and if he fell, there'd be no more support at all. I told him I'd take full responsibility. If things didn't work out, it was my head on the line, I wouldn't get him involved. Then he turned grave and told me he'd given this a lot of thought, and that it was better for me to be outside the palace than inside. Since so many of my brothers and sisters had joined the Boxers, I could use my status as an outsider to pull them together in the service of the monarchy and lead them in the direction of 'support the Qing, annihilate the foreigners.' "

"Were you responsible for that slogan?' "

"You got that right. As a Tang, I know nothing but loyalty to the nation. As in the Three Kingdoms, I recognized Cao, but not Han. A war of resistance requires the officials and the commoners to bond into a single thread. . . ."

"That slogan alone is reason enough to label you a turncoat, a traitor in the ranks."

Bai Du and Yuanbao stood in the temple entrance, their hands clasped, necks thrust out, eyes staring, while a little monk in a black cassock painted moles between their brows and on the tips of their noses with a brush dripping with red ink. Then they joined the ranks of worshippers who made their slow way, each step followed by a kowtow, starting and stopping, toward a prayer hall where incense smoke curled into the air.

A bell rang out sonorously, wooden clappers banged loudly. A Buddha with curly hair, large, fleshy ears, and a full, round face reclined on a flower-strewn lotus throne, his eyes closed, a benign smile on his face. Behind the statue stood a chorus of monks, young and old, swaying from side to side as they intoned scriptures in modulated cadences.

The worshipers, male and female, young and old, fell to the ground at the feet of the Buddha, filled with reverence and awe. After banging their heads on the floor, as if pulverizing cloves of garlic, they stood up and formed a circle around the lotus throne, then left reluctantly, covering their noses as tears streamed down their faces. Those who stood their ground were dragged away by monks to keep them from interfering with the observers lined up behind them.

A group of sobbing nuns was lined up at the exit, each holding a spittoon. Everyone who passed was supposed to shake hands with the nuns, toss coins noisily into their spittoons, and say something consoling. Some emotional women even wrapped their arms around the nuns and sobbed along with them.

Bai Du and Yuanbao walked into the hall, where they bowed respectfully to the reclining Buddha, then knelt and kowtowed three times. Once they were back on their feet, they walked up next to the statue and stared at it with heartfelt emotion. Then, instead of making a circle around the hall and leaving, they took out rolls of coins and rained them down into the large spittoon at the base of the lotus throne; the spittoon sang out happily as a covey of golden birds hopped out from the floral base of the throne, chirping and looking all around.

Suddenly the hall fell silent: no movement, no sobbing, no chanting. The heavy silence was broken by strains from a pipe organ, and amid the somber ambience of the prayer hall, the Buddha slowly sat up, turning to face Bai Du and Yuanbao. The throne turned with him.

"Howdy, folks." The Great Buddha's eyes sparkled, his mouth opened and closed, emitting a tinkling sound. "Here for a game of chess or some Ping-Pong?"

Bai Du fell to her knees: "Almighty God, we are not here to play chess or Ping-Pong. We seek your love and charity, and we give our thanks for the food you have bestowed upon us, keeping us from hunger, and for the clothing that keeps us warm. . . ."

"My child, you needn't thank me. No ass-kissing to your God. He knows that the more fervently you praise Him, the greedier your demands upon Him."

"Your Holiness, since you can see everything, I'll make this short."

Bai Du pushed Yuanbao up close.

"Please look at this man before you; tell him where he's from and where he's going. Cleanse his contaminated soul and restore in him the pure heart of a child."

"Ashes to ashes and dust to dust. Your physical body must undergo pain and suffering, yet your soul may not be saved. Give unto me your lambs and your calves. I will show you the way to happiness. Refrain from lying and peeping into women's baths. Anytime you receive ill-gotten gains, you will have accepted a gate pass to Hell. Anytime you give your last cornmeal cake to someone hungrier than you, you will have deposited a tidy sum of U.S. dollars in Heaven's bank. Love your enemy, and when he slaps the left cheek of your bottom, offer up the right. Keep a civil tongue, be courteous and self-disciplined. Give up your seat on a bus cross streets only in the crosswalk stop at a red light go on the green buy and sell at fair prices do not take a needle or thread from the masses turn in everything captured be prepared to struggle against evil people and evil deeds . . ."

"God, this sounds awfully familiar."

"My child, even God can use a cliché once in a while. . . . Things are much better these days, not just somewhat. . . . My, how time flies, another year has passed. . . ."

"If you have nothing more to say, God, that ought to just about do it."

"My child, even God has occupational ethics to consider.

You gave enough for ten minutes, so God is obliged to speak for ten minutes. He will not shortchange you."

"God, since we still have some time, why not go ahead and check his health?"

"My child, God will give you a quick rundown. He's got a touchy stomach, caught colds easily as a child, and suffers from diarrhea every time he eats a cucumber."

"Almighty God, how do you know all that about me?"

"My child, your God isn't God for nothing."

"Oh, no!" The Great Buddha's voice had changed, and even though he was still smiling benignly, there was fear in his voice. His eyes turned shifty, as if searching for something, then settled on Bai Du. "My child, what sort of person have you brought to me? Why does he look so weird?"

"What has frightened you, God?"

"Look for yourself, my child. This person is possessed. I'll let you off this time, but don't push me, or I'll get you for disrespect later."

"Have mercy, God, save this pitiful disciple, show your powers of exorcism."

"I've never seen a demon like that. We travel in different circles. You must seek out the Immortal Zhang. I've heard she has great powers, a specialist in exorcising demons, a real wizard."

"Migh—ty—!"

The monks shouted in unison.

Confounded by this turn of events, Bai Du grabbed Yuanbao's arm and made tracks.

That evening, as the sun was setting, Bai Du and Sun Guoren stood in an unlighted room, studying and pondering Yuanbao.

As his face grew increasingly blurred, he paced the room silently. The yellow haze from streetlights outside produced ghostly shadows.

"Don't listen to that old monk, you two." Yuanbao was getting goose bumps under his two companions' gaze, and rushed to his own defense. "I grew up under the red flag, just like you. I've been steeped in milk and honey, and bathed in sunlight, so how could I be possessed?"

"Don't come any closer," Bai Du cautioned him, holding out her hands. "Maybe not physically, but who knows about your heart and soul?"

"I know," Yuanbao insisted, thumping his chest. "My heart is a couple of ounces of flesh, filled with pure thoughts."

"I still say exorcism is needed," Sun said. "If your thoughts are so pure, there's nothing to be afraid of. If it's as he said, you can be transformed; if not, you can be strengthened. We must guard against sinister possibilities."

"Impossible!" Yuanbao complained. "Ever since I was a kid, I've taken Pagoda Candy worm medicine. And if a measly roundworm can't survive inside me, a living demon doesn't stand a chance."

"How much do you know about the Immortal Zhang?" Bai Du asked Sun.

"Quite a bit." he replied. "An old woman who lives at Su Family Heap in Beijing's Haidian district. Stolen by a demon as a child, she wasn't returned for a whole year. If anyone can drive the thing out, she can. She knows every demon south of the Great Wall and north of the Yellow River, knows them by name."

"Is she human, or is she a demon herself?"

"Somewhere between man and demon. She mixes easily with them both. And even though she doesn't work like other people, she eats people food. Back when the Japanese demons were passing through minefields laid by the Eighth Route Army, they tied her to a goat and sent the two of them across first."

"There's a demon, I know there is. I smelled it the minute I walked in."

A rustic, bound-foot old woman all in white—white robe, white slippers, white hair—and carrying a wooden, tasseled sword, strode grandly into Yuanbao's dorm room, casting glances from side to side and sniffing the air.

Yuanbao jumped to his feet and said ingratiatingly, "Open the window and air the room out before you start sniffing around. I just shit my pants."

"You could smash rotten eggs all around the room, and I could still smell the demon in you," the old woman said with a contemptuous snort. She continued her inspection of the room, looking into every nook and cranny.

Sun Guoren, a cigarette dangling from his mouth, eyed the old woman, then turned to look at Bai Du, an enigmatic grin on his face.

Glaring back at him, Bai Du followed the old woman around the room, not sharing Sun's glee.

The old woman reached out to touch the windowsill. Her white glove was sullied by the thick layer of dust. "This room is filthy. No wonder there's a demon here."

"Here's what we'll do," she said, turning to face the other occupants. "First, we determine who the demon is; then we'll figure out who's best to get rid of it. Demons aren't afraid of just anybody. Like people, they have their own particular mortal enemies."

"Go right ahead. You hold the magic in this room," Sun said. "Stand back, everybody, and give her room to do her thing."

"Do you have a cassette player?" The old woman produced a tape cassette. "We need to play this first."

"Yes, we have. I got one just for you," Sun said as he fetched a player, inserted the cassette, and pushed the Play button. Funereal music filled the room, and when they looked over at the old woman, she was already swaying to the music, eyes closed, waving her wooden sword in the air, and humming to the melody. Then she began to sing:

Ah, how splendid . . . the storm has passed, the sky is clear again. . . .
I look to the left right ahead behind see nothing but a sea of people
*   and traffic jams*
I see a village but not the people in it
My tears splash like eggs thrown into a grove of artemisia. . . .

The music sped up, now tense, now relaxed, the melody getting weirder by the minute, her words growing increasingly disjointed, until they made no sense at all.

The old woman's dance also grew frenetic—hips shaking, arms swirling, shoulders heaving. One minute she soared like a hawk; the next she reached into a well for the moon like a monkey, or did a split, with her rear foot touching the back of her head. Her sword twirled like a silver chain, chilled air hugged her body, soughing icily. Whether her head lurched downward or was tucked between her legs, her every word rang out clearly, gloomy yet vigorous. She was a dragon; she was a dog.

"Swords glint for a thousand *li* vengeful eyes fill nine cities maybe you cannot open your eyes any man of true mettle should battle for years amid the storms of war. . . ."

"This must be one helluva spirit," Sun Guoren whispered to Yuanbao.

"That's what I was thinking."

The old woman began the inquisition:

"Zhang Three, tell me, where is your home? . . . Why have you left your home and your beloved wife? . . . There's no enmity between us, so why did you make me lose face and live a life of shame?"

"There, I know who it is," she said as she abruptly broke off her routine and returned to normal. She wiped the sweat from her face and turned to Bai Du, who was recording everything on a second machine. "Rewind the tape," she said. "Turn up the volume, and listen."

Bai Du rewound the tape, turned the volume all the way up, and hit the Play button. The old woman's song filled the room.

"Zhang Three, tell me, where is your home?"

The loud hum from the tape recorder suddenly gave way to the weak, distant sound of a male voice. It evoked a mixture of sadness and anger, but was clear and distinct.

"Tangyang in Henan Province."

The old woman's voice: "Why have you left your home and your beloved wife?"

"... Wind and Waves Arbor ..."

"My God, it's Yue Fei—Yue Fei!" everyone in the room blurted out.

"There's no enmity between us, so why did you make me lose face and live a life of shame?"

"Go with your feelings...."

"Go with your feelings?" Yuanbao erupted. "What the fuck does he mean by that? What possible similarity in feelings could there be between a great general like him and a small potato like me?"

"I beg the immortal to show the way," Bai Du entreated the old woman.

"What is your ethnicity?" she asked as she lit a cigarette, looking at Yuanbao out of the corner of her eye.

"Me?" Yuanbao thought for a moment. "Manchu."

"That explains it. General Yue's feud is with you non-Han people."

"But the five ethnic groups formed a single republic long ago. We were all but wiped out by you folks once."

"But General Yue doesn't know that."

"Maybe he knows, but he let his emotions get in the way."

"Immortal," Bai Du said with a frown, "would you talk to Mr. Yue for us? Yuanbao belongs to the three lower banners, and has never participated in any military action. I think the old gentleman would feel better attaching himself to a member of the Manchu royalty."

"Easier said than done. Everyone here is aware of General Yue's martial abilities. Unless he wants to leave, trying to get him to do so by force might well exceed the powers of all the deities combined."

"Bring Jin Wushu!"

"It's worth a try," the old woman said as she dropped her cigarette to the floor and ground it out with her foot. "This lad's going to have to suffer a bit," she said with a look at Yuanbao. "String him up!" she demanded.

Yuanbao was hung from an overhead beam, arms and legs bound, over a blazing fire. The old woman, dressed in white armor, sword in hand, made as if on horseback. Galloping up to a spot directly beneath Yuanbao, she brandished her sword and reined in her horse; her eyebrows arched up menacingly, her eyes widened, and she shouted:

"I am Jin Wushu, Fourth Prince of the State of Jin. You, there, Yue. Dismount and surrender, and be quick about it!"

"Jin Wushu can go fuck himself!" Yuanbao cursed as the thin bindings cut into his flesh. "Who the fuck do you think you are? Jin Wushu, my eye! You're no better than the dirty sole of a shoe."

"How dare you curse me, get a taste of my sword!"

A frenzy of hacks at Yuanbao exploded from the old woman. Poor Yuanbao yelped, "Go easy with that thing, old woman!"

Yuanbao lay faceup, tied to a bench. The old woman sat astride him, smacking him on the rump with one hand, scratching his mouth and pinching his cheek with the other.

"I am Zhao Gou, prince of the Great Song dynasty. Retreat, and be quick about it, Yue!"

Yuanbao glared at the old woman, his eyes red with anger. "You'd better never let me up from here, because if you do, I'll burn down your house!"

"You've got a smart mouth! I always knew that sooner or later we'd be arrayed against each other."

The old woman slapped him.

"No good, I can't talk it out of him and I can't beat it out of him. The bones of Yue Fei are hard as steel," the old woman said breathlessly, as she rolled up her sleeves and picked up her sword.

As Yuanbao lay bound to the bench, Sun Guoren piled bricks onto his feet. Poor Yuanbao screamed bloody murder:

"I'll get you one of these days, you bunch of assassins!"

"Rip out his fingernails! Brand him with a red-hot poker! Rub salt in his wounds!" the old woman said to Sun, gnashing her teeth.

"None of this is working," the exasperated old woman said finally to Bai Du. "I guess the only thing left is to wrap him up, coat him in oil, and burn him at the stake."

"Think harder. Isn't there someone we haven't summoned so far?" Bai Du asked.

"I've asked everyone who might come. Wait a minute! . . ." The old woman smacked herself on the forehead. "How could I have forgotten him? Stop everything and give me some room." She straightened her clothes and, as her head began to sway, she flicked her wide sleeves and goose-stepped her way up to Yuanbao.

"Generalissimo Yue, do you know who I am? I am Qin Kuai, prime minister of the Great Song dynasty."

Straining to lift his head, Yuanbao stared at the old woman. "Prime Minister, spare me . . ."

Yuanbao passed out.

"All right, now you're talking!" Everyone clapped and jumped up and down. "Prime Minister Qin, we've found the right person."

Yuanbao's bonds were loosened and he was lifted off the bench. Sun Guoren sprayed water in his face. Yuanbao came to; his eyes snapped open.

"How do you feel?" Bai Du asked him solicitously.

"This old woman must have worked in the torture chamber of the Sino-U.S. Intelligence Agency during the war," Yuanbao blurted out before losing consciousness again.

"What possessed you to treat Comrade Yuanbao like that?" Zhao Hangyu railed at Bai Du as they rushed along the hospital corridor. "Under certain circumstances, a punch or two might have been called for, but within limits. Like a mother spanking her child."

"That's exactly what we did, a mother spanking her child."

Zhao was all smiles when he stepped into Yuanbao's hospital room. He reached out with both arms. "Sorry I'm late, Comrade Yuanbao. We've put you through hell."

Yuanbao's lips quivered before he burst into tears and, like a little boy, buried his head in Zhao's embrace. Holding Yuanbao with one arm, Zhao patted his gauze-swathed head with his free hand.

"Go ahead, cry, get it out of your system. Once you're outside, there can be no crying, not a single tear to show the world."

Zhao gave Bai Du a sign with his eyes for her to leave the room.

Bai Du slipped into the corridor, where she leaned against the door frame to catch her breath and calm herself. Then she turned and went back in, where she was treated to the sight of Yuanbao and Zhao chatting and laughing together.

Zhao was beating a rhythm with his hand and singing, joined by a radiant-faced Yuanbao, who was gazing out the window at the sunny sky:

"The little chick goes peep-peep-peep, the young swain seeks a lovely bride . . ."

"Look at you two, one old man and one young one," Bai Du said with a smile.

"Say there, Yuanbao," Zhao said, "it makes sense that Generalissimo Yue possessed your body, and not because of that tale of rubbish the old witch spun about a feud with the Manchus. He had the words 'Loyalty to the Nation' tattooed on his back, and that's where the two of you are alike. You share in his glory. You must learn from Generalissimo Yue. Treat your comrades with the warmth of spring, and your enemies with the harshness of winter, cruel and relentless."

"So we shouldn't drive Generalissimo Yue away if he returns, is that it?"

"That's what I think. How about you, Bai Du? It's worth a try."

"Our friend has undergone a true test, and has come away stronger than ever."

The praise invigorated Yuanbao, who jumped down off the bed, flexed the muscles of his good arm, and shouted, "I can eat ten pounds of meat and shoot an arrow from the strongest bow."

"Mama!" Zhao and Bai Du nodded in enthusiastic agreement. "The skinniest camel is bigger than any horse. A single hair on your leg is thicker than our waist."

An array of wristwatches, gym shoes, tea mugs, cigarette lighters, stationery, and other objects, each with its own numbered card, was displayed atop a rectangular table covered with red cloth.

The auditorium was packed with men and women of all ages, craning their necks to see the objects on the stage.

A bell rang out, and the presiding officer emerged from the wing, in coat and tails, wearing white gloves. The audience broke out in applause, to which he responded with a deep bow, then stepped up to the microphone and picked up a gavel.

A large man in the same attire, holding a wooden pointer, took his place behind the table, to which the audience responded with another round of applause.

"I declare the auction open," he announced. "Item number one, a wristwatch."

The man behind him picked up the watch with his pointer to show to the audience.

Gripping the podium with both hands, the presiding

officer turned to look at the item. "We have here a Gemstone wristwatch with a stainless steel back, worn by Tang Yuanbao for eight years, accompanying him through good times and bad, witness to many important historical events. Who'll open the bidding at eighty yuan?"

Thunderous silence.

"Seventy-five."

Not a murmur.

"Seventy, then."

And so it went.

"Twenty-five yuan."

In the back of the hall, a woman's hand, rings on nearly every finger, went up.

Bang! The presiding officer's gavel hit the podium. He pointed to the woman. "Sold, for twenty-five yuan!"

With a flick of his pointer, the man behind the table sent the wristwatch soaring above the audience, landing precisely in the woman's lap.

"Item number two, a pair of plastic Liberation sandals that adorned the feet of Tang Yuanbao for eight years, taking him down the perilous road of life. . . . Who will give me three-twenty for the pair?"

"Did the owner have athlete's foot?" one of the auction-goers shouted from his seat. "They're not worth that much if he did."

"The answer is no," the presiding officer replied courteously. "I've been told that, except for normal sweating, Tang Yuanbao's feet showed no visible defects."

"I'll give you two-fifty," the man said.

"Sold, for two-fifty!"

As the gavel came down a second time, the pair of plastic

sandals soared above the audience and landed in the new owner's lap.

"Item number three, a pair of army boxer shorts. The original owner suffered neither from syphilis nor AIDS. He was free of hemorrhoids and ringworm, never wet the bed, never had a wet dream; except for a slight discoloration, they're spotless. These two holes in the back are a unique design, carefully crafted so the wearer can put them on backward, if he wants, speeding up the dressing and undressing process to keep lice away and the bedbugs from finding a home, like no other underpants in the world . . . one-seventy is what we're asking."

The auction progressed.

"Item fifteen is a self-criticism in Tang Yuanbao's own hand, dealing with how he had bullied some of his young classmates. . . . You can have it for ninety-nine cents. . . ."

Liu Shunming, a sack of flour slung over his shoulder, pulled back a door curtain and entered the shack, followed by Zhao Hangyu and some men in army greatcoats. "Our leader has come to see you, ma'am," Liu said to Yuanbao's mother, who was sitting on the bed playing poker with some other old ladies. He laid down his sack of flour.

Zhao Hangyu walked up and shook hands with her. "Please don't get up; I just came to wish you a happy new year."

"It's so nice of you to think of me, busy as you are. But you really didn't need to come. I'm more uneasy seeing you than you are seeing me."

The shabby interior of the shack saddened Zhao. "After all these years," he said, "the lives of the masses haven't improved much."

"This has been a bad year. We were doing better before."

The visitors sat around a table in the shack making stuffed dumplings. Zhao Hangyu put the finishing touches on a perfect little dumpling and asked Yuanbao's mother, "Is there anything you need, ma'am? Like some winter clothing?"

"I've scavenged enough here and there to keep me from freezing."

"You need to have faith. Maybe if you ran over and helped with the rebuilding, you know, gave them a hand, you'd have all the food and clothing you could ask for."

"I can't allow myself to rely on others. . . ."

"I'll come see you often."

"You'd do better putting me out of your mind altogether."

"Don't talk like that," said Liu Shunming.

"Take it easy." Zhao Hangyu stopped Liu from losing his cool. "I understand why the masses are complaining. We haven't done our job well enough."

"May I be so bold as to ask, does the government know what you're up to?"

"What kind of people do you think we are, ma'am?"

"I don't know what to say about a big, well-fed fellow like you, but Commander Liu here reminds me of a bandit in the revolutionary play *Taking Tiger Mountain*."

A statue of old man Tang in a fighting stance, front leg bent at the knee, rear leg at a stiff angle, sword raised menacingly over his head, fire in his eyes, stood at the museum entrance. Some of the shackled men behind him had lowered their powerful heads, while others were raising wine cups and howling at the heavens. Foreign soldiers and Manchu officials groveled and clawed the ground at their feet.

"Three swords hung above the heads of the poor in the damnable old society. . . ."

Tang Yuanfeng, pointer in hand, was standing in front of some photographs in the exhibition hall, lecturing to a crowd of children with red bandannas around their necks.

"Take the province of Shandong, for instance. Among the three hundred sixty or more households in Liyuan Hamlet, in the heart of Guan County, only twenty-eight owned a hundred or more acres of land. Or take Beijing. In the area south of the Xidan Archway, on either side of the Xuanwu Gate, over a hundred families paid rent to the West Warehouse Church. Back then a popular song went, 'The foreigners entered China, their lackeys stood up. Braced by the imperialist forces, they took up the foreign religion and knew no shame as they replaced the portraits of our ancestors.' "

Zhao Hangyu led Liu Shunming, Sun Guoren, and the others up to a spot behind the children and looked at Yuanbao's sister with gloom in their eyes.

"Just look at her, a real pro at that."

"Oppression anywhere will give rise to resistance." Yuanfeng struck her pointer against one of the photographs. "See here: Fearful thunder that rocked the world! In 1899, in western Shandong, the Boxers mounted an insurrection in Pingyuan County. . . ."

As she launched into her explanation, Yuanfeng pointed to more photographs and to objects in the glass display cases.

"Here you have a teapot and a bench used by the Boxer warriors when they rested after practicing their martial arts. . . . This is a photograph of the Boxer chief, Tang Guotao, enjoying life after Liberation. . . ."

The children, bright-eyed and eager for knowledge, followed the movements of her pointer and copied down every word in little notebooks.

"This large rectangular table was used by the Boxer leaders for their strategy sessions. . . . Here we have an iron wok used by Red Lanterns to make flatcakes for the warriors who slaughtered the enemy at the battle at Langfang. Notice the black marks caused by explosions of imperialist artillery. . . ."

"I'll be goddamned. Every piece of the Tangs' junk is now a museum piece."

"This is an undershirt worn by a Boxer warrior . . . a wine bottle used by one of the Boxer warriors. . . . This photograph shows the ruins of the house belonging to Tang Guotao and his family, which was destroyed by the imperialists. Now look over here, at examples of the lordly, luxurious, loose, and idle lifestyles of the imperialists and feudal emperors. Here you see a black cassock worn by imperialist missionaries and one of their Bibles, with which they poisoned the minds of the Chinese people. . . . Here we have a pair of ivory chopsticks and a gold-etched ricebowl used by the feudal emperor. . . ."

"Study these well, learn from them," Zhao Hangyu said emotionally as he surveyed the objects displayed in front of him. "This is art," he continued, "displayed openly, a complete collection, imaginatively arranged."

"Now look at part four. A single spark can start a prairie fire. The Chinese race can never be killed off, nor frightened into submission. Twenty years later, in the city of Nanchang, the sounds of war once again rocked the entire world. . . . Note the Hanyang rifle used by a soldier in the Red Army. . . ."

Zhao and his henchmen left the group of children to tour the other wings of the museum—where items from China's revolutionary history and documented achievements of socialist construction were on display—before tactfully returning to where they had started.

Contingents of youngsters, each under the supervision of their teachers, streamed in and out of the museum wings.

"Every one of those little darlings is money in the pocket," Zhao said with a sigh, pointing to the children with his chin, his hands clasped behind his back. "I'll bet the popsicle peddlers around town are losing a bundle these days."

His followers held their tongues.

"How much did we take in from the auction?"

"A little over a hundred," Sun Guoren admitted forlornly.

"Now I'm not criticizing you people when I say that raising money is an art form. We gained the upper hand when we took our captive alive. And what did you do about it? You made a mess of things, that's what!"

Bong bong bong—A little monkey in a full-length robe with a rope tied around its neck circled the area beating a cymbal. The presiding officer stood in the center of the ring, flicking his sleeves and brandishing his fists at the circle of bystanders.

"If you've got the money, toss it over; if not, just enjoy the show. This person has asked, 'What kind of show are you going to give us?' And I say, Showing you how the Eighth Route Army routed the Japs wouldn't be anything new. How about this? I'm going to show you something you've never seen before."

"Ohhh—" The crowd roared.

"Yes, that's right," the presiding officer said with a deadpan look, his heart not so much as skipping a beat. "This person just said, 'Quit your boasting. What could my buddies and I not possibly have seen before? Arson, burglary, skyjacking, bank robbery, the four great dangers, the four great acts of courage, the four great revulsions, the four great delicacies—go ahead, count 'em!' So I say, Not so fast. How does the old adage go? *Give only the hint of a smile to strangers; don't let them see what's in your heart.* There are skies beyond this sky, mountains beyond that mountain; nothing is too bizarre for this vast world, the universe is boundless. How about the SST or test-tube babies? Life is mysterious and endless, so let's not be in too big a hurry to boast. There's no limit to man's innate ability to explore."

There was a smattering of applause from the circle of onlookers.

"Thank you," the presiding officer said with a cocky flick of his hair. "This person," he continued in a different tone of voice, "said, 'You're spraying saliva all over the place, like clouds and mist covering mountains, nothing but a load of bullshit. You wouldn't be looking to transfer money from our pockets to yours, would you? We know that trick, because we've been playing it since we were kids. It's old hat.' And I say, That's where you're wrong. You don't know how lucky you are. For the first time in your lives, you've met up with a person who loves the truth and hates money. But it's easy to understand why you don't believe me, since I myself don't. Whether it's real or phony, whether it will stand the test of time or pass from view ignominiously, let others judge. If it's your money I'm after, I'm a son of a bitch! All I seek is the rare opportunity to meet you. All I want is to have a good time. What can I say? We were fated to meet."

"Hey, what I want to know is what you're going to show us! If you want a soapbox, go to Hyde Park!" one of the bystanders shouted.

"This person asked, 'Why must you insist on talking instead of giving us a demonstration? We've been standing here for half an hour and we haven't seen a thing.' I say, Talking and demonstrating both have their place. But the martial arts are more than just talk. There, I've had my say, so now it's time to start the show, which is why you're here. I have one request: If you like what you see, your donation will be appreciated."

"What are you gawking at? Stand aside, make room."

Behind the shack, Yuanbao, bundled in an army greatcoat, stood amid a five-legged goat, a three-legged chicken, a pig with horns, and a two-headed snake, while Bai Du painted his eyebrows.

They were surrounded by gawking children.

"How dare you treat the masses like that," Bai Du criticized Yuanbao. "Don't forget who nurtured us. Without the masses, you'd be a big fat zero."

"It's time," the presiding officer announced as he flew over from the staging area. "If we don't start pretty soon, they're going to tear the place apart."

"Okay, let's start." Bai Du took charge. "Everyone do what you're supposed to: lights, music—then curtain."

Amid strains from the score of "Little Sister, Stride Forward Boldly," the five-legged goat ran out pulling a wagon with a furtive-looking, near-sighted, squirming monkey. They were followed by the horned pig, grunting loudly as it lumbered along.

Next came the three-legged chicken, flapping its wings wildly as it landed in the middle of the stage before tossing back its head, thrusting out its chest, and strutting off.

Off to one side, the presiding officer announced exultantly through a megaphone, "If you don't watch, you'll never know; if you do, it's a thrilling show!"

A bear in overalls and a white bandanna emerged, walking on its hind legs and pushing a handcart loaded with bricks. A bespectacled ape with its hair parted down the middle walked out reading a book and cracking melon seeds.

"Dear friends," the presiding officer said passionately, "if what you've just seen hasn't flabbergasted you, I ask you to feast your eyes on the last species to emerge onto our stage. . . ."

The music stopped and was followed by a drum roll as Yuanbao made a vigorous entrance, a greatcoat draped over his shoulders. He stopped and stood ramrod straight, shrugged off the greatcoat and posed for his audience, arms and legs bared for all to see.

More music, louder than ever, drove all the other animals off the stage, which now belonged solely to a smiling Yuanbao.

"What you see before you, this living creature, is a man," the presiding officer announced proudly. "A bona fide, genuine human being. Feel free to touch him, or pinch him, if you'd like, to see if I'm telling the truth. As the popular saying goes, *A three-legged toad is easy to find, a true two-legged man is seldom seen.* Legends of human beings have made the rounds in our country for over two thousand years. But hearing is one thing and seeing is another. Finally, your eyes are going to be given the treat they deserve."

People rushed up to the stage to reach out and touch or grab Yuanbao.

"He *is* different," the discussion began. "Just look at the quality of that skin."

"Look, see how hard he's breathing."

They laughed, they talked, they looked to their hearts' content, and they tossed coins into the hat at Yuanbao's feet.

The music turned joyous, and all the animals returned to the front of the stage, where they formed a line. Those with hands waved hats to the onlookers. But they were ignored; the people were too busy tossing coins to Yuanbao.

"Not a bad show today. We got to see a real human being."

"I hope the guy can hold on a little longer than the others. Not long ago, a penguin arrived at the zoo and died of heatstroke in only a few days."

After a brief but animated discussion, the crowd dispersed.

When Zhao Hangyu drove past the circus tent, what he saw was people lined up under a billboard announcing "Human Body Exhibit." They were patiently waiting for no-shows to turn back their tickets.

"What are they doing?" Zhao asked Sun Guoren, who was sitting next to him.

"Waiting to see a human-body exhibit," Sun answered cautiously.

"How vulgar can you get, taking advantage of the common folks' search for novelties. I don't believe there's such a thing as a 'human' on this earth. It's like a dog-meat peddler hanging out a goat's head. Probably just some monkey with a skin disease."

"What's on display is our own Tang Yuanbao."

Zhao Hangyu was dumbstruck.

"How dare they try to pull a fast one on the masses like that? Phony trademarks are illegal."

"As I see it, we need to sum up the first stage of our work."

10

The same round table had been set up on the stage. The presiding officer, Bai Du, Sun Guoren, Liu Shunming, and others sat with lowered heads.

Zhao Hangyu paced the stage, hands clasped behind his back, followed by a spotlight, which bathed him in brilliance.

"Our work has borne fruit, but problems remain. Some of our comrades' grasp of policy is inadequate, as is their understanding of organizational needs. Once the call for a hundred flowers to bloom is raised, they wash their hands of the matter, and out come all the feudal superstitions and nasty vulgarities you can imagine."

"But didn't you say that anything goes, as long as it works to his advantage?" Bai Du replied, stiffening her back. "As far as I'm concerned, we did our work in accordance with that principle. Anything reactionary or obscene we refused to touch, but that's where we drew the line. Our litmus test was how the masses felt. We put our trust in their ability to distinguish between beauty and ugliness."

"I hear you took Tang Yuanbao to some sort of rally, and by so doing we got complaints from a mental hospital, with inmates asking exactly whom we're supporting. And where our sympathies lie. Even asking why we've taken sides with Trotskyites. Those are not frivolous questions. They demanded that I produce a written guarantee, which I had no choice but to do. I've reminded the comrades over and over that we are a popular organization and that our responsibility is to do our job and do it well, and to stay the hell away from matters over which we have no control."

"When I took him, there was no declaration one way or the other. And I had no prior knowledge that they were a bunch of Trotskyites, holdovers from the Gang of Four. All I wanted was for Yuanbao to be exposed to some people who hold firmly to their political views, passionate, spirited people. It's not like I had a lot of options. I made contacts all over the place, but all everyone talked about was their visits to America. Except for this particular mental hospital, and one or two other places interested in the affairs of Germany. By the time we realized we were off the track, it was too late. But that doesn't mean our heads were in the clouds, Yuanbao in particular, and I admire him for the way he took on his detractors in direct confrontation."

"All right, let's not look for scapegoats. What's past is past, but your leaders want to remind you of something. We are faced with problems that demand our vigilance if we are not to make a serious mistake and fall flat on our faces. Don't wait for something to happen, then blame your leaders for not warning you. Getting to where we are today has been no easy matter, something we should value highly, something worth safeguarding. Don't destroy that over something someone said or over any one individual. That would be stupid, and wouldn't give you a chance to show what you're made of, now would it? Avoid the appearance of being more liberated than anyone, and hold your tongue. Don't come across as a person who doesn't have to worry about being spanked. Anybody can call people names. The way I see it, even if I told you exactly what to do, you'd screw it up. When the Nationalists were in power, I swore at more people than you did—and a guy could have lost his head that way back then. Oh, sure, writers have talent and deserve protection. . . ."

Zhao walked back to the table, where he put on his glasses, licked his finger, and flipped through his outline.

"I've gotten a bit off the mark—so now let me announce the decisions of the MobCom Directorate: The first stage of Tang Yuanbao's training was a disaster, and the Directorate finds it necessary to reorganize the leadership of the work detail. We are removing Comrade Bai Du as primary contractor and selecting a more appropriate candidate for her job. Second, Comrade Liu Shunming's cover has been blown, raising doubts among the masses. The MobCom Directorate therefore recommends that he be relieved as Commander of the Tanzi Lane Security Detachment and reassigned." Picking up a document, he read in a firm voice, "Here are the decisions of the MobCom Directorate!"

Everyone rose and stood at attention.

"Comrade Liu Shunming will assume supervision of Tang Yuanbao's training, and Comrade Sun Guoren will be the new Commander of Tanzi Lane Security. Comrade Bai Du is to be reassigned to the Planning Department as researcher with the title of envoy, at a salary of three hundred silver dollars a month. I look forward to the dedicated cooperation of all comrades. Pro patria."

Zhao laid down the orders, took off his glasses, and smiled.

"Is everyone satisfied with this arrangement?"

"Yes, completely."

Bai Du sat with a long face, while Liu Shunming and Sun Guoren beamed.

"By the way, Shunming, I have one more decision to announce. You need to be mentally prepared. The organization has decided that, in order to redeem our influence in Tanzi Lane and rebuild our prestige there, we need to supplement the announcement of your dismissal from the post by taking you into custody."

"I hereby order the arrest of Liu Shunming, a swindler who passed himself off as a government worker in order to oppress the people!"

This announcement was shouted by Sun Guoren at a "Leniency to Those Who Confess and Severity to Those Who Resist" rally in Tanzi Lane.

Liu Shunming, seated in the front row, was jerked to his feet by two security officers. With three clicks of an abacus, his hat was whisked off his head, his badge of leadership and epaulets removed; then he was disarmed, stripped of his uniform, and unceremoniously dragged away.

"Liu Shunming, the son of a Hunan peasant, has always been an idler, never holding down a proper job. After leaving his village last February, he drifted from place to place, always getting into trouble, and passing himself off as a soldier from

Wang Zhen's Three-hundred-ninety-fifth Brigade. Earlier, during the Jinggangshan period, he was troubled by doubts and began to waver. He asked the question, 'How long can the red flag wave?' How can we possibly keep somebody like him in a position of leadership?"

Zhao Hangyu, Walkman earphones plugged into his ears and a stern look on his face, addressed the citizens of Tanzi Lane.

"Without heaven, how could there be an earth? Without you, how could there be us? In feudal times, officials held sway over the common people. . . . Beyond the window leaves on the tree rustle/Could it be the sound of human suffering? . . . I will smash the rice bowl of anyone who neglects the people's work. . . . You revere your parents for sacrificing all for you, and I . . . erecting a red embroidered tower and throwing down a red embroidered ball . . . ball, ball, hitting a leather ball . . . and hitting me in the head . . ."

"Ha ha—" The crowd laughed heartily. "Give us an aria from 'The Horny Widow Visits Her Husband's Grave.' "

Noting only the laughter and not the shout, Zhao Hangyu was beside himself with glee.

"If you must know, the more you see of me, the more you'll realize that there's nothing to fear. I'm easy to get along with and wise in the ways of the world. I want only to be your friend. I'll give you my phone number. Call anytime for anything. A leaky roof, a stopped-up toilet, no time to feed your kids since you're holding down two jobs, whatever's on your mind. I see visitors every Thursday. Call my hotline at one-one-four."

A loud whistle from someone with two fingers in his mouth split the air.

"Get down from there, you piece of shit!"

"Can the act!"

"Bring that smile down here to me, and bring my troubles with you . . ."

Zhao Hangyu flashed a warm smile at the masses and began doing a folk dance.

"I hear a police siren, my feet weigh a ton/I see the tears in my mother's eyes, and my heart fills with remorse . . ."

"Get some pliers and adjust it a bit. You're way out of tune."

"Thank you very much," Zhao Hangyu blew a kiss to the audience. Holding the microphone and dragging the cord behind him, he paced the stage as if deep in thought.

"Hanging around a dance hall all day long, wandering the streets aimlessly . . ."

"What the hell is that?"

With sad eyes, Zhao Hangyu gazed up at the sky. "I saw a movie when I was young, and learned that a prison is where revolutionaries are locked up. . . ."

"They've made space for you at the prison."

"Thank you, you are the true heroes!" With obvious emotion, Zhao reached out to the masses. He stepped down off the stage and shook the hand of an unfortunate individual sitting in the front row. Then he mounted the stage again and sang some more:

"Where, oh where, is springtime? Where, oh where, is springtime? . . ."

"Won't anyone take charge of this guy?" an angry member of the audience demanded of Sun Guoren and the others, who sat red-faced on the rostrum, shifting their eyes to avoid the scene in front of them.

"I—" Zhao Hangyu thumped his chest and announced to the masses, "—love all of you!" Tears spilled down his cheeks.

Utterly embarrassed, Sun walked reluctantly up to Zhao Hangyu and, with a flurry of gestures, tried to explain the situation to him.

By this time, the masses, under the leadership of Blackie, were already showing their dissatisfaction with a loud, rhythmic chorus of boos.

"Show him what you think, let's hear it!"

"Boo! Boo!"

"Give him a bedpan, that's what he needs—"

"Go home and wash your underwear!"

But Zhao Hangyu was oblivious to what Sun was saying. In a final act of desperation, Sun warded off all Zhao's attempts at resistance and jerked the Walkman cords out of his ears.

As if waking from a dream, Zhao Hangyu finally realized what the masses were shouting.

"Get down get down get down! Get off get off get off!" A booming, syncopated shout from the masses, accompanied by a sea of brandished fists.

"How can they treat me like this?" Zhao asked Sun with obvious disappointment. Then he turned to the masses. "How can you treat me like this?"

Those seated in the front rows made faces at him.

"Piss in a basin, then take a look at your reflection!"

"Reach down and see if there's hair on your cock!"

Paling at the insults, Zhao Hangyu hurled back one of his own: "You goddamned bunch of ingrates!"

The masses hissed to show their contempt, then kept up their taunts: "Get down from there! No one wants to see you!"

Sun Guoren, driven by loyalty, coaxed Zhao, "Maybe you ought to get down off the stage. As they say, 'A gentleman always gets his revenge, even if it takes ten years.'"

But Zhao Hangyu held on to the microphone for dear life, refusing to give it up to Sun.

"I'm not getting down off anything. I'm willing to listen to reason, but you can't push me around. I'll be the one who decides if I get down or not, and I sure won't do it to a chorus of boos."

"I'm not getting down!" he screamed at the masses below the stage. "I am *not* getting down!"

In the car, Zhao Hangyu, so angry his hands shook, said to Sun Guoren, "The residents of Tanzi Lane have shit for brains. Some of their thinking borders on heresy. Their animosity toward us is clear as day. We need to determine if there are bad elements or instigators among them. We'll murder some and arrest the others, if we have to! Then we can educate those who have fallen under their influence, raise their consciousness. We can't allow these dangerous tendencies to undermine our work."

"They really went too far in their treatment of you, old Zhao," Liu Shunming, now in civilian clothes, remarked. "No one's stopping them from making suggestions. If I've made mistakes, I'll face the music, whether it's apologizing, saying I'm sorry, asking for forgiveness, or making compensation. But there's no call to take it out on you, old Zhao, is there? You have to doubt their motives for acting the way they did."

"Taking it out on me is no big deal, since I was prepared for mudslinging when I took on this job. Life or death, glory or insults have never been a consideration. What bothers me is the blind immaturity of the masses. They think that by subjecting me to their vilification, peace will reign throughout the world. If that were the case, I'd willingly offer up my head in apology to my fellow countrymen."

Zhao Hangyu smiled a weary, dejected smile.

"Have you ever heard this fable from Aesop? Once upon a time, a bunch of leaderless frogs begged God to send them a king, and He answered their prayers by sending down a block of wood. Concerned and disappointed that the silent block of wood was incapable of taking care of business, they went up to see God and asked Him to exchange the wood for a king. So he gave them a king, an animal who feasted exclusively on frogs—ha ha ha."

Zhao Hangyu laughed at his own little joke.

"What time is it?"

"Don't ask. It's a long time yet till dawn, and you can forget about getting any sleep tonight."

11

In the interrogation room, old man Tang could barely keep his eyes open. The fat man sitting behind the desk was wide awake and full of energy.

"How about a cigarette?"

"Not yet. You can have one when it's time for *me* to go to bed. Now hurry up and come clean about your history."

"It'd take me all night, and I still couldn't tell you everything. Can't we stop now and pick it up from here tomorrow? I don't expect to ever leave this place anyway, so you can take as long as you need, the rest of my life, if you want."

"Maybe you've got the time, but I haven't. Do you think yours is the only case I have? You've got the rest of the night to make a clean breast of things, and that's all. Count yourself lucky. There are people just begging to talk to me, but I determine their guilt or innocence without giving them a chance to open their mouths."

"Thank you, from the bottom of my heart."

"You can thank me by not wasting my time. Now tell me exactly what happened during the attack on the foreign concession at Purple Bamboo Grove."

"What does the book say?"

"It says you fought with no regard for your own safety, that you forged ahead with demonic courage. 'We frightened the imperialists out of their wits, sent them running with their tails between their legs. But it was too late, they couldn't get away.'"

"This time the book got it right."

"That goes without saying. But what I don't understand is, since you had things so well in hand, why didn't you finish the job at Purple Bamboo Grove?"

"We didn't?"

"No. The book says you were forced to fight your way out of Tianjin, take up positions on the periphery, and continue the fight there."

"Is this the same book?"

"It is."

"Then, it's right, and there's no contradiction. The imperialists couldn't get away, that's what the book says, right? It doesn't say we killed them all. And since they couldn't get away, they had to keep fighting, and after a while, it was time for us to get away, which is what we did."

"What I want to know, then, is, who blocked the imperialists from getting away?"

"Cao Futian. He gave orders to wipe them out."

"What did you do?"

"At the time . . . at the time, I had my troops block the imperialists' escape route and fight to the death."

"So what you're saying is, Cao Futian gave the order, and you carried it out."

"I sure did!"

"I guessed as much. So now tell me why you wouldn't let the imperialists get away. I wasn't overstating the issue when I said it was intentional, did I?"

"I wanted to kill them."

"Kill them? Who was it you really wanted to kill?"

"I know what you're getting at. Don't say you think I wanted to see my own countrymen killed."

"I don't care who you wanted killed, I just want to get at the truth. The imperialists were armed with rifles and cannons. You knew that, didn't you?"

"I knew."

"Do you also know what weapons the Boxer warriors had at their disposal?"

"Yes. They had swords and spears."

"And do you know which is deadlier—rifles and cannons or swords and spears?"

"Of course. Swords and spears are no match for rifles and cannons."

"Since you know that, your intentions were crystal clear."

"Of course my intentions were clear—to kill the foreigners! And that includes those we could kill and those we couldn't. If a toad hops onto your foot, it scares you whether it bites you or not. You have to be an idiot to sleep on a cold brick bed, since it's built to have a fire underneath. If we'd wiped our asses with a window screen, the imperialists would have seen right through us."

"The issue is clear as day, so you can dispense with the empty boasts. Now let's move to the second item . . ."

"What's clear as day? I don't think you understand one bit."

"That issue is closed. Let's move on. My next question is, according to old records, on at least one occasion you rustled a peasant's livestock. . . ."

"I did not."

"Don't be pigheaded! Did you or did you not tell your subordinates to commandeer all the farm oxen from Gao Family Village during the busy season?"

"I commandeered those animals to lay land mines in the foreign concession."

"I don't care why you did it. I have just one question. Did you pay for the oxen?"

"You're being unreasonable."

"Who's being unreasonable?"

"Who? Gramps says he's right, Grandma says she's right. I've got my way of looking at things, you've got yours. And right now we're talking about mine."

"Tang Yuanbao, did you see Director Zhao's order?"

"I saw it."

Liu Shunming, dressed in a Western suit and holding his hands over his privates, stood stiffly in front of Yuanbao as he coldly admonished him. The new team stood equally stiffly behind him, a line of beautiful women, all of them a head taller than Liu.

"From today on, you are to take orders from me. I will orchestrate your every move. Let's dispense with the nastiness first. Since I took on this job, nothing anyone says is going to bother me. Life or death, glory or insults, have never been a consideration. Get ready for trouble, prepare yourself for danger. Don't think things are going to be as easy as they were with Bai Du."

As he paced the floor, Liu kept stopping to look over at Yuanbao.

"I place great store in loyalty; so long as you do as I say, we'll get along just fine. But if you disobey me, don't blame me for showing my mean side. You could have the heart of the old man in the sky, and if cutting it out or slicing it up was called for, that's what I'd do."

"I'll do as you say, why wouldn't I? I just want to be left alone."

"Now that's what I want to hear."

Liu Shunming smiled, raised up on his toes, and patted Yuanbao on the shoulder.

"Stick with me, and you won't be sorry. I've always taken good care of my cadres. If you don't believe me, ask them; they're right behind me."

"Every word's the truth," the girls said in unison. "Commander Liu has never treated us like outsiders."

"Don't call me Commander Liu," he said with a smile and a modest wave of his hands. "Since I've stepped down, you can just call me old Liu."

Tang Yuanbao straightened his new suit in a full-length mirror, turning from side to side, even looking at his back.

Liu Shunming, still in his pajamas, appeared in the mirror beside him. "What do you say? A good fit?"

"I love it," Yuanbao said with a bashful smile as he turned around. "But it cost so much. I can't help feeling . . . you know."

Liu Shunming laughed. "For you, anything."

One of the serving girls walked up with a pot of coffee, a pitcher of cream, and a sugar bowl.

"Come on, let's go back to bed," Liu said, tugging at Yuanbao. "We have to drink this coffee in bed."

"I haven't brushed my teeth," Yuanbao said.

"For this, everything has to be natural. Otherwise, it's all wrong."

Liu pulled back the covers, climbed into bed, and leaned against the headboard. After taking off his suit, Yuanbao joined him.

The serving girl brought the coffee over. "Sugar?"

"Not for me," Liu said affectionately, taking the cup from her. "Thank you," he said with a nod.

"Me either," Yuanbao said as he took the other cup. He, too, nodded and said, "Thank you."

Holding their saucers in one hand and cups in the other, the two men sipped their coffee, teeth hidden behind their lips, then jiggled their cups to churn up the grounds and exchanged satisfied smiles.

"Like it?"

"It's delicious."

"How does it compare with bean milk?"

"Night and day."

"Now you can see that my style is different than most people's, can't you?"

"I sure can."

After finishing his coffee, Liu Shunming chewed on the grounds and smacked his lips contentedly.

"I plan to Westernize you from head to toe. We learn from the barbarians how to defeat them. We'll take it one step at a time. You have to learn all the etiquette and customs of civilized society. Naturally, if your background weren't so wanting, we'd be speaking English already."

"Oh, I already know the basics—How doo yoo doo?"

" 'Sanking you belly mooch.' That'll never do. My English isn't very good either. I can't seem to lose my French accent."

"It sounded pretty good to me. What do we do next, my dear?"

"We have breakfast with some extraordinary people, that's what."

In a grand, sun-splashed dining hall, a party of neatly dressed boys and girls sat at a long table covered by a white tablecloth, snow-white bibs tucked under their necks, knives in one hand, forks in the other, as they dug in fashionably, quietly, unhurriedly cutting up fried eggs on the plates in front of them. The muted sounds of cutlery were accompanied by whispered "Thank you's," "Pardon me's," and "Be my guest's."

A gentleman in miniature sat at the head of the table. Looking to be no more than five or six years old, he nonetheless was the most stylish, most poised member of the party. Suddenly he frowned and, in a show of impatience, threw down his knife and fork, tore off his bib, and lashed out at the half-eaten eggs in front of him:

"They're overcooked, their nutritional value ruined."

"Want to send them back for some more?" Liu Shunming asked apologetically.

"Forget it. I could send them back a hundred times, and they'd still taste the same. I'll just make do. I guess I expected too much."

"How about some appetizers?" Yuanbao asked warmly.

The little gentleman responded with a quick glance at Yuanbao, then looked away. Liu Shunming stared daggers at Yuanbao, who lowered his head, ashamed of himself.

"I just returned from America," the little gentleman announced to the other youngsters around the table, "where I visited a number of places, mostly in the South. I had hoped to travel a bit more, but since I had to hurry back for a meeting, I cut short my trip. I had a conversation with the head of the American Arts Council, and had a chance to see Mickey and Minnie. They send their regards. When the conversation turned to literature, they told me that American writers have plenty to worry about, since so many readers are turning to popular works, and a significant number of serious writers have all but given up writing. They're quite envious of the prosperity our writers enjoy, with their steady salary and all. They praise us to the skies, a poor country willing to support a whole cadre of writers. That could never happen in America. They pay close attention to Chinese literature, which, they say, is the hope of literature all over the world."

"See there, did you hear that? If that's what the Americans are saying, what sense does it make for us to feel inferior?"

"It's all up to us. We can't let our people down."

Liu Shunming and Yuanbao exchanged glances and sighs of veneration, then turned to admire the little gentleman at the head of the table.

"Go on, please."

"In my view, Chinese literature has a long way to go before it takes its rightful place on the world stage." The little gentleman deliberately cleaned his teeth with a toothpick. "Most of our young writers don't measure up. Back in my time, any writer you named had at least a nodding acquaintance with a foreign language. Some had actually taught in a girls' middle school, knew their way around a Western meal, and, in almost every case, had taken private lessons in something. Chinese studies, Western studies, they could handle them both, and quite adeptly. That's what's missing from today's writers. Oh, sure, they make a lot of noise, call themselves new wave, a little modernism here, some root-seeking there, but if you ask me, those so-called modernists are just playing games with our scraps. When we were young, we knew what it meant to do something new. I admit that social conditions were a lot better back then, what with opium dens, whorehouses, gambling casinos, you name it. And America? A dark society, you say? They couldn't hold a candle to our old China. When you talk about eating, drinking, whoring, gambling, and smoking, that China of ours led the rest of the world; we were the gold standard. I've watched some of those hard-core videos that everybody shamelessly salivates over, and I haven't seen anything that couldn't have come from that old novel of ours, *The Golden Lotus*. What I'm saying is, don't be so quick to show off, since we're all more experienced than you, and have a better foundation in being playboys, practicing our evil ways, hooliganism, sedition, stuff like that. You young people nowadays, with all your bluster, think you're so superior. You look down on everybody. But tell me, how many of you could possibly fit the definition of royalty? Back then, we were all the sons and daughters of powerful landlords. At the very least, our fathers served the Qing as Grain Commissioner or Transportation Administrator. What are we competing about, you ask? Being superfluous? Being empty? Being well fed but having nothing to do? The label 'superfluous men' fits us perfectly."

"You're right, you're absolutely right. These youngsters simply don't understand the concept of declining gracefully," said Liu Shunming.

"Whether it fits or not," the little gentleman said, "they steal the first hat in sight and wear it themselves, leaving the old comrades bareheaded. You have every right to live, but so do others."

"They all figure, the more hats the better."

"And it's wrong. That path doesn't stand a chance of saving China," the little gentleman said with genuine emotion. "Back then, we didn't leave home and set out on the path to socialism. No, we had our doubts, plenty of them. We took a wait-and-see attitude, and vacillated between the need for a constitution, for reforms, for a republic. We tried them all, and none of them worked. Don't get the idea that the capitalist system is some panacea leading to a progressive society. Even if you signed Beijing over to Reagan, I doubt he could turn things around. About the most he could accomplish is to place a few more trash cans around the city and throw up a few highway overpasses."

"I believe what you're saying. The Chinese people may seem naïve, but we can be damned sneaky. Dynasties come and dynasties go, but even the Tang emperors and the Song rulers failed to make honest folk out of the Chinese people."

"I tell you from the bottom of my heart, the Communist Party hasn't done badly. I doubt that any other party could have done as well."

"I support the Communist Party, that goes without saying."

"Gentlemen, I say, and ladies, have you had enough to eat?" Liu Shunming looked around the table, where the diners were by now chatting among themselves. He rose from the table, clapped his hands to get their attention, and said, "If everybody's finished, let's retire to the parlor for after-dinner drinks and entertainment provided by a young lady at the piano. You may continue your conversations there. But before you leave, I have something to say. We invited you here today to solicit your views on literature, so please try to confine your discussions to literary topics. We've been extremely pleased with what you've said so far, but please use the little time remaining to best advantage. If there are other things you'd like to discuss, feel free to do so after today's meeting. Or, if you'd like, we can call another meeting on a different topic some other day."

"I want whiskey—on the rocks," the little gentleman said, a long cigar in his mouth. Keeping one hand in the pocket of his vest, he used his other to take a glass from the tray proffered by one of the serving girls and sipped it expertly. He and the young ladies stood around in twos and threes holding glasses in smiling conversations. Some congregated around a grand piano, listening to the recital. The notes washed over their heads in all their loveliness.

"How old are you?" the little gentleman asked Yuanbao after Liu Shunming had introduced them and they had shaken hands.

"Twenty-seven."

"So young. Not bad, not bad at all. Even at your young age, you've accomplished enough to be hanging out with us."

"Oh, but you've been hanging out here much longer than I."

"I'm old," the little gentleman said, pointing to his head. "I haven't got it up here anymore. People of your generation have it all over me. Once people get up in years, no one likes to hear what they have to say."

"That's not so. What you said at the dining table moved me to tears. Couldn't you see how my eyes were fixed on you the whole time? On my way here to the parlor I couldn't help thinking how ordinary talk sounded so much better coming from you. It underwent a complete change. That's something I should learn."

"If you only knew. Old Ma was once the Chairman of the Myna Bird Association. Those birds can talk just like humans, so you can imagine what old Ma could do."

"No wonder; just as I thought. Ordinary people can't measure up even if they try."

"Flattery will get you nowhere. I may be getting on in years, but that hasn't affected my mind. I can still tell the difference between talk that's honest and that which isn't. I don't care if all of you think I haven't got a fresh thought in my head, *that* won't shut me up. I'll tell my story to anyone who'll listen. I have no objections to you folks learning from America, so long as you learn something worthwhile. Morality plays a major role in American society, and their artists aren't hell-bent on producing stuff that flies in the face of tradition or is out of the mainstream. Take Hollywood movies, for instance. They're a lot more didactic than anything we produce, but it's done so well it pleases rather than repels. Now that's something worth learning from them—subliminal education. Is something progressive just because it opposes authority or tradition? I don't think so. It's far more taxing to a writer's talent and creativity to figure out how to sing the praises of authority or tradition and attract rather than repel your audience."

When the piano recital ended, the little gentlemen and ladies applauded, bringing an end to the conversation. Liu Shunming and Tang Yuanbao joined the little gentleman in applauding the young pianist. Then two boys took the young woman's place at the piano and knocked out a four-handed rendition of "Hunting Tigers on the Mountain."

"Eyes fixed on America, whose moon is rounder than ours. I ask you, how many people have a real understanding of America? America has hippies. Does that mean we should have them, too? That's different from our wanting an atomic bomb because other countries have one."

Some of the boys called out to Liu Shunming, who left with a "Will you excuse me?"

Just as Tang Yuanbao turned to watch Liu go, the little gentleman dragged him off to the side, keeping his back to the guests and continuing with what he was saying.

"On this latest trip to America, I saw some things that really got to me. Bank robbers stand in line with everyone else, not making their move until they're at the teller's window. No line-crashing for them. Now that's what I call being civilized. That sort of behavior is the greatest loss we suffered during the Cultural Revolution. If good people won't even stand in line, how can we measure up to other countries? Then there's the ethnic question. America isn't a republic with five nationalities. It's the one place where people of all races go to live, the world's melting pot. What more can you say? Here in China we're no match for them. If we don't find a way to solve these two problems, all this dialogue about joining the ranks of advanced nations is nothing but empty talk."

"What were you talking to him about?" the boys asked Liu Shunming. They all kept one hand in their vest pockets and held cocktail glasses in the other; they cast contemptuous glances over at the little gentleman, who was still rattling on.

"That's all he ever does, chase his American dream, and we're beginning to wonder if he's changed allegiances and is now a member of the American Communist Party."

"Call your buddy over here. Let the guy tell his story to the wall, and just ignore him. It's the same old problem, and you're the ones who caused it."

"How would that look?" Liu Shunming asked, feeling awkward. "Aren't we Chinese always talking about saving up good deeds for the next life?"

"If you're embarrassed to call him, we'll do it."

The boys called out to Yuanbao, who turned around. They waved to him, so he apologized to the little gentleman and walked over.

"Tired? You must be."

One of the boys said with a sneer, "You need to pick the right occasion to demonstrate revolutionary humanism."

"You're right. I was starting to get nervous, and I was hoping you'd call me over."

"This is my latest work," Liu Shunming said to the boys as he patted Yuanbao on the back. "What do you think? Spicy or bland?"

"Looks like an angry young man to me."

"I don't think so. More like a member of the lost generation."

"His legs are sort of like structural realism."

"But he's dressed like a postmodernist."

The boys, unable to agree on anything, volunteered their various opinions.

"He looks a little like former president Syngman Rhee of South Korea, but not as handsome."

"Up close he looks like an Aliston refrigerator, except they're cross-eyed, while he's sort of walleyed."

"Shallow, pretentious, sneaky," one of them said critically. "Our kids are a lot better than him."

But some of the others came to his defense, arguing spiritedly with his detractors. "Oh, so what you're saying is, the kids in your families are humans, while the rest of us are turtle spawn, is that it?"

"Stop that, no bickering allowed," Liu Shunming insisted, raising his voice and clapping his hands. "What do you say we play a game? The rules are simple. Each of you is to say something to Yuanbao, but you can't repeat anything someone else has said. It has to be original."

The boys quieted down for a moment, then started:

"Angry young man."

"Member of the lost generation."

"Structure . . . structure . . . structural realist."

"Postmodernist."

The little gentleman stood all alone at the window in the study, playing with a myna bird in a cage.

"Myna myna, say Chairman so-and-so."

A vast warehouse for books; as far as the eye could see, nothing but books, filling every corner.

Liu Shunming led Yuanbao inside, carefully negotiating every step like a Seeing Eye dog. They threaded their way among the stacks, gazing up at books piled to the ceiling. Yuanbao's eyes were filled with awe and confusion.

12

"Sort of like Heaven, wouldn't you say?"

"I've never been to Heaven."

"Well, now you can say you have," Liu said somberly. "Heaven is just like this."

"Really? No wonder some people are willing to go to Hell." In a somber tone to match Liu Shunming's, Yuanbao asked, "Should I be excited?"

"So excited you nearly choke to death! You should be so excited you can hardly contain yourself. And you should feel sublime. Just think who you're with."

"Are sublime feelings the same as feeling dizzy?"

"Pretty much. They're like sisters."

"Then that's what I feel."

"In this place you can become the person you want to be. Anything can be gotten from books. In books there are rooms of gold, in books there is jadelike beauty."

"Are they really that good?"

"You bet. You don't think all those bullshitters were born that way, do you? So tell me, what kind of person do you want to be?"

"An intellectual," Yuanbao said with a bashful look at Liu Shunming. "Am I asking too much? That's my only wish. You don't know how much I envy . . ."

"There's no need to be embarrassed," Liu said with a smile. "I've never met anyone who didn't want to be an intellectual. What could be better? Wherever you go you can hold forth, and you can live a life filled with rich spiritual rewards."

"That's right. And you don't have to fight the foreigners, just engage them in a battle of wits."

"A lifetime of being the conscience and the standard-bearer at the same time. You sure know how to choose a model," Liu said with a laugh, looking at Yuanbao. "Okay, whatever you say."

"So now am I an intellectual?" Yuanbao asked excitedly. "I feel like going out and holding forth."

"Do you think that all you have to do is say it to make it so?" Liu muttered. "You have to strip off several layers before you can become an intellectual. Let me ask you, have you ever heard of an intellectual who doesn't have a history written in blood and tears?"

"I can stand hard work, and miseries don't scare me."

"Okay, let's start from the beginning—bullshitting. Tell the citizens of our great country all about your relationship with books."

Liu Shunming's words no sooner died out than the room was flooded with light. The tall, ponderous book stacks suddenly parted to reveal a rainbow of colors, as a movie camera the size of a cannon rolled up in front of Yuanbao. A host of men and women in windbreakers and glasses, and carrying scripts, strode up; even more men and women in windbreakers and glasses emerged from behind the stacks, carrying a variety of objects. They quickly busied themselves putting the stage in order, measuring the light, and setting up lights.

"This is the director," Liu Shunming said to Tang Yuanbao. "Your master for the time being. Do as she says. Whether or not you get your wish of becoming an intellectual depends entirely on her."

Liu turned and walked off. Yuanbao nodded to the director and all the people in windbreakers, then bowed deeply. The people in windbreakers, busy with whatever they were doing, didn't even look at him. Yuanbao's feelings of inferiority were magnified.

Liu Shunming emerged from the set, and had no sooner lit a cigarette than he was surrounded by a crowd.

"I'm from the toothpaste factory. We'd like to get Tang Yuanbao to advertise our product."

"I'm from the distillery. . . ."

"We make face cream. . . ."

"Don't waste your breath!" Liu cut them off with a wave of his hand. "He gets a hundred thousand per ad. If you've got the money, let's see it. If not, go jerk off."

"How about lowering your price a little?"

"Okay, thirty thousand. How's that?"

Liu walked off, followed by a gaggle of wagging tongues.

"Do we need to go over your lines?" the director asked Yuanbao.

"I don't think so. All I have to do is convince the people of the country to love these books, right?"

"That's right. I can see you're a born actor. What I want you to do is tell the people of the country they're making a huge mistake if they don't buy these books. You need to create a mind-set that people can be idle, but books cannot. If books pile up in bookstores and don't sell, that is a national shame."

"I see what you mean. I'm to turn books into a necessary commodity."

"Let's run through it." The director turned and walked off. She picked up a book—a prop—and tossed it to Yuanbao. "Go ahead, you're on."

Yuanbao caught the book in both hands, but it was so unexpectedly heavy, it nearly bowled him over. "This is one heavy book. It must be crammed full of knowledge."

Yuanbao stood the book up on the floor, then struck a pose similar to the one he used at home when he worked out with a block of stone. He started to take off his shirt.

"No, leave it on!" the director shouted. Then she sized him up. "On second thought, it clashes with the book. Okay, you can take it off. Hey, there, one of you people drape your windbreaker over his shoulders."

One of the men took off his windbreaker and handed it to Yuanbao. He was wearing a second windbreaker under the first one.

"Hold on a second," the director said. "He needs a pair of glasses. I can't stand that look in his eyes, sort of wild, not very intelligent."

The director removed the glasses from a person next to her. The person had a second pair of glasses behind the first pair.

The director placed the glasses on the bridge of Yuanbao's nose, then sized him up again. "That's better, sort of misty."

Yuanbao took a step and nearly fell on his face.

"What the hell? Are those for myopia? Anyone got a pair with plain glass?"

"We're all myopic," they replied.

"I can't believe it." The director sighed and took off her own glasses. "Try mine," she said. "They're plain glass."

Yuanbao put on the glasses, straightened his windbreaker, and held up the book in both hands.

"Look at me. No, no, it's all wrong." The director walked up to him. "What are you holding there?"

"A book."

"No, you're not. How can that be a book? It's a torch, a torch to lead humanity forward, it's the fire Prometheus stole, it's the sun, which warms us and makes us happy, it's blazing rays of sunlight—it is not a book. Now remember that! Let's try it again."

Yuanbao held up the book again; the director raised her hands to show him with dramatic gestures what she wanted. "Move it back and forth," she said, "back and forth, lightly, from left to right. You're bringing light into a world of darkness and chaos, you're calling out to the people to come into the light, to shout and jump for joy in the sun's rays. Now, left foot, right foot, left, right. . . . Cut!"

She remained dissatisfied. "Still not right, too vulgar. You haven't read that book, have you?"

"No."

"That's right, no one has. That's because it's made out of a brick."

Cupping her chin in her hand, she slouched over, frowned, and paced the floor.

"Let's do it this way. Pretend you *have* read the book, that in fact you wrote it. It's a combination of the Bible and *The Second Sex.*"

"Got it," Yuanbao said as he held the book up one more time.

The director clapped her hands. "Back and forth, back and forth, reserved yet bold and unrestrained, passionate but diffident, solemn yet joyful. Like God looking down on earth. Here's the message you want to give: I'm not selling this book, I'm here to save you."

While she was giving Yuanbao directions to wave the book in his hands, she was saying to a photographer: "Take one . . . Action!"

"Wave, back and forth . . ." The director waved her hands along with Yuanbao. *Click click* went the shutter.

Pop. A puff of white smoke rose in the air when a flashbulb went off.

"Cut!" The director stopped moving and wiped her sweaty forehead. "That'll do."

Yuanbao put down the book and walked up to the director. "Madame director," he said, "I was in a different world just then. I didn't see myself as God, but as a little boy."

"I couldn't tell," she said. "Besides, who knows what God looks like?"

"No, I mean it; this is big. I don't want you to have any regrets, so let's do it one more time."

"Don't get too wrapped up in this. If you want your picture taken, we can do that later."

"He acted like it was the real thing," the photographer said with a sneer.

"What do you mean, *like* the real thing? It *was* real," Yuanbao argued. "I'm sorry, madame director. When I'm acting a part, I need to forget who I am in real life. It's a performance."

"That's it, you hit the nail right on the head," the director said to Yuanbao comfortingly. "That's what it takes to be an actor. But don't take yourself too seriously. You did great, but this is just the first of many scenes. Let's go to the next one."

"Whatever part you give me, I'll perform it flawlessly," Yuanbao crowed as he walked back to his spot.

The director took her place again and told him what she wanted:

"This time put the book under your arm. You know how to do that? That's right, snug up against your armpit. Now, raise your free hand in the air and wave it as you turn to look behind you. Good! Now, what's that tucked under your arm?"

"A satchel of dynamite," Yuanbao replied à la Dong Cunrui, the fictional PLA hero, prepared for the ultimate sacrifice.

"You're quite the clever little devil," the director said approvingly. "You're right on the money; that's a satchel of dynamite under your arm, and you're going to blow up the pillbox of the benighted and clear a path to victory for your comrades. Now let's hear you say this: 'I can't live without books.' "

"I can't live without books!" Yuanbao repeated the words passionately, hugging the satchel of dynamite to his chest.

"Press the book up against your face with both hands—my

mother gave me birth, but books have brought light to my heart."

"My mother gave me birth, but books have brought light to my heart."

"What do I lack? Ah, I lack the perfect book."

"What do I lack? Ah, I lack the perfect book."

"Just look how uncultured you are—point to the camera with your finger."

"Just look how uncultured you are!"

"What do you think?" the director turned and smiled at the sound man. "How's the sound?" she asked. "Play it back for me."

The sound man rewound the tape and turned up the volume. The room swelled with the grating voice of Yuanbao:

"I can't live without books!"

"Just look how uncultured you are!"

"It sounds like he's struggling with himself, doesn't it?" the director asked the people nearby, after a brief pause.

"A little bit. And I detect an abusive tone in his voice."

"His voice doesn't cut it," the sound man said, hands in his pockets. "We'll have to dub in somebody else's voice."

"It didn't sound that bad to me," Yuanbao disagreed. "I was just a little nervous, that's all."

"Then go get somebody else," the director said to the sound man. "For now let's hear him count."

"I don't want you to read the script this time," she said to Yuanbao. "One number for each word in the script. Script man, what's next?"

"I only read the most expensive books. Seven words."

"Okay, count from one to seven for me," the director said to Yuanbao. "Take one. Places, everybody."

"One two three four five six seven," Yuanbao said into the camera. "Madame director, something was missing that time. Oh, damn, I forgot the book. No wonder it didn't feel right."

"Forget it, I can edit in a close-up of the book." The director shook hands with Yuanbao. "Thank you, that was a fine piece of acting. Have you done this before?"

"My first time, at least like this."

"Then you're a born actor."

"I've always been good at refining my talents. Ever since I was a kid I've admired and been in awe of movie stars who can convince you that make-believe is real. I told myself that when I grew up I wanted to be just like them, professionally and personally."

"Keep working at it, you'll get there someday."

Yuanbao's book promotion was playing on the TV screen in Bai Du's living room. Yuanbao's mood went from wide-eyed anger to desperate sadness to pensiveness, and was occasionally characterized by a long, drawn-out sigh. The advertising managers who had banged their heads against Liu Shunming's intransigence formed a distraught circle around Bai Du.

"You were once his superior. Won't you put in a word for us, give us some face?"

"Yuanbao is a treasure belonging to the entire Chinese race. How could he possibly become the exclusive property of any one firm? Either everyone gets a piece of him, or no one does. Back when MobCom was being organized, we helped out as much as we could. You can't dump us by the roadside like a bunch of beggars now that the good times have arrived."

"Ai—" Bai Du heaved a loud sigh as she stood up. "You folks should take the long view," she said. "Why is it so important to have Yuanbao in person? Since a video of him is already available, why can't each of you use that as source material? With expert editing, you can add some text for your own products, and no one will be able to tell the difference. Not only will that be cheaper and entail a lot less work, but the end result could well be better than shooting a new ad in the flesh. Can't any of you tell that he hardly moves at all? Remove the background and erase the sound track, and you could convince people that he's having an attack of hysteria."

"Fuck, why the hell didn't I think of that?"

"You said it. All packaged and ready to go."

"You're all too naïve," Bai Du said as she looked into their excited faces. They were like people who had just awakened from a dream. "Much too naïve."

Not a cloud in the sky. A herd of horses is galloping alongside a crystal-clear mountain stream of icy water swirling around bottles of cola brand soft drink. Yuanbao, hugging a book to his chest. A close-up. He throws the book into the stream and fishes out a bottle of cola. A close-up of his face. Yuanbao says, "I can't live without cola."

An elegantly furnished home, complete with every imaginable electric appliance, except in one empty corner. Yuanbao hugs a book to his chest, deep in thought. "What do I lack?" he asks. A refrigerator descends from nowhere and is slotted into the empty corner. "Ah, I lack the perfect refrigerator."

Yuanbao hugs a book to his chest and points off camera. "There's more to life than reading books." The camera shifts to a scene of men and women drinking wine from an array of colorful bottles. "The true hero drinks without getting drunk!" a voice says.

Liu Shunming threw back the covers and climbed out of bed. Standing there naked, fists clenched, he stared in absolute stupefaction at one commercial after another, verbalizing his disbelief in a single repeated utterance: "Oh, my God!"

Yuanbao buries his face in a book and says with profound emotion: "Whenever I get tired of reading, my thoughts turn to the East and to Chill-Way refrigerators."

The director threw back the covers and climbed out of bed. Standing there naked, fists clenched, she stared in absolute stupefaction at one commercial after another, verbalizing her disbelief in a single repeated utterance: "Oh, that motherfucker!"

Perfume bottles, bath oil, cosmetics, a feast for the eyes. Foamy, clear saltwater spray; tender, lovely skin; a pair of fetching eyes; the camera sweeps past an array of skin products and stops at a bar of translucent, velvety bath soap.

Yuanbao looks into the camera and says with an air of tranquility: "Lux is the only bath soap I use."

13

Liu Shunming, eyes bloodshot, sat on the edge of the bed, a damp towel wrapped around his head. "You betrayed my trust," he said to Yuanbao, who stood penitently in front of him. "You've ruined me. How will I face my literary friends?"

Tears welled up in Liu's eyes, but he kept them from spilling out by force of will. "You've ruined yourself, too," he said. "You can forget your dream of becoming an intellectual. They've booted us both out."

"I accept the consequences of my actions. None of this was your fault." Yuanbao was so angry he could barely contain himself.

"How many people are as reasonable as you? The intellectuals are mad as hell. They say I should have kept a tighter rein on you."

"I'll go talk to them. It doesn't matter if they boot me out, but you're an essential part of their circle. You're a true intellectual, and I can't imagine what you'd be if you weren't a member."

"You don't have to fight my battles. Whether I'm a

member of their intellectual circle or not, I'll continue to place strict demands on myself. I'll be content if you become one too, one day."

"Yes, I will, I promise. They might be able to have their way with my body, but they'll never capture my heart."

"Keep working hard at your drills; don't slack off. While I've been laid up sick these past few days, I've given a lot of thought to your training schedule, and I can see there are problems with your boxing moves. Since you want to pass your technique on to future generations, you can't be content with simply applying it. Form is important, too. A true work of art must be both functional and attractive, something that stands the test of time. If all you manage is a bunch of wild punches, you'll be a laughingstock even if you win."

"I agree completely. So what changes are needed?"

"I've thought this over carefully, and in the process, I've abandoned gymnastic exercises and Peking opera acrobatics as inadequate for our purposes. At most, these kindred skills are patchwork enhancements of form and movement, a far cry from truly revolutionary changes. What I'm saying is, enhancing these movements still leaves you with recognizable boxing techniques, and that's about it. Not much to brag about. What's needed is a complete overhaul. Otherwise, forget about change altogether and leave things as they are."

"You're right. If an old lady stays a virgin, no alien invader has ever broached her fortification."

"No, you're missing the point. I'm saying we need change, radical change that turns heaven and earth upside down, a complete rebirth."

"That's right, an old lady stays a virgin—for what?"

"That way there's no need for concern. A turtle tries to

make a meal out of a tiger. If it's successful, it's an historic event. If not, it draws its head into its shell and remains turtle spawn."

"That's right, if an old lady is still a virgin—that's her choice."

"I've made up my mind. We'll blend Big Dream Boxing and ballet. You might as well learn something new. There's no better food than stuffed dumplings, and no better game than mahjong. You and me, we're top of the line."

"That's right. A chimney warms the room, your hindquarters warm the bed. Change is better than no change any day."

"I've decided to get you the best possible teacher and find a quiet spot for you to work out with no interruptions. But you'll have to really work hard for me and turn yourself into someone who will make those intellectuals' eyes pop. With you around, we eat tofu; without you we can't even chew soybeans."

"But where will you find a quiet spot?"

The Museum of Modern Art. Walls were covered with worn-out clothing sprayed with paint, torn cardboard in a mishmash of shapes, and montages of human figures, body parts photographs, maps, and paintings, some like explosions, some like whirlpools, and some like splashes, all slapped and pasted together helter-skelter.

The center of the exhibition hall was decorated by tires, beat-up tables and rickety chairs, a crumpled car, and a scarred window frame. There were also some naked men and women with painted faces and bodies, some standing, some seated, and some walking around striking weird poses, but with blank looks on their faces.

Liu Shunming, still showing the effects of his illness, walked into the hall ahead of Yuanbao, the ballet instructor—an anemic-looking old woman whose chin was as pointy as a dagger—and a bunch of girls she'd brought with her.

The caretaker, a tubby, slovenly old man, walked up and asked hoarsely, "Who you looking for?"

"We've hired this hall," Liu said. "We need space to move around."

"Ah, you must be those good folks who bought up all the tickets. Now I know. Thanks to you, I've got some cornmeal cakes to nibble on."

"In a few minutes, old friend, we'd like you to stand at the door and keep the riffraff out. We don't want anyone to disturb our artists while they're working."

"Don't worry, no one would come in here if you paid them. We went out on the street three separate times to rope in a bunch of modernists, then chained the door behind them so they couldn't get away. They climbed out through the window. You won't find a quieter, more secluded place anywhere in Beijing. Not even the criminal element shows up here."

The old fellow hobbled off.

"Let's not waste time," the ballet instructor said earnestly. "There's lots to do."

Liu Shunming walked over to a usable flush toilet, put the seat down, and sat down to observe a row of colorfully striped backsides.

Yuanbao, the old instructor, and the girls undressed and hung their shirts and pants alongside the worn-out clothing on the wall. Then, dressed in leotards, they formed a line.

The old instructor reached behind her and took out a rattan switch, dipped it into the water in one of the toilets, and tested it against her palm a couple of times before walking down the line and smacking the legs of Yuanbao and the girls.

"Stand straight. Feet together, bodies taut, stomach in, chests out, heads high . . ."

She pointed to problem areas, and wherever her finger pointed, the switch followed.

Once Yuanbao and the girls had formed a straight line, the old instructor took out a handful of pencils and inserted one into each and every crotch.

"Hold them right there, squeeze. The first thing we have to work on is the strength of your inner thighs. Don't let your pencils drop, or you'll get three whacks." She walked up to each of them in turn, a menacing grin on her face. "Don't get the idea that ballet is something you can pick up easily. If I don't take you all to the brink of death more than once, I won't have met my responsibility to you."

The pencil in Yuanbao's crotch dropped to the floor. She followed through on her "three-whack" threat before picking up the pencil and reinserting it. But as soon as she let go of it, it was on the floor again. Three more whacks. Another reinsertion, but with the same result.

"Too thin for you?"

"A little. Why don't we try a basketball."

"I don't have one. What do you think of me?"

"You're a little too thin, too."

"I can see you've worked out before." Gnashing her teeth, she barked, "All right, open stance." She dragged Yuanbao out of line and kicked his feet to spread them, then went around behind and jumped onto his shoulders, putting all her weight into it.

"Now let's work on bending."

Pa pa. She smacked him on the hands.

"Grab your thighs with both hands and stick your head between your legs. Look at me. Smile."

Yuanbao stuck his head as far as it would go and looked up at his own navel. He smiled.

"Good boy, you've got what it takes. Okay, straighten up. Let's try twirling on one leg."

She pinched his shoulder hard, and he began to spin like a top. She stood off to the side, clapping her hands and shouting: "Spin! Spin! Spin! Don't stop!"

Yuanbao spun like a whirlwind, until he was just a blur through which only a pair of eyes showed from time to time.

The old instructor stared at Yuanbao for a long, long time, as a crafty grin spread across her face. "Okay, not bad. Now let's do a dance for two, called a pas de deux. The rest of you stay where you are and hold on to those pencils," she commanded as she spun around to look at the girls, who were about to topple over. Then she snuggled up to Yuanbao, looked into his face, and said, "Put your arm around my waist."

She began to glide like a swan, lowering her head as if preening her feathers. She raised her leg high into the air and waved one hand gracefully back and forth across her mouth; with her other hand she clutched and tore at Yuanbao's mouth.

"Pay attention to my hands," she said. "Now spin me around. Carry me off in your arms. Now lower me gently, then pick me up again. . . . Stop."

Yuanbao let go of the old instructor, who turned to him and said, "Did you get a good look at my movements?"

"Yes," he answered.

"Good. Now you try it. I'll be the man this time."

She reached out and grabbed him by the waist, as if holding back a wagon about to slide down a hill. "Your hand!" she shouted. "Your hand, raise your hand!"

Yuanbao put one of his hands up to the old instructor's mouth and moved his fingers as if scooping out a handful of mud, then kneading it into a ball.

"You're too heavy," she said, letting him down breathlessly. "You're going to have to lose thirty pounds, at least. No more food for you, and I'm going to get you an emetic."

"Anything to make you happy."

"As for you," she said to the girls, "remove those pencils and bend backward as far as you can go. Don't straighten up till I tell you to."

They did as they were told, creating a row of little flyovers.

The old instructor lay on her side, pillowing her head on her arm and curling one leg. The other leg stuck out straight, giving the impression of someone lying drunk in a flower bed.

"Come here," she called to Yuanbao. "Lift me up . . . not like I was a dead baby. One arm under my foot, the other under the leg. That's it. Get a good grip on my thigh; now lift me up. Keep your arms straight. . . ."

As if raising a flagpole, Yuanbao lifted her up by an ankle and a thigh, and held her high over his head. Her hands floated gracefully in the air, her head rocked back and forth; she struck every pose in her repertoire, from death throes to agonized swoons, unwilling to continue but unable to stop, dancing and twisting and spinning until sweat poured down her face, tears ran down her cheeks, and snot dripped from her nose. Yuanbao's face was bathed in sweat.

Liu Shunming, still sitting on a toilet, applauded politely.

The girls stuck their heads out from under their crotches,

cracking melon seeds and chattering away in awestruck praise of the old instructor.

"Thank you," she said as she jumped out of Yuanbao's grasp. "You're the perfect dance partner." With that she turned and walked over to the wall to retrieve her clothes. But just as she reached up, there was a shout behind her.

"Hey, what do you think you're doing?"

The tubby, slovenly caretaker came hobbling up, fire in his eyes, and glared at the old instructor.

"Getting my clothes."

"Getting your clothes?" He looked the half-naked woman up and down, then pointed to the articles of clothing on the wall. "You think you can just take these down? If you can't afford to buy your own clothes, stay naked. Stealing them is not an option."

"What do you mean, stealing? They're mine; I hung them there."

"Old-timer," Yuanbao walked up to explain the situation, "this lady isn't stealing anything. All our clothes are hung up there, not just hers. When we entered a while ago, you saw we were all dressed, didn't you?"

"Don't try to pull a fast one on me, young man," the caretaker said. "I may be old, but I'm not stupid. And I've been a museum caretaker for more than a few years. If you're sick long enough, you become an expert on medicine. I can still tell the difference between clothing and art. Look up there and tell me, which of that is clothing and which is art?"

The girls all turned their eyes to the wall and, sure enough, they couldn't pick out their clothes from the objets d'art on the wall. All just as bright and gaudy, forming a seamless display.

"That answers that. I won't characterize you as a bunch of

swindlers so long as you leave—now." He began hustling them out the door. "You're not youngsters, especially you, madam. You're seventy if you're a day, so it's about time for you to get a new rice bowl and earn a decent living."

"But, but we were dressed when we came in," Yuanbao continued to argue as he was being bum-rushed out the door.

"You've got no complaints, since you're still wearing bathing suits. There are plenty of people out on the streets without a stitch of clothing. You should know that at your age. Once something goes up on our walls it becomes something else, and that's where it stays."

Liu Shunming stood up and started tiptoeing away. The old caretaker spotted him.

"Where do you thing you're going?"

"Back where I came from," Liu answered truthfully.

"And where might that be?" The old caretaker blocked his way and backed him up to the toilet. "Since you're a designated toilet sitter," he said as he pushed him down on the seat, "don't get any funny ideas about skipping out."

"I'm not part of the display," Liu insisted as he squirmed on the seat. The old caretaker held him so he couldn't get up.

"That's not for you to say. My orders are clear: No one disturbs anything in the museum, and I mean anything."

After shooing Yuanbao and the others out the door, the old caretaker locked it behind them. Liu Shunming jumped up and ran to the window, where he clawed at the glass and gazed forlornly at his liberated comrades.

Meanwhile, Yuanbao and the girls hugged themselves and huddled together, then paced back and forth in front of the art museum steps, embarrassed to be seen by anyone.

The old instructor, on the other hand, strode proudly up

and down the street, a grin on her face and daggerlike defiance in her eyes as she returned the gaze of anyone who dared to look at her twice. Those who did wilted under her malignant gaze, their reaction quickly turning from ridicule to terror. Some people, made uncomfortable by the sight and unable to shake off the feeling, actually stripped down to their underwear and, emboldened by their own near nudity, fell in behind the old ballet instructor, where they in turn glared defiantly at anyone who looked their way.

Yuanbao, like a coach exhorting his athletes, barked out orders as he led the girls in a quick-step march home. No one paid them any attention.

Under the streetlights, in one corner after another, young men and women in windbreakers and eyeglasses, individually or in groups, walked around like ghostly figures hugging thick books to their chests and holding bottles of cola. Some stared in wide-eyed anger, others had pensive looks on their faces, and others just seemed troubled.

In a dark, shadowy corner, two old ladies wearing red armbands were whispering. "See there, down that road? Those students are up to something again."

"Gentlemen, I say, gentlemen, it's time to get up."

A hotel attendant in a long Chinese gown stood respectfully at the head of the bed and called out softly.

Zhao Hangyu and Sun Guoren, in bed together, snored on.

"Gentlemen, I say, gentlemen, wake-up time."

Zhao's eyes snapped open in alarm, and he quickly sat up. He began to sweat. His mouth dry as a bone, he managed to say, "Where am I?"

"In the palace," the attendant said with a smile. "Not on the executioner's block."

"Ah—" Zhao let out a sigh of relief and took a deep breath to calm himself. "I was sleeping like a baby," he said, a note of impatience creeping into his voice. "What's the idea of waking me up?"

"It's time," the attendant said, pointing to a clock on the nightstand. "Two A.M. You told me to let you sleep for two hours, then get you up so you can switch rooms."

"Oh, now I remember." Zhao shook Sun Guoren. "Wake up, get up. Now we switch to a Qing-style dragon bed."

Zhao and a sleepy-eyed Sun Guoren climbed off their Simmons mattress and followed the attendant out of the French-style hotel suite into the corridor, which was brightly lit and seemingly endless, with mirrors on the walls and crystal chandeliers overhead. Elegant rooms, all different, opened off the corridor. They were led into a fancy suite with antique Chinese furniture. They climbed into the oversize canopied bed and were asleep as soon as their heads hit the pillows.

Sun, as he was passing into dreamland, had the presence of mind to instruct the attendant: "Wake us at four o'clock to move into the Islamic Mosque."

"Did you ask me why I held back my troops?" old man Tang, by now completely confused, asked the bald, fat man sitting behind the interrogation table.

14

"I was just thinking that the imperialists must have been formidable opponents."

Old man Tang sat up straight and frowned as he tried to dredge up the past. "After we got out of Tianjin," he stammered, "I boarded a ship that took me down the Chaobai River to Gao Family Village, so I could join up with the forces of Liu Nineteen. Now I get seasick just looking at water, and I spent the entire two-hour trip throwing up, even though there wasn't a breath of wind or a ripple on the river. Even after I went ashore, my legs were still rubbery. Before the effects of my seasickness had disappeared, I threw myself into the battle at Beiwa. Commander Liu put some of his best troops under my command and told me to take the men into a sorghum field and wait until I heard gunfire, then count to one hundred and eight before springing an ambush, cutting off the Allied forces' path of retreat. When shots rang out, the Allied forces came charging past me with their rifles and swords, chests thrown out and bellies taut. I was impressed by the way they shouted themselves hoarse as they fought, and I couldn't help thinking that even though they were a bunch of blond, blue-eyed soldiers, they were human beings, just like me. Here I was, seasick after a measly two-hour boat ride on a placid river, while they'd spent days on a ship crossing an ocean just to fight us. As I say, I was impressed. And while I was thinking those thoughts, the battle ended; Liu Nineteen had been captured, trussed up, and spirited away."

"How much time do you think passed? Beijing time."

"How much time could have passed? Tens of thousands of foreigners fighting tens of thousands of farmers in the span of human history is a mere blink of an eye. Besides, I wasn't wearing a watch."

"Then what did you do?"

"Me? The main body of our troops had been wiped out, so what could a hundred or so soldiers accomplish? All I could do is say, 'Brothers, scatter and run for your lives.' "

"Just like that, you dispersed your troops?"

"Just like that. By splitting up and breaking through enemy lines, we could keep the torch of revolution burning."

"That was a criminal act; you know that, don't you?"

"I know nothing of the sort. To knock a wall down, everybody has to push. When the sky falls, it's held up by the tallest heads. Burning houses are the best to loot. You can't break a rock by throwing an egg at it. I did nothing in violation of military strategy. In fact, that's exactly how we won our early victories."

"When you meet a weakling, your anger can't be contained;

when you meet a worthy man, you can't make your legs run fast enough. Is that a fair description of you?"

"Absolutely. And if you put it that way, you've done nothing wrong either."

"Keep a civil tongue! Don't forget where you are."

"How could I dare forget? If I did, there'd be no place for you anywhere between heaven and earth."

"You old traitor, how did you manage to keep from being ferreted out all these years?"

"I'm good at hiding, especially from small fry like you. The truth is, if I felt like it, I could stand alongside the likes of you for generations without giving myself away."

"I think you're tired of living."

"If you'd lived as long as I have—over a hundred years—in hiding, you'd be tired, too, and you'd sure as hell leap out into the open."

"Where's your leader?"

"At an exhibition."

Bai Du and Sun Guoren stood facing Yuanbao, who was shabbily dressed and pale as a ghost, a bundle of nerves and jittery as hell.

"Who sent him? We've got an inspection coming up. I thought he was going to find time to help you warm up. So what possessed him to go out looking for personal publicity?"

"Shunming couldn't help himself; he was detained. Maybe they thought he looked like somebody else."

"Bullshit! There are laws, you know. Is old Zhao aware of this?"

Sun Guoren sighed. "Don't ask. He's already falling apart.

In a single night he slept in eight different rooms and was a nervous wreck by the time the sun came up."

"Ah, life, how it wears you down," Bai Du said. "Here's what we'll do. You try to work things out with whatever organization detained Shunming. Find a way to cut him loose. At a time like this, we can't manage without him. I'll take Yuanbao out for something to eat. There's going to be a sneak preview, and he can't go out half starved."

"Can you think of an excuse to delay the preview?"

"Afraid not. The stockholders have given us an ultimatum. If we don't produce results this time, they're threatening to take us to court for swindling them out of their money."

"How did old Zhao react to that? Did he try to get them to change their minds?"

"He pounded the table and raised hell, but so what? He can sweet-talk them all he wants, but without anything to show for all the money spent, who'd believe his story? The stockholders cast all matters of face aside, and when a person doesn't care about face, it's hard to put anything over on him."

"A mouse can only see an inch in front of its face. We said we were all in the same boat; then those people jumped ship before we were halfway home."

"How are you holding up?" Bai Du asked Yuanbao, whose droopy eyelids showed his exhaustion. "Think you can drag yourself to the nearest restaurant?"

"I could use some malted milk extract."

"Where am I supposed to get a nice tonic like that?" Bai Du took a look around the virtually empty room. "Liu Shunming pawned everything we had for your precious Western meals. For now you'll have to make do with some sugar water."

Bai Du scrounged up a nearly empty sugar bowl and dumped its contents into a glass, then filled it with water and handed it to Yuanbao, who gulped it down in one breath. Licking his lips, he held out the glass. "More."

"This isn't going to work," Sun Guoren said as he cupped Yuanbao's chin to look into his mouth. "He needs nourishment, real nourishment. If we send him out like this, he'll be knocked right back into our arms. He won't pass muster."

"Pull yourself together, Yuanbao," Bai Du demanded as she tried to shake him out of his lethargy. "Don't fall apart on us now. It's only been three days since you ate. The Great Wall hasn't eaten a bite for thousands of years, and it's standing as tall as ever."

"The only things in China visible from the moon are you and the Great Wall," Sun said tearfully.

"I'd like to eat a whole chicken."

"Okay, that's what you'll get. Anything else? As long as it's produced in China, we'll take it out of the tiger's mouth if we have to, and give it to you. To hell with the rest of the Chinese people." Then, drying her eyes, Bai Du stood up and said to Sun, "Yuanbao's getting a decent meal, even if we have to sell pots and pans for scrap metal to pay for it."

A dirty, run-down little diner. Yuanbao, bundled in an army greatcoat, but still shivering, stumbled in the door, supported by Sun Guoren and Bai Du. They sat at a grimy, rickety table.

"Waiter," Sun demanded impatiently as he rapped his knuckles on the table, "bring some food."

A woman seated behind the cash register eyed the three customers, then looked up at the illustrated menu pasted on a sheet of glass above her. She called out to the owner and pointed with her chin to the three people sitting around the table, mumbling something to him. He took off his apron, rolled up his sleeves, and walked over.

"You from MobCom?"

"How did you know?" Sun asked excitedly. "This," he said, pointing at Yuanbao, "is Tang Yuanbao, China's recently anointed superhero. You must have seen him on TV."

"You're Tang Yuanbao?" a young fellow drinking with a couple of friends at the next table turned to ask Yuanbao. "I thought you looked familiar."

"What do you guys do?" Sun Guoren asked with a friendly smile.

"Not a damned thing," the fellow replied. "Just hang out." He returned to his drink.

The owner shook hands with Yuanbao and said to Sun, "You want something to eat, I take it."

"That's right," Bai Du said. "I'm surprised you had to ask. And we're in a hurry."

"How's this, you three mug me instead?"

"What are you talking about?" Sun Guoren was clearly annoyed. "We're here to eat. Why should we mug you?"

"We don't have any food," the proprietor said heavily. "But I've got my life. Now we can all join hands and jump into a cauldron, or we can roll on a pincushion together—you decide. Either way I'm not going to help you out with any food."

"You're afraid we'll stiff you with the bill, is that it?" Bai Du saw what the problem was. "Well, I want you to know we've got the money."

"Okay, let's see it." The owner stuck out his hand. "Pay up front."

"I've never heard of demanding a deposit on a lousy meal!"

Sun bellowed, his face white with anger. "This is racial discrimination! Well, I'm telling you that this is our country, too."

"Why don't you trust us?" Bai Du asked the owner. "Do we look like people who'd skip out on a bill?"

"I won't lie to you. We've received word from people in the restaurant business to be on guard against you three. Your names are on a circular distributed by restaurant owners as freeloaders. Now, I don't know if you've tricked other restaurants out of free meals, but I do know that the manager of the Treasure Palate jumped off a building because of you."

"Come on, let's go," Sun said angrily. "We're not eating in any place that treats us like tramps."

"Leave if you want, sir, but you'll find the same reception everywhere. Circulars with your physical descriptions are posted in every restaurant in the city."

"Ah, hell, we'll pay up front," Bai Du said as she reached into her purse, took out some money, and handed it to the owner. "Sooner or later, all you short-order cooks will regret not giving us a hand when we needed it."

"I'm terribly sorry," the owner apologized as he counted the money. Satisfied with the amount, he shoved it into his pocket. "I've got no choice. I'm still young, and the last thing I need is to go bankrupt without having any idea why. Now, what can I get you?"

"Something very nourishing: donkey dick, dog kidney, pork loin, whatever you've got, so long as it's from the lower body. Chop up some onions and garlic to go with it."

Yuanbao stuffed himself, one huge mouthful after another, until his cheeks puffed out as if he had a mouthful of Ping-Pong balls. He was staring at the plate in front of him.

Bai Du and Sun Guoren watched him eat, their hearts nearly

breaking as they gazed longingly at the forbidden food. Every morsel belonged to Yuanbao.

"The boy's famished."

"Take it easy, not so fast. Those aren't chicken feet; they're your own fingers."

Yuanbao finished every scrap in front of him, and hunger was still written all over his face.

"Proprietor, bring another order of everything," Bai Du yelled.

Pretty soon more food appeared on the table; it, too, quickly disappeared down Yuanbao's gullet, and he was still greedy for more.

"I'm still hungry."

"Too bad. We're out of money, thanks to you."

"I'm not full yet."

"Now what? Go ask the owner if he'll donate to the cause."

"I'm sure he'll just ask us to mug him again. There has to be something we can do. Is there some way to fill him up without eating?"

"Some people are so ugly that one look makes you lose your appetite."

"Come on, use your head. A rich national heritage like ours must have something."

"I've got it! Isn't there some sort of fasting technique in *qigong* exercises?"

With one of Yuanbao's hands on a live wire and the other on a ground wire, the *qigong* master flipped on a switch. Yuanbao suddenly turned transparent. His body shook, flames emerged from his fingertips, and he screamed bloody murder:

"Ow—ow—!"

The *qigong* master flipped the switch off. "Still hungry?" he asked.

"No, I'm not hungry," Yuanbao answered weakly.

"This fasting technique is everything it's cracked up to be," Sun Guoren said, a frightened look in his eyes.

"What fasting technique?" the *qigong* master asked. "That was electric shock treatment, to energize him. Not everyone knows how to carry out a fast. It's in the domain of spirit masters. For the rest of us, a little electricity, some chicken blood, and there goes the appetite, for a while at least."

"You mean it doesn't last?"

"No, it's just a stopgap measure."

"In other words, he's going to be hungry again tonight? Screaming for more food?"

"If he does, another shock will take care of it. Three times a day, two hundred and twenty volts each time. As time goes on, you'll have to increase the voltage, since his desire for food will grow."

"You won't hear me saying I'm hungry," Yuanbao said tearfully. "No more shocks. I'll never complain about being hungry again."

Bai Du walked up to Yuanbao, holding a hypodermic needle filled with a sticky red liquid in one hand and a cotton ball soaked in iodine in the other. She told him to roll up his sleeve and said in a coaxing voice, "Listen to me. This is chicken blood. Once this gets into your system, you'll be as good as new." She located a vein on the inside of his elbow, daubed the spot with iodine, tossed aside the cotton ball, fanned the spot with her hand, and jabbed the needle in.

• • •

"Now do as I say, and drink this bowl of baby urine. It'll calm your heart and ease your breathing. It's not toxic. Do you think we want to hurt you—it's for your own good. Well, what do you say, don't you feel great?"

"I feel wonderful," Yuanbao said, his eyes closed, as he lay on a carrying pole.

A watch tower with a snowy white canopy stood on a mountain slope opposite a hilly, marshy wilderness through which flowed a small, shrub-lined river.

15

Watermelons, bottles of soda, and cigarettes were laid out in the tower.

Zhao Hangyu and a hundred or so stockholders, including the corporate manager, the agricultural entrepreneur, and the private businessman, all in straw hats and sunglasses, entered the tower, fanning themselves against the heat, and took their seats. Bai Du and two girls handed out binoculars and asked everyone to sign the guest book.

The guests focused their binoculars and looked out at the wilderness, scanning the area from one end to the other.

"The performance will begin in a moment," Zhao announced. "Focus your attention on the outcropping over there. That's where he'll leap into view."

"My, it's awfully high. What safety measures have been taken?"

"None at all. His skill is his only safety net."

"I'm impressed. He must have remarkable skills. They should have sent him to defend Wolf's Fang Mountain during the War of Resistance."

"Little Bai," Zhao Hangyu turned to Bai Du. "Tell them we're ready."

On the outcropping across the way, Sun Guoren was wrapping up his last-minute inspection of Tang Yuanbao, who was in full battle dress, with a rifle slung over his back and hand grenades hanging from his belt.

"Button up your collar. Tighten your belt. Take off your shoes. This is going to be a barefoot exercise."

Yuanbao slipped out of his shoes, which Sun stuffed into Yuanbao's backpack.

"Don't forget, the whole Chinese race is depending on you. Advance boldly. Stare death calmly in the face. When you return triumphant, I'll put you up for a decoration."

"If I don't return, tell them not to cry."

"Let them cry if they feel like it. There'll be nothing else they can do for you."

"Make sure they understand that I dedicate my life to the people, and that even my death cannot pay back their trust in me."

"I'll tell them to fix the blame for your death on the imperialists, revisionists, and counter-revolutionaries."

Two red signal flares split the sky above the mountain across the way.

"It's time," Sun told Yuanbao. "If there's nothing more you want to tell me, you're on."

Yuanbao stepped heavily out onto the outcropping and looked down at a world that was spinning around.

"Don't you dare chicken out!" Sun growled.

"Long live the solidarity of all people of the world!" Yuanbao shouted. Closing his eyes and steeling his heart, he leaped into the air.

Sun watched Yuanbao leap off the outcropping, then crawl and roll down to the arroyo below. "He's entered the battlefield!" he reported to a troop of security personnel dressed as enemy soldiers hidden in the shrubbery. "Don't forget, whatever he dishes out, you take it. Any one of you who so much as harms a hair on his head will answer to me when you get back!"

"Let's do it!" The security men threaded their way along a ditch that was head high and took up their positions.

A wave of excitement swept over the watch tower when the score from an old war movie blasted from a loudspeaker—rifle fire and explosions from big guns thundering to the accompaniment of a grand symphony. All binoculars were trained on the scene below.

The observers were watching as Yuanbao leaped from the outcropping and dropped like a feather into the brambles below. A moment later, he stood up, half dazed and covered with dirt, slapped himself twice to shake off the cobwebs, and then took off running. He crawled on his belly until he saw something hidden in the grass; then he stood up to run at a crouch. Suddenly a hulking figure rose from behind a knoll and grabbed him around the waist. With an easy, practiced move, he flipped the man high into the air, like tossing a bale of hay; the poor fellow landed on the ground and lay there without moving. Yuanbao then ran under a tree, where another hulking figure

jumped on his back, only to be flipped over and land unconscious at his feet.

Yuanbao weaved his way through the stand of trees and
clambered over the hilly terrain; with difficulty he forded the
marsh, jumped over a series of water-filled trenches, and climbed
over precipices. All along the way he engaged and vanquished
the enemy as he forged his way toward the watch tower.

He jumped into a raging river and swam for all he was
worth. A river demon sprang up in front of him, engaging him
in a bitter struggle. They fought for their lives, sinking beneath
the water one minute and bobbing to the surface the next,
choking on the water and gasping for air, clawing at each
other's water-soaked face, until finally the water demon slipped
beneath the water and didn't reappear.

Exhausted and waterlogged, Yuanbao crawled up onto the
opposite bank, where he was met by four or five hulking figures with drawn bayonets. He took them on, one at a time, a
remarkable display of disarming the enemy with his bare
hands.

Once he had dispatched the armed men, he jumped into a
second river, again swimming as hard as he could. Another
demon popped up in front of him, and another bitter struggle
ensued. He no sooner crawled up onto the bank than four or
five more hulking figures with drawn bayonets surrounded
him. Again, he dispatched them with his bare hands. . . .

Cannon fire thundered, raining shells down on Yuanbao,
who never stopped running. Dirt flew into the air, craters
opened up all around him. Flattening himself on the ground,
he was swallowed up by flames and clouds of smoke; but as
soon as the smoke cleared, he was up and running again.

A column of enemy tanks rumbled toward him at a snail's pace, forming a wall of steel directly ahead, like a firing squad in front of a condemned man. Gun turrets turned until they were aimed at Yuanbao—they all fired at the same time. Yuanbao, standing directly in front of the tanks as the smoke cleared, put his fists to work. Each mighty punch sent smoke billowing out of the tanks, from which the crews scrambled out through the hatch, only to be knocked unconscious by a waiting Yuanbao, puffs of red smoke rising from their helmets. One of the tanks steamrolled over Yuanbao's body—he tipped it over, stood up, and dusted himself off.

He was running again, slashing and killing as he went. Nothing could stop him. By now he was hobbling, but a look of triumph showed on his face. Flames erupted from a gas cannister ahead of him; he ran into the flames, reached down, and turned off the valve.

On he ran, heading straight for a burning building. He charged into the sea of flames and emerged from the other side swathed in flames. He turned, puffed out his cheeks, and blew with all his might. With a few waves of his arms, the flames flickered and died, leaving behind nothing but cinders.

And still he kept running, until a brick wall rose in front of him. He backed off a few steps, secured his footing, lowered his head, and ran right through the wall . . . he kept running, leaving the wall standing with a gaping hole in the shape of a human figure.

He ran toward the watch tower, his steps light, as if flying on winged feet. He left behind him a road strewn with grass- and dirt-covered pits designed to trap him. He danced across nail-studded iron bars glowing bright red, like a ballet master in action. He crossed a lake like a water skier, kicking up sprays of water, then ran toward the watch tower, which drew closer, loomed larger, grew clearer, until the observers could see every piece of military equipment he carried and the smile on his face; they even heard the sound of his rifle hitting him on the back, the clatter of grenades at his belt, and the slapping of his bare feet on the rocky ground.

The watch tower seethed with excitement; people lowered their binoculars and stood to watch Yuanbao with their naked eyes as he ran toward them. Breaking into applause, they began to shout:

"Give me a hoo—"

"Hoo—!"

"Now give me a ray—"

"Ray—!"

"Altogether now, what do you say?"

"Hoo—ray!"

Applause and loud cheers were swirling in the air when Yuanbao reached his destination. Applause washed over him, flower petals rained down on him as he strutted back and forth, smiling and waving at the cheering crowd above.

Bai Du and the two girls ran down to wrap a towel around his shoulders, then thrust a bouquet of flowers into his hands and bundled him off to the rest area.

A gaggle of reporters with TV and still cameras rushed up to take pictures from every angle, their flashbulbs setting up a string of dazzling lights.

Pop pop, a string of dazzling lights.

A gaggle of photographers clicked the shutters of their cameras as they backed into the hall. Haloed in the bright light of exploding flashbulbs, Zhao Hangyu and a hundred stockholders applauded as they strode into the hall, broad smiles on their faces.

Yuanbao, a towel draped over his shoulders, stood bashfully and all alone on a riser that looked like a scaffold.

Zhao and the stockholders cast their eyes up as they walked by, heralding him with their applause, craning their necks to look at him even after they'd passed. At last they formed a circle around him, one of benevolent smiles and clapping hands. The corporate manager stepped up to get a closer look at the grenades hanging from his belt. "Are those the weapons that brought you victory?" he asked.

Sun Guoren squeezed out of the line and answered for him: "He didn't use a single weapon, boss. Those are just for show. All he needed was his red heart and two tough, callused hands to emerge triumphant."

"No kidding!" the man exclaimed. He lifted up one of Yuanbao's hands and rubbed the calluses with open admiration. "Just like a bear's paw. If this palm were on anyone else's hand, he'd be a cripple."

"Show the bosses your feet." Sun lifted one of Yuanbao's feet, the sole facing up so the stockholders could get a good look. "All these calluses grew by themselves; he didn't rough them up. Come touch them if you don't believe me."

Pale, chubby fingers reached out and pushed down on the sole of Yuanbao's foot. Sighs of astonishment followed.

"It's tougher than a donkey's hoof."

"How did you get so good?" the peasant entrepreneuer asked Yuanbao.

Sun gave a hand signal, and two hulking men carried in a punching bag.

"He works out on this every day, and once he grew used to hitting it, he was able to take any punch thrown at him."

The corporate manager, bursting with excitement, jabbed the air a couple of times in front of the bag, then kicked it. "Great!" he reported loudly to the crowd. "With a warrior like him, we don't have to worry about anybody getting tough with us!"

"Come on, gather round, it's picture time," Zhao Hangyu stepped up to announce. "Let's take a group photo."

The stockholders clambered onto the riser and stood shoulder to shoulder, hands behind their backs, chests out, stomachs taut, tight, serious looks on their faces. Bai Du and her helpers moved some chairs up in front for Zhao, the corporate manager, the agricultural entrepreneur, and one or two other leading stockholders.

Yuanbao was forced down on the floor in front of the riser, but there was no room for him to get his footing. By then the photographers were taking pictures right and left, and everyone was too busy posing to pay him any attention. It was the corporate manager who happened to spot him standing forlornly off to the side. He waved and called to him, "Come, come, come, stand next to me. How could we leave out our star?"

Yuanbao walked up to the front row, but there was neither room to stand or to sit.

Pointing to his feet, the corporate manager said, "Kneel in front of me and I'll put my hands on your shoulders.'

"One knee or two?"

"One. How would it look if you knelt on both knees?"

Everyone stared into the cameras, as flashbulbs erupted again. In the afterglow of the dazzling lights, a photographer sidled up to Bai Du as he fiddled with his malfunctioning camera and whispered, "I thought we were going to see a martial-arts demonstration. Who turned it into a war game?"

"You see exactly what we want you to see," Bai Du replied flatly. "I'll answer your questions on the day we fail to put on a show for you."

On the flickering TV screen, anchorman Luo Jing, who was gazing off-screen, quickly turned to face the camera.

"This afternoon," he said, "there was a martial-arts demonstration in Beijing's western suburbs. China's number-one superhero, Tang Yuanbao, showed his magical skills in a sneak preview organized by the All-China Mobilization Committee. Within a circumference of thirty miles, he routed the enemy as if they didn't exist. He tamed four tall mountains, forded four rivers, smoothed out four marshes, vanquished forty opponents, snuffed out four raging fires, even broke through four brick walls, drawing gasps of astonishment from over four hundred observers. Now let's go to our correspondent Re Heman for details."

A series of video clips of Yuanbao climbing mountains and fording rivers, putting out fires, and engaging in hand-to-hand combat flashed onto the screen, interspersed with shots of the observers on the watch tower gazing through binoculars, mouths hanging slack and hands trembling.

A voice-over:

According to experts in the field, China has not seen another individual with the incredible restraint or unmatched skills of Tang Yuanbao. They consider him a national treasure, someone whose safeguarding is absolutely essential. They stress that Tang

174

Yuanbao must be studied carefully to see what makes him so special, for that may well hold possibilities in enhancing the quality of the Chinese race. A spokesman for MobCom revealed that this spectacular demonstration followed a month of controlled fasting. During that time, he received daily electric shock treatments, twice-daily injections of chicken blood, and a cup of infant's urine, and he thrived. This development makes it imperative for us to reevaluate a return to some of our traditional health preservation techniques, which, for too long, have been written off as old wives' tales. Experts have pointed out that members of MobCom relied upon the most austere surroundings and primitive methods in their fostering of the startling Tang Yuanbao, and if the nation takes the important steps of providing superior conditions and incorporating everything learned to initiate measures of accelerated talent development with uniquely Chinese characteristics, then the creation of an army of Tang Yuanbaos will not be the ravings of a lunatic. This issue will be the focus of next week's program "Observe and Ponder." We hope you will tune in . . .

In the clip, the tank that had run over Yuanbao was tipped over, its gun turret pointing backward into the air. Yuanbao casually crawled out from under, dusted himself off, turned slowly toward the camera, and began to run. . . .

"Pinch me, pinch me," a battle-scarred old general urged his daughter as he sat dumbstruck in front of the TV. "I must be dreaming."

Firecrackers exploded all over the city, rising to form a shimmering rainbow of colors, then floating to earth like snowflakes.

The bespectacled members of MobCom, flaming brooms or mops in their hands, stood at the entrances to public housing complexes and shouted at the top of their lungs:

"Come outside, everybody! Hit the streets, hit the streets . . ."

Boys and girls with rifles slung over their backs and hand grenades hanging from their belts streamed barefoot and high-spirited out of the buildings, quickly forming a human tide of silent demonstrators. At the first intersection they met up with another detachment of marchers, boys and girls decked out exactly the same. They joined forces amid war whoops and embraces, and marched down the street singing "The Internationale":

"The Internationale is sure to become a reality."

The headquarters of MobCom was ablaze with lights; the leadership of the organization sat around a conference room table in tense session.

Zhao Hangyu, who had called the meeting, announced excitedly, "Our sneak preview was an unprecedented success. The reaction by society in general was magnificent. Congratulatory telegrams and donations have flooded in, virtually overwhelming us. We need to strike while the iron's hot, go for broke, fight to undertake as many activities as possible, and rake in the money."

Liu Shunming, pale and drawn, said, "The people's will is our key."

"That's right!" Zhao continued. "Now we must launch a fervid 'study Yuanbao, overtake Yuanbao' campaign, and fill our lives with sunlight . . ."

A pair of eyeglasses with a sweaty forehead charged into the room. "They're coming," he stammered, "they're coming . . ."

"Who's coming?" Sun Guoren grabbed the man and shouted in his ear. "The police?"

"The masses . . . the masses are coming, they're coming to congratulate us . . ." Eyeglasses pointed to the window.

The sounds of a vast human gathering swelled in the square outside the window: footsteps, shouts, loud singing, a deafening clamor.

Zhao Hangyu jumped up and kicked his chair away, then ran to the window, where he stuck his head out and blew the crowd a kiss.

A sea of black heads turned up the volume; all those boys and girls waved back.

Then Zhao looked above him, where he saw Yuanbao waving to the crowd with one hand and keeping the other in the pocket of his pajamas. He turned and walked sullenly back to the conference room to announce unhappily, "Let's get on with the meeting. . . . I think we'd better put a stop to all this publicity on Yuanbao's behalf. We don't want things to get out of hand. . . ."

"Thank you, Yuanbao, for bringing glory to China," someone shouted up to Yuanbao, who was still standing at the window. Hot tears filled Yuanbao's eyes. Choked with gratitude, he waved again to the crowd below.

The red-eyed boys and girls lowered their heads to dry their tears, then looked up again and gaped at their hero.

"Comrades, fellow countrymen." The crowd grew quiet. "I am a lucky man," Yuanbao said before choking up again. A groundswell of applause rose from the square; tears of emotion ran unchecked down every face.

"Give us something to really cheer about!" the rifle-toting boys and girls shouted as one.

"Something to really cheer about?" Yuanbao wiped his runny nose and dried his tears. "My sons," he shouted, "my sons, ideals are not the exclusive property of old men. My sons, do not give way to the aged; my sons, my sons, why haven't you brought your hooked swords?"

"Something stronger!" the crowd roared.

". . . Put me to death!" Yuanbao replied.

"He's getting more outrageous by the minute." Zhao Hangyu held his face like a man with a toothache, plugging his ears so he didn't have to listen to the dialogue between the masses and Yuanbao. "This Tang Yuanbao doesn't know the first thing about communicating. Send a couple of guys up there to pull him away from the window. From now on, he's not to have another dialogue with the masses. Everything will fall apart if we're not careful."

"What worries me most is that Yuanbao might start sticking up his tail, you know, get cocky," Liu Shunming said. "We won't be able to control him at all if that happens."

"Don't worry about that," Sun Guoren said. "We made him, and we can break him."

"The publicity should focus on how we took a pile of shit and a puddle of piss and turned it into somebody. We must make this clear to the masses," Zhao Hangyu said.

Yuanbao had been whisked away from the window, but the crowd below continued shouting excitedly:

"We want Yuanbao! Give us Yuanbao!"

A phalanx of police cars sped into the square from all directions, sirens wailing, spotlights sweeping the area. The police quickly surrounded the crowd as the loudspeaker atop one of the cars blared, "Everyone down on the ground, lay down your weapons! Now, put your hands behind your heads and walk this way. . . ."

The masses in the square hit the ground like toppled grain stalks.

"You're under arrest," two stern-looking policemen said to Yuanbao.

16

"For what?" Yuanbao asked as he let himself be
handcuffed.

"For inciting unrest." They produced an arrest war-
rant and told Yuanbao to sign it. Then they hustled
him through the door and into a waiting squad car,
which drove off with its siren wailing.

"Tang Yuanbao's display was no accident."

Zhao Hangyu, his face glowing with health, sat in
the TV studio chatting with the hostess with fervid assurance.

"He's the fruit of much hard work. If you'd seen him
before, you'd have known that he was as common as they
come. But once he came under our wing, we put him on
a strict diet and a comprehensive training schedule, and
slowly but surely, one step at a time, we broadened his
field of vision, nurtured a whole range of interests, drawing nourishment from the treasure house of civilization—

domestic and foreign, ancient and modern—until he was transformed into the man you see today: persistent and indomitable, unyielding, indestructible, a man who laughs at physical hardships and attacks . . ."

"I'd like to add something," the *qigong* master broke in. "Tang Yuanbao's supernatural tolerance and his prodigious force and talents are inextricably tied to the practice of *qigong*. When I first met him, he was little more than a body wracked with illness, so paper-thin he couldn't stand up to a simple gust of wind. But after my painstaking treatment regimen and *qigong* exercises, he was a new man in no time. A ruddy complexion, walking on flying feet, someone who can put on weight without the benefit of food or drink and get a rich tan indoors, out of the sun . . ."

"That came later," Zhao Hangyu interrupted the *qigong* master, a smile on his face. "Prior to that, we worked on him nonstop."

"As far as I'm concerned," said the little gentleman, who had been sitting off to the side listening, "all I've heard you talk about so far are his physical qualities. No one disputes the fact that he's in fine shape physically, and I agree that he has supernatural tolerance and can stand up to any force. But what I find so appealing about Tang Yuanbao, his uniqueness, what makes him worthy of our attention and study, is his character, his loyalty and honesty, his spirit of willingness to bow his head and carry the children of the nation on his back. You don't see much of that these days. In fact, it's no exaggeration to say you'd have difficulty finding anyone quite like him."

The little gentleman took out a cigarette and lit it. "And that sets me wondering, why is he like he is? Easy to manipulate, never complaining, totally devoid of pride."

"Selfless, always placing the public good before his own!" the hostess added.

The little gentleman glanced at her, took a drag on his cigarette, and continued, "I don't think it's that simple. I haven't spent much time with Yuanbao; in fact, we met just once. But that was enough for me to see that he's a terrific listener, modest to a fault, quite bashful actually. That, I think, is a key factor in all this. He doesn't know how to say no. As long as it benefits him, he's for it, unlike so many young people who eat only what they like. How can they get any nutrients that way? Only by standing on the shoulders of a giant can you see far off in the distance. That, in a nutshell, is what makes Tang Yuanbao a clever man. He takes his place on our shoulders."

"The creation of Tang Yuanbao was no accident," said the director, still wearing her windbreaker. "I disagree with what our diminutive friend just said. Tang Yuanbao is not unique, but is the personification of so many young people. They grew to adulthood not through the efforts of other people, but through books! They are the amalgamation of all the quintessential thoughts and deeds and words in recorded history. Books have given them courage, wisdom, models for emulation, and aspirations. I can see in them traces of ancient Rome's wrestlers and of Christ on the Cross. A few days ago, a Central TV newscast raised a question: Would it be possible to create a legion of Tang Yuanbaos? Or words to that effect. I say it is. But before we create a legion of Tang Yuanbaos, we must create a legion of books. Books are humanity's friends. Without them, we would still be groping our way through the dark. . . ."

"I'm opposed to putting Tang Yuanbao on too high a pedestal," the ballet instructor said indignantly. "I have no idea why MobCom wanted to nurture someone like him, then praise him to the skies. I've only met Tang Yuanbao once in my life, but that was enough for me to see that he is a bad person, someone without a shred of decency. He pretends to be honest and kind, but treachery lurks in his heart. He's utterly shameless; there's a dagger hidden behind his smile, and he's a low-down weasel. Compared to all those self-respecting young people who are willing to work hard for the good of the country, he is despicable and vulgar, and I could never trust or have any good feelings for anyone who has abandoned his self-respect and treats himself as anything but human. If someone like that is made into a model for our young people, I fear for the future of the country. I am of the opinion that the creators of Tang Yuanbao are frivolous individuals, and just by looking at Tang Yuanbao you can see that they are people of bad taste who are winning over the masses with claptrap. For the time being I'll refrain from saying they have a hidden agenda. This is not the least bit funny. Don't treat something so nauseating as simply amusing. You may not want to hear this, but it is a humiliating insult to the nation's youth. I wish to ask Tang Yuanbao's creators, how much of the man is genuine? Instead of portraying all the conscientious, hard-working young people from all walks of life, who carry out their duties without complaint, you focus your attention on this disgusting specimen. Is that something worthy of the times? Where, I ask you, is your sense of duty, your sense of purpose? Where are you leading the youth of today?"

"May I respond to the comrade's concerns?" Bai Du said. "First, we had one goal in mind when we created and nurtured Tang Yuanbao, and that is to bring glory to the nation, to emerge victorious in an international free-style wrestling meet, and to hoist the five-star flag. Second, we devised a training strategy and regimen based upon Yuanbao's situation and condition, with no thought to whether or not it could be applied to the broad masses of China's youth. Wanting all of China's youth to follow his lead was not something we considered—it never crossed our mind. The truth is, Tang Yuanbao is Tang Yuanbao, period. No one can learn from his example. And it was never our intention to make a joke out of him or win over the people with claptrap. Needless to say, we never tried to use him to insult or humiliate the broad masses of young people, or to make them appear ugly. It goes without saying that in nurturing Tang Yuanbao, we had no precedent to follow, and as we groped along with our hands in the mud, inevitably the fish and shrimp got all jumbled together. There were many twists and turns, and sometimes the situation got out of hand or we went astray. We learned many lessons the hard way. As for your question of whether Tang Yuanbao is genuine or not, I don't know the answer, because everyone wears a mask sometimes. We don't have to like each other, but we need to be tolerant. I don't like you, for instance, but you won't hear me saying that your existence is a humiliating insult to women."

"This has been a lively discussion," the hostess said, "with clear distinctions among the points of view. What say we end the show not with more critiques of Tang Yuanbao, but by addressing this question: If Tang Yuanbao represents the current generation of youth, how do we go about bringing about the emergence of even more Tang Yuanbaos?"

"I believe we should affirm Tang Yuanbao, though I don't understand his private behavior, and have no idea what he's thinking deep down. That said, I think that the courage he showed the other day in that utterly fearless sneak preview was admirable in the extreme."

"Whether he represents the current generation of young people or not is something we can discuss later, but we should not find fault with him. I'm not lying when I say that I am shamed by any comparison with him. You could bury me in gold and he'd still have more courage than I, a man unconcerned with matters of life and death or honor and disgrace."

"I still think you people have put him on too high a pedestal, and that you've fallen under the spell of his false image. It's not because he possesses lofty beliefs that he's able to go through fire and water without regard for his own safety."

"I consider Tang Yuanbao worthy of being called China's top superhero. Now that may not be a particularly scientific conclusion, and I'm not remotely interested in what motivates him. To me his behavior commands deep respect. A moment ago, one of the comrades here said he was shamed by any comparison with Tang Yuanbao. Well, so am I. Who here today thinks himself Tang Yuanbao's equal? In my view, every one of us is too much in love with himself. If China were fortunate enough to have a legion of Tang Yuanbaos and fewer of the likes of you and me, it'd be in much better shape than it is now. As to the question of how we can bring about even more Tang Yuanbaos, I need time to think. Does burying your nose in books automatically make you smart? I don't think so: Is there anyone among us who isn't a bookworm? Although I haven't thought this through yet, shouldn't we be doing something with genetic engineering? It's incredibly reliable and effective. Modern technology has already made great strides in the science of human cloning. . . ."

"This is a matter of great concern, for if we're not careful, we could produce a generation of idiots. . . ."

"I have one request," Tang Yuanbao said tearfully to the two policemen. "Lock me up with rapists and thieves. I do not want to be a political criminal."

* * *

"A telegram from 008."

Zhao Hangyu, Sun Guoren, Liu Shunming, and the others had just sat down to eat. Silently chewing their food, they listened apathetically as the secretary read the telegram.

FROM EXTENSIVE NEWS COVERAGE STOP FAT MAN LEARNED OF PLANS TO PIT HIM AGAINST A BILLION HOSTILE PEOPLE STOP GAVE UP ALL HOPE STOP EARLY THIS MORNING COMMITTED SUICIDE BY CARBON MONOXIDE POISONING STOP DEAD AND GONE STOP NATIONAL HUMILIATION CLEANSED STOP HALLELUJAH STOP JUMP FOR JOY STOP AWAITING INSTRUCTIONS STOP SHOULD I TAKE PHOTOS OF FUNERAL FOR OUR COUNTRYMEN STOP 008.

"He's dead?" Liu Shunming recoiled, his mouth full. "How could he be? Why couldn't he have just come over to see how he fared?"

Zhao Hangyu kept eating, despondently now, and didn't say a word.

"Because he knew he was outmatched, see?" Sun Guoren said. "Now, at least, we've managed to save face."

"What the hell do you know?" Zhao spoke up as he stared blankly at the ceiling. "We may have saved face, but at the cost of a smashed rice bowl."

"How's that?"

"Without an adversary, what's left for MobCom to do?"

That hit Sun and Liu like a clap of thunder.

"Send 008 a telegram," Zhao said to the secretary.

DO NOT LET THIS NEWS GET OUT STOP THE DEATH OF FATSO MUST NOT BE REVEALED IN COUNTRY STOP CEASE ALL COMMUNICATIONS BETWEEN CHINA AND FRANCE STOP INCLUDING TELEPHONE TELEGRAPH POSTAL STOP.

"What does that solve?"

After the secretary walked out, Sun said anxiously, "Frightening a foreigner to death brings great glory to the Chinese people. When the newspapers hear about it, they'll splash it all over the front page."

"Back to work," Zhao said as he jumped to his feet. "We take things one day at a time. Mobilize the troops to pore over newspapers and magazines, domestic and foreign, to find out if any Chinese competitor in any field has suffered defeat recently."

"There are so many, we'll never see the end of them," Liu Shunming said. "I haven't heard of a single event where we've had a winner this year, except maybe in Ping-Pong."

"Find me the worst of the lot, someone beaten so badly even his underwear got lost."

"Will do."

"Come back here," Zhao called to Sun and Liu, who had just turned to start the search. "Where's Yuanbao? Send someone to keep an eye on him. We can't let him out there on his own."

"Oh, he was arrested last night. I was so busy I forgot to report that to you."

"It looks like our government's gotten the news already. Good. With the cooperation of the government, we have nothing to fear."

"We've looked everywhere and can't find a single loser in a men's event," Liu Shunming said to Zhao Hangyu, waving a thick stack of newspapers in front of him. "That's because none of them even made the prelims."

With a creased forehead Zhao Hangyu wracked his brains for an idea. All of a sudden he looked up and said to Liu Shunming, "Well, then, how about women's events?"

"I am resolutely opposed to neutering Yuan-bao!" Bai Du spun around at the window and announced to Zhao, Sun, and Liu, who were seated around the conference table. Her lips were quivering, as she fought to control her emotions. "I am resolutely opposed to neutering Yuanbao," she repeated. "Gentlemen, I've cut a swath through this world for several decades, and have earned my reputation as a wicked, merciless woman. But what you want to do, I'm sorry, it disgusts me. This is going much too far."

"Then how do you propose we stem this raging tide?" Zhao Hangyu asked her. "Everyone knows our backs are against the wall."

"I don't know. I'm too confused at the moment to come up with a better idea."

"We can't just stand idly by and watch all our hard work come to nothing."

"Struggle demands sacrifice. We're not a bunch of sweet old ladies, but we're not out to get anyone either. I'm sure that everyone at this table would gladly give up his most prized possession if necessary—we've already given up plenty of face."

"But think about Yuanbao. He's so young, and he'll lose it forever, before he's even had a chance to use it. That will scar him for life. His soul will bleed for the rest of his days. He has the right to use his body any way he sees fit."

"If he's to have the perfect face, he's going to have to give up something. It's an agonizing choice he'll have to make sooner or later."

"You once said that in all of China his is the only true and living face."

"It still is. We don't want to cripple him—unless, of course, you think that women are crippled by definition."

"There's no loss of face in this, and it's not going to turn him into some sort of freak. None of the millions of women in the world have one, and I haven't heard any complaints from them. Oh, once in a while, there may be a slight note of regret, but they go on living their normal lives, filled with confidence."

"In fact, they're often livelier, different from other people in an upbeat way."

"You lose something, you gain something."

"All the proletariat lost was their chains, and they gained the world."

"I understand the logic, but emotionally I can't turn the corner. Are you sure that after you've neutered him he won't turn weird, and that he'll retain his strength and courage?"

"It's worth a try. There's only one way to find out. Things couldn't get any worse, after all. If instead of an Amazon warrior we wind up with some Thai transvestite, all we do is lower the flag, put away the drums, and close down MobCom. Then we figure out a way to stage a comeback."

"We can't let our flagpole topple. You not only have to turn the corner, you have to take charge personally of the work involving Yuanbao, convince him to happily accept the decision by the organization. If you won't, we have no choice but to remove you from MobCom's Directorate."

"Is that an organizational decision?"

"Yes, the Directorate was unanimous, and sent us three to come talk to you."

"Then I must bow to the wishes of the organization. But I have misgivings."

"We have no problem with that, but the organization insists that you carry out your instructions to the letter."

"I have one last request, and that is, if the sex change does not turn out as expected, I beg you not to attempt a reattachment."

"Why must you have such a low opinion of us? I want you to know that this was an agonizing decision. Many of the comrades actually wept, saying they were letting Yuanbao down."

"We, all of us, have razor-sharp tongues but hearts made of tofu. If we weren't in this predicament, with emotions taking a backseat to practical needs, and weren't forced to serve the greater good, do you really think we could turn into what we've become—beasts in human form?"

"Little Bai," Zhao Hangyu said as he put his arm around her shoulder and walked her around the room, "you must concentrate on the arduous task before you. It may sound easy, but it won't *be* easy. Except for a eunuch, who wouldn't be upset by being castrated? You have to convince him that it's the thing to do, make him *want* to do it, let him know that women are people, too. As a comrade *and* a woman, you're in the best position to do that. It's people who make the difference. Just think, we even turned the emperor around. Now can Tang Yuanbao be harder to transform than an emperor?"

The cell door clanged open; a policeman stood in the patch of sunlight admitted by the skylight and shouted into the darkness:

"Tang Yuanbao, front and center, and bring your bedding with you."

In the prison reception room, the warden looked at Bai Du and said sternly, "I'll accept your explanation, but I'm warning you, since you're a popular organization, you must stay within the bounds of acceptable speech and behavior. Don't let your work stray into the realm of government activities. More important, don't create the impression among the masses that you've been given leave to represent the government."

"Yes, of course."

"Don't let smugness get the better of you, and watch what you say. Whatever you do, do it right, whether it's organizing a competition or training competitors. Tap the inner resources of people and the difficulties they face instead of hammering away here and pounding away there, going off in tangents. Where social ills are concerned, discuss them if you will, but remember that public ridicule will get you nowhere."

"You're right. We'll make it a point to attend to our business and nothing else."

"That's not what I'm saying. You can attend to matters dealing with other people, but in a proper manner, and with honorable intentions. A sense of responsibility toward society is a good thing, but if it takes on a caustic, sarcastic, even a malevolent character, and evolves into slander and innuendo, that's bad."

"I'll make sure they watch themselves."

"What do you mean *they*? I want *you* to watch yourself. I'm talking to you."

"I'll watch myself."

"Just saying it isn't enough. I want action. I know your type. You give assurances in public, and quickly violate them in private."

"Not this time. We'll dedicate ourselves to identical public and private behavior. When the competition with the foreigners finally takes place, we'll give you two comp tickets, so you can continue giving us the benefit of your wisdom."

"I may go; I may not. I'm not all that interested in taking part in these quarrels with foreigners. I've got my hands full with domestic affairs."

The warden stood up and shook hands with Bai Du. As he saw her to the door, he said, "I'm letting you off with a warning this time. But the next time Tang Yuanbao gets into trouble, I'll throw the book at both of you. You made him what he is, after all."

"I'll be careful to keep him away from situations that might make him think he can pop off like that again."

"Be a stern mentor and use his talents with discretion."

Yuanbao was standing alone at the prison gate, looking bewildered.

Bai Du, after walking out of the prison building, her purse under her arm, went up to Yuanbao, who smiled when he saw her.

"You've got the nerve to smile?" she complained. "After I had to sit there and be lectured to? From now on, don't go off half-cocked like that, because you won't be the only one to suffer. Next time they'll make an example out of me, too. Let's go."

Bai Du and Yuanbao no sooner walked through the gate than they were surrounded by a gaggle of reporters and people with nothing better to do. The street was bathed in sunlight and crowded with vehicular traffic. Yuanbao was blinded by the light. Opening his lusterless eyes as wide as he could and looking downcast, he fell in behind Bai Du as she elbowed her way through the crowd.

"Are you sorry for what you did?"

"Will you repeat your actions if you get the chance?"

"Do you think you've been treated unfairly, that the authorities misinterpreted your intentions?"

The reporters fired questions at him as he passed through the gauntlet. Maintaining his silence, he left it to Bai Du to say, "No comment."

Yuanbao sat quietly eating at a table with a white tablecloth in a brightly lit, comfortably appointed room. You could have heard a pin drop, except for the occasional clink of cutlery. The table was spread with an abundance of rich, appealing food.

Yuanbao ate without a hint of emotion, but before long, he began to weep; tears snaked down his cheeks.

Bai Du, who was sitting across from him, rested her face in her hands and watched him, but said and did nothing.

Yuanbao reached up to dry his tears, then returned to his food, keeping his head lowered to avoid looking at Bai Du.

This went on for a while, until he finally laid down his utensils, looked up, and said cooly, "I'm full."

She stirred, nodded, and said, "You're full."

"Now what?" Yuanbao asked as he jerked off his bib, tossed it to the floor, and walked to the end of the table, where he picked up a cigarette, struck several matches violently, and finally lit up.

"Now we do nothing," she said, her head lowered, as she fiddled with a fork, spinning it around on the tablecloth. "You can do anything you want."

"You must be joking. How can there be nothing to do?" Yuanbao blew out a mouthful of smoke and gazed out the window. "I can do anything I want? What am I capable of doing? There's nothing I want to do—but you guys probably want to do plenty."

"No, nothing," she said. "You're a free man. We release you from your vow. From now on you're free to go where you want and do what you like. You're your own boss."

Yuanbao stared at Bai Du for a long moment, as his cigarette burned down and the ash kept dropping to the floor. He walked back to the table and sat down, stubbed out his cigarette in an ashtray, and said flatly:

"I have no place to go."

"How could you have said that to Yuanbao? Who gave you the right?" Zhao Hangyu pounded the table and screamed at Bai Du, standing right in her face. "This is nothing less than naked betrayal!"

"I think she's completely departed from the MobCom position," said Liu Shunming, who was sitting off to one side.

"She's out! Cancel her membership!" Zhao screeched hysterically to the members of the Directorate seated around the conference table. "Any objections? None—the motion is passed!"

"Fine with me," Bai Du said calmly. "That saves me the trouble of resigning."

"Get the hell out of here! I don't want to look at you another second, and don't come looking for me ever again, not in a hundred years."

"I won't, not even *after* a hundred years. And if I'm nothing but ashes, I don't want to be scattered anywhere near yours." Bai Du turned and stormed out of the conference room.

"Stinking whore!" Zhao cursed at her retreating back. "I'll remember this even if you turn to water or pus!" He sat down dejectedly and covered his eyes. "How could I have been so blind," he said with grief and indignation, "not to have seen that we were sleeping next to a lovely snake in the grass? She betrayed my trust. After a disappointment like this, how will I ever trust anyone again?"

"Don't let it get to you, Director Zhao," Liu Shunming said cautiously. "She's gone, but you've still got us."

"Let old Zhao rest a while," Sun Guoren said as he helped Zhao Hangyu to his feet and led him away from the conference table. "This has really hit him hard." He helped him lie down on a sofa and told one of the girls to rest his head in her lap and gently fan him.

"The meeting isn't over yet," Sun said as he sat down in Zhao's chair. "We haven't finished discussing the matter of Tang Yuanbao. I'll take over as chair for now."

"I have a motion," Liu Shunming said. "Bai Du's gone, but we can't give up our work on Tang Yuanbao. We need a capable, reliable person to undo the damage she's inflicted. It's a heavy responsibility, and who we choose is critical. Sun Guoren is the logical choice."

"No no no," Sun Guoren demurred urgently. "Not me, I'm the wrong man."

"Don't be so modest."

"I'm not being modest. My duties at Tanzi Lane give me no time for anything else. I suggest we choose someone a notch above me—Liu Shunming—to take over Bai Du's duties. He's up to the job, and he's overseen Tang Yuanbao in the past. Rather than bring in someone new, who would have to start from scratch, we should send a comrade who's familiar with Yuanbao."

"No no, not me. I screwed things up the last time."

". . . any objections? None—the motion is passed."

"Yuanbao, pack up your things, you're moving,"
Liu Shunming said.

18

"Moving where? What's wrong with this place?"
Yuanbao got slowly out of bed and began packing.

"You need a change of scenery," Liu said. "A place
better suited to remolding."

Yuanbao said nothing.

"You're about to try out a new and quite wonderful
life, one I'm sure you'll enjoy."

Picking up some of Yuanbao's belongings, Liu led
him downstairs, where an automobile waited. They got
in the car and drove away.

On a university campus, students chatting and laughing
in small groups stopped to watch the car drive up to a
dormitory, where the balconies were filled with
women's underwear and an array of other feminine
items. A bevy of students, lying or standing on the bal-
cony, gazed down at Yuanbao's car and twittered like

mother hens. Some eyed him out of curiosity, others sent lovely giggles raining down.

"Let's go," Liu Shunming said as he picked up Yuanbao's bedding and dragged him out of the car. "Upstairs."

Every basin- or book-carrying girl they passed stared in bewilderment, then turned and watched them continue up the stairs, wondering what was going on.

When they reached the top floor, they walked down the hall as girls in every doorway watched their progress with smiles and grins. A group of four girls, elegantly dressed and lovely beyond description, formed a welcoming committee in one of the doorways.

"These are your new quarters," Liu said. "And these are your new teachers. You'll be staying with them, so introductions are in order. This is Miss Zhou," he began, "Miss Wu, Miss Zheng, and Miss Wang."

Yuanbao shook hands all around. "I'm Tang Yuanbao, 'yuan' as in 'yuanshuai' [generalissimo], 'bao' as in 'baozi' [leopard]."

"Welcome to our room," the girl at the end said. "We hope you'll be happy here."

"Miss Wang is in charge," Liu took pains to point out. "From now on, if you have any questions or don't understand something, she's the one to ask."

"But if I can't make myself clear, feel free to ask the others."

"There's no need to hold back with us," the three girls said in unison.

"Here are the rules," Liu said to Yuanbao once they were inside the room. "You must respect your new teachers. As a group, you're pretty much on your own. But no undue attention to any one of them. Take full advantage of this wonderful learning opportunity. Each of your new teachers possesses many virtues, so observe them carefully and pay attention. After a while, I'll be back to test you to see what you've learned."

"We'll help each other and learn from one another," Miss Wang said earnestly.

"This is a teachers college, so you students must be thrilled to have a chance to put what you've learned into practice."

The dean of students had called a meeting of key members of the college's Party, Youth League, and student body leaders in the auditorium.

"The MobCom comrades have shown their trust in us by sending Tang Yuanbao for training. It is a distinct honor. I expect you all to work with MobCom, looking after Tang Yuanbao in all matters, large and small, and showing your good breeding and high aspirations. Become an influence on Tang Yuanbao's life, bit by bit. Remolding another human being is arduous work, much harder than giving birth to a new one. Tang Yuanbao is a man of many talents, which means we have a lot of work ahead of us. But I want to make one point absolutely clear, and that is, none of you is to get emotionally involved in what we're doing. You boys are not to get jealous over the fact that he can stay in the girls' dorm and you cannot. He's on a mission. And you girls, don't let your thoughts run wild, for obvious and important reasons. If you let your thoughts stray, the comrades from MobCom will be the losers, and all our efforts will be wasted. Anyone seen displaying any of these tendencies will be expelled immediately, and the words 'does not yield to assignment' may be entered in your dossier."

"Key members of the Party and Youth League will be in charge," interjected the head of the college, who was sitting off to the side. "This is important work, and must be treated as such. Red stars and demerits will be distributed, and these marks will appear on your final exams. They will be taken into consideration when we choose our 'Three Good' students and in determining student stipends. No one without red stars will graduate. If you can't teach a Tang Yuanbao, how do you expect to go out into society as a teacher?"

"Thank you, one and all, for your support," Sun Guoren rose to express his gratitude as MobCom representative. "We put a lot of thought into this before deciding to seek the help of your fine institution and its students. We considered other organizations, including a textile mill and a hospital, but decided against them, either because they lacked sophistication or constituted an environment ill-suited to learning. We share a feeling that among all the various professions, students are the most patriotic."

"You'll sleep here, on the top bunk next to the window," Miss Wang informed Yuanbao, as she helped him spread out his bedding. "That way, you'll be able to observe everything we do in the room."

"Fine by me. I can sleep anywhere."

"No no, we each have our own bed. No sleeping around."

"Personally, we don't care," Miss Zhou said. "But we don't want your reputation ruined."

"I can't imagine how any of you could ruin my reputation," Yuanbao replied, sitting on his bunk with a blank look.

Not knowing what to say, the girls just exchanged glances.

Finally, Miss Wang broke the silence. "I say we all lighten up." She smiled. "Yuanbao is one of us, so from now on we treat him like a sister. Just carry on as before, whether it's washing up or brushing our teeth or snacking or gossiping."

That breathed new life into the girls, who went back to looking in the mirror and nibbling on melon seeds and lazing around.

The college cafeteria was packed, with long lines at every window.

Yuanbao was squeezed in among Misses Zhou, Wu, Zheng, and Wang, all tapping their lunchboxes lightly as they walked excitedly into the cafeteria.

"No meat," Miss Wang said to Yuanbao. "It'll make you fat. We'll all settle for tofu."

Affecting effeminate airs as best he could, Yuanbao licked his fingertips and counted out the right number of greasy food coupons, which he handed to the kitchen helper. Then he elbowed his way out of line, holding his tray in both hands, and searched for an empty seat. Some girls at one of the tables scooted over to make room for him; he sat down and began nibbling daintily at his food, puckering up his lips and picking out little pieces, all the while leaning over and whispering to the girls or roaring with laughter, even when his mouth was full, before quickly sitting up straight, sneaking a look around, then returning to his spoon and eating with a supercilious look on his face.

The four girls and Yuanbao skipped gaily down the street, hand in hand, stopping to do some window shopping, then reluctantly moving on after discussing the various goods on display. Then another shop, more window shopping . . .

A fashionable young woman passed them on the street, and all five turned to admire her. When she was out of sight, their looks of envy changed to expressions of critical aloofness. They resumed their stroll and aired their unanimous opinion of the young woman: "That outfit looked terrible on her."

If they saw a shy, ordinary-looking woman in a nice dress, they'd rush up to her.

"Where'd you buy that dress, comrade?"

And when they passed boys loitering on a street corner, they'd turn very prim, walk stiffly, and look straight ahead. But one might say to the others without moving her lips, "Did you see the one on the left?"

Then once they'd put some distance between them and the boys, the others would turn to look, one at a time, then pick up the pace and remark excitedly, "Are you kidding? I didn't think he was good-looking at all."

"Those jeans made his legs look like a pair of drumsticks."

At a department store, the girls took in everything with shining eyes, then stood silently in front of the glittery jewelry counter, biting their lips with ill-concealed envy, carefully scrutinizing every item on display. Finally, red-faced and teary-eyed, their hair slightly mussed, they straightened up and shambled off forlornly despite attempts to appear resolute, lost in their own thoughts.

They regained a measure of confidence as they approached a discount clothing counter, where they elbowed their way up front and frantically dug and tore through the offerings, snatching whatever they could without even asking the price. Then, with the same frantic urgency, they elbowed their way back out of the mob and tucked their new purchases under their chins to show them off to full effect, oblivious to the bumps and shoves from people behind them. Their reactions ran from giggly delight to hangdog disappointment and from relief to ambivalence. "Girls," said Miss Wang, pleased with her selection, but suddenly reminded of Yuanbao's presence, "let's not get too caught up in these bargains. Where'd our student go?"

They looked around. Where was Yuanbao? Finally, they spotted him standing off by himself, an island in the stream of bargain-hunters, looking lost and very much alone.

Suddenly regaining their sense of responsibility, they skillfully made their way upstream and formed a protective moat around him

"Why didn't you stick close to us?" one of them complained.

"I tried, I really did," Yuanbao said, "but I couldn't keep up. The ins and outs of shopping aren't something you can learn just by watching."

"It's not easy being female, don't you think?"

"You can say that again. I'd have an easier time studying to be a circus clown."

"Don't lose hope. You must believe in yourself. You're focusing only on the difficulties of being female and haven't tasted its pleasures."

"After you buy a cute little frock and wear it out on the street, you stand there feeling the warmth of pride. It doesn't get any better than that."

Miss Wang joined the other girls in admiring some lovely skirts on a rack, necks craned, heads tilted upward, eyes wide. When a harried clerk rushed by, she said, "Miss, would you let us see that pink dress, please."

"No, the green one's prettier," Miss Zhou said. "It makes one's skin look milkier."

"I like that yellow one," Miss Wu said. "It looks so fresh, so clean."

"How about the lake-blue one?" Miss Zheng asked. "It says tranquility."

"Which one do you want?" the shopclerk asked impatiently. "Make up your minds."

"Pink."

"Green."

"Yellow."

"Blue."

"Who's it for?"

"Him." Miss Wang pointed to Yuanbao. "Which color do you think would look best on him?"

The clerk stared at Yuanbao, then took a deep breath, turned, and walked off.

"We don't have his size."

"Come here, over here."

The girls dragged Yuanbao up to the cosmetic counter, where they sniffed all the colognes and pointed out different brands of cosmetics. "Tell us what you like," they said, cocking their heads toward Yuanbao. "Which fragrance appeals to you?" They each pointed out their favorite brands:

"How about Orchid Beauty; it has a rich fragrance."

"Au Cher, it turns your skin silky white."

"How come you're not trying Red Bird?"

"I don't care one way or the other," Yuanbao said to Miss Wang. "Do I have to use all these scented products?"

"Women like to smell good."

The beauty salon owner greeted them with a bow and a nod of his head. "Are you young ladies here to have your hair done?"

They stepped aside to bring Yuanbao into view.

"He is," Miss Wang said.

The owner rolled his eyes, but quickly regained his composure. "Come in, please; have a seat."

Yuanbao sat in the stylist's chair, a white apron tied around him, and stared at his image in the mirror. Comb and hair dryer at the ready, the stylist asked tentatively, "How would you like it?"

"Like mine," Miss Wang said, shaking her head to set her short hair flying, à la Yamaguchi Momoe.

Yuanbao stared at himself in the mirror. Freshly permed, he was wearing a slip, and the girls were busily introducing him to the world of cosmetics.

Miss Wang first applied cleansing cream to his forehead, nose, cheeks, and chin, then smoothed it in with the palm of her hand. After gently rubbing foundation into his skin, she applied several coats of powder with a powder puff, turning his face and brows ghostly white.

Miss Zhou worked on his eyebrows, drawing them thin, long, black, and with sexy upward curves. She then turned her attention to his eyes, starting with eyeliner after having him close his eyes.

Miss Wu used a curler to give him long, lush, curving lashes, then topped them off with mascara.

Miss Zheng drew lines alongside his nose with a colored pencil and smoothed the area with her hand, highlighting the arch of his nose. Then, after outlining his mouth with a lip liner pencil, she carefully filled it in with bright red lipstick.

Miss Wang completed the makeover with a touch of rouge on each cheek.

The finished product was a shocker.

The girls were stunned.

"Something's not quite right. Too flashy, maybe?"

"I don't think so. That's pretty much how we do it most of the time."

"His skin's too pale and the lips are too red. And his eyes arch too much."

So they picked up the tools of their trade and did a touch-up.

Yuanbao looked at his new face with no display of emotion. But after a moment, his lips parted into a smile. His mouth looked like a bloodsucker; even his teeth were red. The face powder separated and gathered into clumps, then rained to the floor.

The smile vanished, leaving behind a motley face of greens and purples.

19

"How's he doing?" Zhao Hangyu, drunk as a lord, asked from the passenger seat of the car. "Holding up okay?"

"He's holding up fine," Liu Shunming said, leaning forward. "He's calm and compliant, says okay to everything. He gets along great with the girls and does what they say. Nothing seems to bother him. He's a youngster you can be proud of. All that crap Bai Du fed him doesn't seem to have affected him at all."

"Watch him carefully. It might just be for show. Nobody in his right mind would object to moving in with a bunch of pretty girls. But once he finds out what we've got in mind, will that bring a swift and acrimonious halt to his cooperation or, even worse, take him out of the picture altogether?"

"At the moment that's hard to predict, but I don't think so. Yuanbao is no Bai Du. He's much more tolerant and honest. Obviously, a long process is involved here, so I'm in no hurry to bring him up to speed. I say, let him get good and comfortable in his new environment, get used to things and smell the roses for a while. That'll make it easier when it's time to talk to him about you know what."

"Don't let yourself be lulled into putting too much trust in what his behavior seems to indicate. That's a painful lesson I learned all too well. Who, in fact, is innocent? Who's tolerant and honest? The more innocent someone seems, the deeper the seeds of evil are planted in him. I can see right through people like that. It's a sham, all a sham, an act for somebody else's benefit. Showering him with kindness is a waste of time. It's like trying to make a pet out of a wolf by feeding him well. Then, when you least expect it, he'll take a bite out of your hide. What a bummer. . . . Life's a bummer. Sometimes I feel like breaking down and crying. . . ."

Zhao Hangyu began to sob.

"Snap out of it, old Zhao," Liu Shunming tried to comfort him. "You're taking this too hard. Are you losing the will to live, all because of Bai Du? She isn't worth it."

"Over the past few days, I've awakened from dreams bawling like a baby just about every night. It's so dark I can't see my hand in front of my face, and I keep asking myself, *Where am I?* The words are no sooner out of my mouth than my nose begins to ache and the tears start all over."

"Don't cry too much, it could make you sick."

"What else can I do? All I think of these days is that man lives but a generation; grass dies each season. You're born unsullied and try to leave life the same way . . ."

"Really, old Zhao, you're not thinking what I think you're thinking, are you? We're all counting on you."

"Ah, who can really count on anybody? Parents and children

can't spend their whole lives together, and a good name loses its luster over time. Ultimately, even the universe is slated for destruction, and human beings last for maybe a century. I came into the world naked and will leave it the same way with no regrets."

Burying his face in his hands, Zhao broke down and cried.

Distraught over the words he had just heard, Liu nonetheless forced a smile on his face. "That's putting too negative a spin on things. We revolutionaries are expected to keep going as long as there's breath in our bodies, to fight on till we breathe our last. So long as the wheelbarrow of human liberation stays upright, we keep on pushing. Just think about the two-thirds of the world's population who live in the abyss of suffering. Who but us can save them?"

"They're them and I'm me. What does their suffering have to do with me? And what do my sadness and grief, my pitiful moans and groans, have to do with them? I'm throwing in the towel, no more for me. Eat, drink, and be merry, I say. Summer or winter, spring or fall, I don't care . . . the nights are made for drinking. Tonight I'll get drunk on the banks of the Qin Huai River . . ."

Softly, Zhao began to sing, and suddenly the strains of ancient lyrics emerged:

Once parted, year after year . . .
a dusky haze in a broad southern sky . . .
though I have a thousand feelings, to whom can I bare my tortured
*   soul? . . .*
Doesn't she know, doesn't she know, green leaves should be lush, red
*   petals should be frail? . . .*

The car came to a stop, but Zhao Hangyu kept singing:

An embroidered coverlet on a cold, lonely night
Who is there to share it with? . . .
The frown has disappeared, and now my heart aches . . .

"Care to dance?"

"Love to."

Yuanbao, heavily made up, looked down into the face of a much shorter and terribly frail young man. Spreading his arms, Yuanbao let himself be held around the waist with one arm and by his hand with the other. They glided out onto the dance floor.

The cafeteria was packed with paired-off students silently dancing to the music. The girls were made up like panda bears; the boys looked like extraterrestrials with the lights reflecting off their eyeglasses. The ghostly white face of Yuanbao rose above the crowd, his features poking through the face powder, making him look like a reincarnation of the Song dynasty woman Qin Xianglian, dragging her infant son along with her.

"Are you CP [Communist Party] or CY [China Youth League]?" Yuanbao asked his struggling dance partner.

"Neither."

"Then what organization do you represent? Someone had to send you."

"I was sent by an alliance of people. If I were a member of something, I wouldn't be as bad off as I am. I'm just a hanger-on."

The little guy struggled to move Yuanbao around. Raising Yuanbao's arm, he twirled underneath it, nervously concentrating on his dancing feet as he made his way across the floor. He was tripping all over himself.

"Don't knock yourself out. You have your whole life ahead of you."

"No problem. Ever since I was a kid I've worked on the family farm. I know what it means to work my butt off."

"How about I take the lead?" Yuanbao volunteered.

"No, save your sympathy. I'll dance till I drop."

"But I wouldn't hurt a fly."

"I'm a masochist. And that's my problem, not yours."

"Then keep thinking about a mule turning a millstone, and you'll feel better."

The music ended, and the little guy leaned against Yuanbao to catch his breath. Then he straightened up, thanked Yuanbao for the dance, and, with tears welling up in his eyes, walked off. The dean of students greeted him with a pat on the back, spoke a few words of encouragement, and solemnly entered a red mark in his notebook.

With a wave of the dean's hand, another student-martyr walked up to Yuanbao, who was back in his seat with the other girls.

"What is this, a suicide squad?" Yuanbao asked Miss Wang, beside him.

"Just what do you think *we* are," she asked him, "if not a suicide squad?"

"Apparently made up of two detachments."

As the new recruit approached Yuanbao, he smiled sweetly. Yuanbao smiled back affectionately.

"I've been wanting to meet you," the recruit said as he sat down beside Yuanbao. "Haven't we met before?"

"I recall meeting, too."

"What's your name?"

"Tang, as in the famous Tang tricolored pottery."

"Really? No wonder you looked so special."

"Oh? Am I someone you could like?"

"More than you'll ever know."

"Then how about taking me to dinner? After that, if you're game, we can go to bed," Yuanbao suggested.

"I just want to talk. I'm not looking for action."

"Why so well behaved all of a sudden? You're not like that most of the time."

"You must have me confused with someone else. I'm a model of decorum, so if we don't hit it off, it'll be your fault. You really make a man giddy."

"You can call for your daddy if you want," Yuanbao said, "but after we're finished, if you still think you can just walk away from me, be my guest."

"Is that what you think of men?" the recruit said, keeping his anger in check. "My patience has its limits."

"How about a kiss?"

As Yuanbao puckered up his painted lips, the young recruit jumped to his feet and ran off. An argument between him and the dean of students broke out immediately, but his pleadings fell on deaf ears, as the dean regretfully entered a black mark in his notebook, while the exasperated recruit gazed helplessly at the ceiling.

"Let's dance."

The band started up again, and Miss Wang pulled Yuanbao to his feet. Once she and the other girls had him out onto the dance floor, they began tugging this way and that to the rhythm of music.

A cluster of boys came up, dragged them away from him, and began pairing off.

Seeing the latest recruit standing timidly to the side, unable to get up the nerve to ask for a dance, Yuanbao walked up, spread his arms as an invitation to dance, and said, "You have nothing to be ashamed of."

Graceful music blared from the bandstand with the addition of several synthesizers, their electronic echoes and vibrations creating the sound of cascading ocean waves. As the volume increased, the waves crashed onto the shore, like heavy sighs, then slipped back into the watery vastness. . . .

The hotel lobby had taken on a new look: Two curtains had been lowered at one end, and a T-shaped runway extended out through the space between. Spotlights in the four corners of the ceiling lit up the runway. A banner draped in front of the curtains read:

PRELIMINARY TRIALS OF THE ALL-CAPITAL HIGH SCHOOL AMATEUR MODEL CONTEST.

All three sides of the runway were packed with students and invited guests, Sun Guoren and Liu Shunming among them.

Amid waves of applause, a girl in a swimsuit flounced out from between the curtains and walked proudly down the runway, twirling every few steps to give the audience an eyeful. When she reached the end, she let her figure do the talking, first with her hands on her hips, then holding out her arms squeezing her thighs bending her knees spreading her legs standing straight and tall. After completing her sensual performance, she spun and walked back to the far end, stopping every few steps to twirl and make eye contact with the judges.

Prancing and twirling, she reached the curtains and, with a reluctant last look at the audience, and the most appealing pose she could manage, vanished with a straight face. No one who saw her would soon forget that narrow waist and those flat hips.

The second competitor was Miss Wang, and although she wasn't nearly as flashy, she had everything she needed; at least she tried. A little unsteady in high heels, she walked with an uneven gait, which kept her from wowing her audience. But the look on her face was everything a seasoned pro could ask for. Cool, haughty, exuding beauty too great to absorb. Step by proud step, she walked from east to west and back again, displaying a sense of melancholy.

Miss Zheng stepped out next, swaying her hips, a radiant smile on her lips. She walked as if swept along by the wind; one might have thought she was rushing to take a dip in the ocean, or running to catch a bus. Of course, there are other, even better, ways to describe the effect.

Miss Zhou was next. The wiggle in her hips and the smile on her face failed to mask her nervousness. People in the know could see that she was hoping to make one quick turn and head back; those who weren't might have thought she was about to feed herself to the sharks. There was, in fact, nothing to be afraid of. She could have been standing there naked, and not even the keenest eye in the audience could have seen a thing. Fortunately for her, she was a human being; if she'd been a chicken, whoever bought her would surely have taken her back for a refund, assuming the seller had kept the best parts for himself.

There isn't much to say about Miss Wu, who came out face-first. Except that for her, everyone in attendance lowered their heads in embarrassment, as if guilty of an indiscretion, feeling somehow as if time had suddenly stood still.

The audience was still recovering from Miss Wu's assault

when Yuanbao appeared. The rhythm of the waves faltered: They crashed onto the shore but were in no hurry to return, leaving no room for the next assault on the beach. The sound hung in the air in a way that's hard to describe.

He was wearing a revealing, backless swimsuit as he strolled confidently down the runway, his body in perfect rhythm. When he reached the end, he gazed down at the dignified ladies and gentlemen seated below, to whom he showed off his body. He then turned to give them a view of his backside, tautly showing off its curves, to everyone's utter delight. Not wanting to slight the other viewers, he turned his back to them as well, before heading back the way he'd come, accompanied by their applause.

Yuanbao stopped, turned back, sucked in his gut for all to see, and flashed a captivating smile before turning once again and strutting back to the curtains, his midriff flat as could be.

"Notice anything different?" Liu Shunming asked Sun Guoren.

"Not that I could see. He looked a little weird, that's all. I say, cut it off, and he'll be perfect."

"You're right. He'd be much more comfortable without it."

"There's something sinister about that damned thing. I don't like it."

"Me, either. With it, he seems threatening somehow—even with the smile."

"It makes me uncomfortable. Zhao might have hit the nail on the head when he said he was unreliable. You can know the man and the face, but not his heart. We ought to try to find out what's going on in Yuanbao's head. I'm beginning to think he isn't as simple as he looks, and that maybe we're the ones who are being manipulated, not him."

"If you think it's necessary, I'll go along with testing him."

"I won't rest so long as he remains uncastrated."

The swimsuit competition ended, the music lightened, got livelier and happier, as the finale began.

Yuanbao and the other girls walked out in straw hats and rather ugly domestic gowns and daily wear. As if hunting down Eighth Route Army undercover agents, they stopped and started, every once in a while holding the brims of their hats and gazing left and right. Some of the girls peeled off their tops and carried them over their arms as they walked, then put them back on before they reached the end, where they stopped and spread their arms to show off the dresses underneath, like streetcorner peddlers revealing the brand name and then quickly covering it up and walking away.

Yuanbao held his hat down with one hand, picked up the hem of his skirt with the other, and twirled, causing the skirt to flare out and float in the air.

The judges closed their eyes.

Yuanbao closed his eyes and lay atop the white sheet, stripped to the waist. The heavy window curtains were pulled shut, turning the room dark and murky. The stillness of the room was broken only by the sound of a leaky faucet.

"One, two, three, four, five, six, seven, eight . . . nothing here to disturb you . . . except for the sound of my voice and the dripping water, you hear nothing . . . your eyelids are getting heavy . . . you're getting sleepy . . . I'm going to count now, and I want you to count with me . . . one, your body is being submerged in a current of warmth . . . two, your mind is clouding over . . . three, foggier and foggier . . . four . . . five, you're getting sleepier and sleepier . . . six, swathed in silence . . . seven, you are asleep, deeper and deeper . . . eight . . . nine . . . sleep has claimed your body . . . ten, you are now fast asleep . . . eleven, you can hear nothing but my voice . . . twelve, sleep, have a wonderful sleep . . ."

Yuanbao's breathing was even, his chest rose and fell rhythmically; he was snoring gently.

Liu Shunming and Sun Guoren, both in white lab coats, tiptoed into the room. The hypnotist whispered, "He's asleep. He can answer your questions now."

Liu took a list of questions out of his pocket and handed it to the hypnotist, who looked it over, then sat down beside Yuanbao.

"I'm going to ask you some questions. Are you ready to answer them?"

"Yes," Yuanbao replied happily.

"Do you like all those pretty clothes?"

"Yes."

"Do you like them best on other people, or when you're wearing them?"

"I like them on other people *and* on myself."

"Does it embarrass you to be made up like a woman and wear women's clothing in public?"

"No."

"Why not? A man wearing women's clothing isn't a pretty sight."

"I don't do it to be pretty."

"Why do you do it?"

"Being pretty isn't that important . . ."

"You didn't answer my question. If you don't do it to be pretty, why do you do it?"

"There's no such thing as being pretty. Nobody's pretty.

217

This isn't a matter of being pretty or not. . . ." There was an edge to Yuanbao's voice. "I'm not sure I can explain it, but when I wear women's clothes, I'm neither pretty nor ugly. It's something special, but it isn't wrong. I've never cared much what I wear, never cared at all."

"Have you always had a secret desire to be a woman?"

"No. Oh, maybe I have at one time or another, but never a strong desire. I don't think being a woman is something wonderful, but I don't see anything bad in it either. I've never really weighed the pros and cons. I don't care all that much what I am. Good or bad, whatever you are causes problems for others. I seldom examine myself."

"Are you satisfied with the circumstances in being a man?"

"I can't ask for better ones. I have no complaints, since everything's as it should be."

"How's that?"

"Things are as they are, so there's no need trying to figure them out."

"If you were asked to give up being a man, would you do it?"

"I couldn't make it happen myself, but if others did it, that'd be okay with me. I'm only a man because of other people's labors. I didn't have to do a thing."

"Easy come, easy go, right?"

"Easy or not, there's no way to protect against it. There's no reason for me to hang on to it, since it doesn't belong to me."

"Including your body? And your convictions?"

"Including everything. It all comes from the labors of others, and from their sins. What am I, after all? In your eyes, just another living creature. If you close your eyes, I no longer exist. I only sense my own existence from your reactions. If you're happy, I feel that my life is of value. Don't pay any attention to me; let Comrade Lenin be the first to leave."

"You feel no pain or humiliation? In other words, when you find it necessary to sacrifice yourself for the benefit of others, you actually feel duty-bound not to turn back, unswayed by even a hint of emotion?"

"It never reaches the point where my patience is exhausted."

"Never?"

"My imagination, on the other hand, has reached its limit."

"If a situation arose that did exhaust your patience, if . . . I can't think of a good example at the moment."

"I'd close my eyes."

"How could you deal with it like that? That way . . . um, you're always thinking about others, never yourself."

"It's a long story."

"Let's move on. Back when you were a child and just starting to learn the ways of the world, did you already have a tendency to suppress your personality?"

"Childhood . . ." A slur crept into Yuanbao's voice. "The first time I . . . urine . . . mud . . . fort . . ."

"You built a fort with urine and mud, is that it? Where? In your lane? Out on the street? Under a tree or in your own yard?"

"Under a roadside tree."

"Did that make you sense your own insignificance?"

"I sensed the insignificance of the whole world."

"Was it a feeling of despair?"

"I felt—there was nothing to fear!"

Silence . . .

"Anything else you want to ask?" the hypnotist asked Liu and Sun as he stretched wearily.

Numbly, they shook their heads and walked gingerly out of the room.

"I'm going to bring you out of your sleep in five minutes," the hypnotist said softly to Yuanbao. "You will feel wonderful and full of energy, as if you'd just awakened from a good night's sleep. Your mind will be clear and sharp. I'm going to count backward from five. When I reach one, you will be wide awake and fully rested. All right, here we go. Five . . . four . . . you're starting to wake up, see how energetic you feel . . . your muscles are resilient and powerful . . . three! . . . your head is clearing . . . you can distinguish external sounds . . . two! Now you're wide awake . . . under the influence of happy feelings and a great mood . . . one! Wake up! Be sure not to burp or fart or cough. . . . You must avoid all sudden discharges."

Yuanbao opened his eyes and sat up. A huge, shiny mucous bubble emerged from his nose.

"Do you think there's a problem?"

20

Sun Guoren and Liu Shunming were squatting side by side in an outdoor toilet, their pants legs rolled up, each holding the torn half of a newspaper and smoking a cigarette. Sun kept his voice low as he strained to finish what he was there for.

"I don't see any reason why we should bring our work on Yuanbao to an end at this point," Liu answered. "Even though I feel that his thinking processes are warped, at least he hasn't exhibited any signs of passionate opposition yet."

"You're right. At one point my greatest concern was that he'd harbor resentment against us. But so far, so good. His attitude is somewhat negative, but as long as he doesn't turn reactionary, we might be able to put that to our advantage."

"I'm moved by what he's shown me. Maybe the fact that we Chinese keep fighting through setbacks, that we know how to extricate ourselves from desperate situations, that we're doggedly tenacious, and that we always land on our feet is the main reason why the Chinese race stands tall in the forest of nations—always has and always will."

"You couldn't ask for a finer race, and if we don't finish what we set out to do, we will be unworthy of this land, so richly endowed by nature."

"Otherwise, the blood of all our martyrs will have been spilled in vain."

The two men sighed passionately, then returned to the subject at hand. In a furtive tone of voice, Sun asked Liu, "What's your opinion of Zhao Hangyu?"

"He's okay in my book," Liu replied with a guarded look at Sun. "Sure, he's got his faults, like anyone, but as a leader, we couldn't ask for more."

"You don't get the feeling that his mood has soured recently?" Sun cast an inscrutable glance at Liu, being as ambiguous as he could.

"What do you mean by that? Whatever it is, spit it out. There are no secrets between friends."

"I didn't mean anything special. Ordinarily, people have the right to display their emotions freely. But for someone in a leadership position, wallowing in your emotions can be risky. His influence on our work must transcend the personal. He has to take charge of everything. How does it look for him to always be weeping and gnashing his teeth? He doesn't do any work. He's either eating or drinking and having a good time, or reciting poetry and writing stuff."

"You're right; he is beginning to look like an ordinary citizen," Liu said pensively.

"Actually," Sun said as he dragged on his cigarette, "you've pretty much been running the show lately, and I figure we can manage just as well without somebody else waving his arms for show."

"Better, even."

Sun laughed and gazed meaningfully at Liu. "Since Hangyu is so fond of poetry, I say, let him go ahead and devote himself to literary studies. What do you say?"

Liu also laughed. "He can tend his garden, eat porridge, and live a few extra years. Leave the more troubling affairs for younger people to worry about."

"I'm worried about him," Sun said solicitously. "I don't think he can take any more bad news. He's aged a lot over what Bai Du did."

"China can't lose any more national treasures like him—we need all we can get."

"He's part of an endangered species, and we need to protect him like one."

"Maybe even establish a nature preserve."

They had a good laugh over that while they used their newspaper as toilet paper, pulled up their pants, and stood up.

"How you doing, comrades? Did you have a restful Sunday?"

A smiling Zhao Hangyu walked into the conference room with his briefcase and walked naturally up to the head of the table. Removing his tea glass, a tin of tea leaves, a fountain pen, and a notebook, he waved happily to the people sitting around the table.

"I'm feeling much better these days. The poetry I've been reading has lightened my mood considerably. I've even written a bit myself, which I'll be happy to read to you—ha ha—for your comments and suggestions. Western ginseng is terrific, and I recommend it highly. Go home, try some; you'll find it unique, sort of like wearing a heavy parka, then going out to jog bare-chested in December, and sweating up a storm. Ha ha . . ."

He sat down in the chairman's seat and turned to Sun Guoren. "What's today's meeting about? You made it sound urgent. Why's it so important I attend?"

"You'll know in a few minutes," Sun replied icily from the far end of the table. "Is everyone here?" he asked Liu Shunming. "If so, we can start."

The members of the MobCom Directorate sat hushed around the table.

"What's on the agenda?" Zhao asked, smiling warmly at Sun Guoren. He rapped his knuckles on the table. "I ought to know, since I'm presiding."

"I'm presiding today," Sun said, glancing around the table. "The first order of business is a reassignment of responsibilities. Inasmuch as my duties have changed, creating a vacancy in the Tanzi Lane Security Command, I move that Liu Shunming reassume those duties. Let's put it to a vote. . . ."

"Do you really think it's a good idea for Shunming to take on that job again?" Zhao asked unhurriedly. "Remember, he was arrested the first time."

"Any objections? None? The motion passes unanimously."

Sun then lowered his head and read from a printed document. "The next order of business is my motion to rehabilitate Comrade Liu Shunming and restore to him his fine reputation, to repudiate all slanders and libels forced upon him. Do I hear any objections?"

He raised his head to make eye contact with the people around the table. "None? The motion passes unanimously. The third order of business is a proposal to initiate a campaign within

MobCom to oppose all negative, damaging, backward-looking capitalist thought and behavior, and to eradicate the influence of said thought and behavior. Do I hear any objections?"

"Have you discussed any of this with me?"

"None? The motion passes unanimously."

"This is outrageous!" Zhao Hangyu banged the table. "Who gave you the right to initiate such a campaign? Anything this big requires full notification; it's not something you can decide unilaterally. What about the principles of the organization?"

"On to the fourth item, an expression of gratitude to Comrade Zhao Hangyu . . ."

"A sneak attack, this is clearly a sneak attack." Zhao was convulsed with rage. With trembling hands and a halting voice, he said, "How can you treat a comrade this way . . . before the feudal lords send their armies against the court they have to promulgate an official denunciation . . ."

"Settle down, please, while I read the letter," Liu Shunming said as he stood up holding a sheet of paper. "Esteemed Comrade Zhao Hangyu, we members of the MobCom Directorate take this opportunity to express to you our respect and gratitude. You have been diligent and untiring in the daily workings of MobCom, occupied with a myriad of state affairs, leading a hectic, militaristic life, remaining in the saddle under the most adverse conditions, sapping your energy, worrying yourself to distraction, and devoting every ounce of energy to the liberation of the Chinese people; you have retrieved the golden goblet of national integrity, and have busied yourself with the important work of land redistribution; you have lived gloriously and will die with honor; blood shed in this just cause has produced the flower of victory; in facing down the enemy's swords, you have sought out poetry. Flying across the mountain pass, you raise your glass to toast the bright moon; in dreams the universe is vast, awake one's life is long; after a thousand *li* we raise a tent; at last I must bid you adieu; fine flowers do not often bloom, good times do not last forever; when the time comes to part, then part we must. When it's time to forgive, then forgive one must; when affairs of the world do not reach closure, they must be put aside; flowers wither, water flows, and springtime ends—the world changes. The little boat leaves from here, the rest of one's life is claimed by rivers and oceans. When bright mountain flowers are in full bloom, your laughter will emerge from the thicket . . ."

Liu read the declaration with a quiver in his voice, passion in his face, and tears in his eyes. His listeners were choked with emotion, great doses of melancholy filling their bellies.

Zhao Hangyu, whose towering rage had turned to sorrow, was sobbing uncontrollably.

"Can't I even help you onto your horse and accompany you down the road?"

"You needn't go anywhere," Sun Guoren said as he dried his tears, "except for home. Enjoy life for a change."

"But how can I, when I'm worried you may not be able to handle something so big? This old steed still has a few miles left in him. . . ."

"We may not be perfect, but we're up to the task, surely no less so than you. It's time to escort old Zhao to his home."

Two security men entered the room and stood beside Zhao, one on either side.

There was more he wanted to say, but one look at his escort changed his mind. He stood up docilely and shuffled toward the door.

A round of applause followed him.

Zhao held onto the bannister as he walked down the stairs ahead of the two security men, who merely watched him stumble down, one step at a time.

There was no car waiting for him at the door, only a husky young man on a bicycle with a piece of cloth covering the rack behind him.

"You'll have to go second class," one of his escorts said as he pointed to the bicycle. "We've already taken care of the fare."

The other security man tossed Zhao his beat-up briefcase, which hit him squarely in the chest. The security man and his partner turned and went back into the building.

Hugging his pack to his chest, Zhao Hangyu looked skyward and sighed. "Since I, the legendary strategist Zhou Yu, am here, why bring a Zhuge Liang into this world?"

Yuanbao and the girls sat in the front row of the lecture hall, their eyes glazed and glittery, radiating childlike innocence as they gazed up at the podium, behind which stood a skinny and very animated lecturer, who normally choked with laughter over his own lively lectures.

The lecturer adjusted his glasses, looked down at his notes, then raised his head.

"Now that I've concluded my opening remarks, let's turn to the topic at hand: Who creates history?"

He looked with self-satisfaction into the eyes of his student audience.

"Who has an answer to my question?"

The fifth girl stood up. "The masses," she replied.

"Wro—ng. You may sit down. How about the hermaphrodite in the front row; what do you say?"

Yuanbao pointed to himself. "Me?"

"Yes, you. Are you a boy or a girl? I can't tell. But I don't like your looks."

Yuanbao stood up. "Books create history."

"Wr—ong again," the lecturer said decisively. "Books are written by people."

"Then it's the people who write the books."

"Non—sense! Sit down. Anyone else?"

"Emperors and kings and generals and ministers."

"Stu—pid! That explanation is dead and buried; no one believes it anymore!" The lecturer swept the hall with his eyes. "Does anyone know? No? Then I'll tell you. History is created by women . . . heh heh." He luxuriated in the reaction to his comment.

"Which came first, the chicken or the egg? Think about it. The chicken, of course. A chicken can be seen as just another bird, yet if the egg is laid not by a chicken, but by some other bird, it can't be a chicken's egg. History is an egg, an egg laid by women. The masses, all heroes, writers of books—can you find a single one among them who wasn't the child of a woman? Even if she was a whore. When we look at China's history, every time there's a crisis, it's a woman who steps forward to disperse the fog steady the course set history on the path of development. From Dan Ji of the Yin dynasty to Bao Si of the Ji Zhou, from Xi Shi to Lü Zhi, Wang Zhaojun, Zhao Feiyan, Yang Yuhuan, Wu Zetian, and others, to feminized figures like Zhao Gao, Gao Lishi, Wei Zhongxian, Little An, Little Li, and a whole bunch of people born as or converted into women. While they could not bear the burdens of state-hood or rule with an iron fist, one word from them brought the nation to glory or ruin. They fulfilled a function that class enemies wished to fulfill but couldn't and accomplished things that class enemies wanted to accomplish but failed to. Thus they invested our history with impropriety, threw prosperity and decline into chaos, bequeathing to us no end of remorseful sighs, fanciful thoughts, and unanswered questions. They provided us with another type of historical development: You can conquer the world either by sitting on the back of a horse or by lying on your back in bed.

"In *The Art of Warfare*, Sun-tzu wrote, 'Defeating the enemy without engaging him in battle is the sign of a great general.' I say, 'Reaping a harvest without working in the field is the sign of a true sage.' All you students, you female students, is this not praise indeed? Don't shrink in the face of the rantings of men, all this talk of the authority of the husband or of male superiority. They have dreamed up these tricks for their own psychological equilibrium, because they are afraid of you. Why, I ask you, don't the police arrest good people but concentrate instead on hooligans and thieves? Isn't it because they fear the damage these people can inflict on society? And so, although you travel the world as members of the weaker sex, there is nothing to stop you from doing as you please, just like men. Throw off your sense of inferiority! What do we say of women? That they are far more savage and cruel than men. . . ."

The lecturer released a long, leisurely, resonant fart. He was deeply ashamed.

"Pardon me, I'm so sorry. That was terribly impolite, please forgive me."

"Don't sweat it," Miss Wang consoled him on behalf of the students. "Our last speaker shit his pants, and that didn't bother us."

"Don't you understand that what they want to do is destroy you?"

The audience had filed out, leaving the lecture hall to Yuanbao and Bai Du, who was dressed as a man. They were in the last row. Bai Du was both extremely worked up and extraordinarily morose.

"This is a well thought-out scheme with a clear purpose in mind. You must put as much distance as possible between you and them, or it's all over for you."

With palpable indifference, Yuanbao scanned the rows of empty seats, as if everything she said was going in one ear and out the other. He didn't say a word.

"I came prepared," she said. "Tomorrow night, say you have to go to the bathroom. You change into these clothes I've brought with me and climb over the wall behind the bathroom. I'll be there waiting at eight o'clock."

Bai Du took a policeman's uniform out of her bag.

"No one will hassle you in these."

Yuanbao glanced at the uniform without a trace of emotion, and didn't reach out to take it from her.

"Will you do it or not? If you don't like this plan, we can think up something else. I can have a patrol car drive up to the college and take you away in custody . . ."

"I'm not leaving," Yuanbao said flatly. "Thanks for the concern, but I'm staying."

"What's there to keep you? Is there anyone here who actually treats you as a human? They're all using you for their own purposes, and they'll destroy you in the process. They'll turn you into whatever their hearts desire. I can't believe you don't feel any rage or humiliation. How can you possibly just sit there and take it?"

"If I hear you right, you're saying there is a sanctuary somewhere in this world?"

"Don't you think so?"

Silence.

"We can go to West Mountain, or to the liberated areas. . . . The sky there is blue, the water green, with fresh flowers in full bloom. Everyone has food to eat and clothes to wear. There's no oppression, no exploitation. You're free to do what you wish, a place where life is lived with a song."

"You don't have to work?"

"No. The streets are paved with gold, and all you have to do is bend down to pick it up."

"It sounds like America to me."

"Pretty much, close enough. The only difference is that there are no presidential campaigns. You don't have to answer to anyone."

"I'm not sure I could get used to never answering to anyone."

"How sad. We poor, benighted Chinese."

"Up your . . . I mean, up my mother's you-know-what! How could I be such a useless specimen, useless and stupid. Gooey mud doesn't stick to a wall. If you dug a gold or silver pit right at my feet, I wouldn't have the guts to close my eyes and jump in. You've all been so good to me, and I've let you down. How can I ever face all the people who've been so caring to me? Hell, why don't I just slap myself in the face?"

"Does that mean you've decided to leave?"

"No, I'm not in the mood. Just consider me one of those two-cent chicken asses, not even worth considering, good or bad. I'm not worth shit. Whether I live or die shouldn't bother anybody."

"You're human, and you ought to see yourself that way. . . . I feel crappy."

"Don't feel crappy; I'm not human, never have been."

"I do feel crappy, I have to. Don't think I don't understand you. I'm partly to blame for turning you into what you are today."

"Save that for a deathbed confession," Yuanbao said.

"No, I want to say it now."

"Why be so hard on yourself?"

"You have to think about the future. You can't play the clown all your life. Sooner or later, the real play has to begin. What the people really like to see are emperors and kings, generals and ministers, gifted scholars and beautiful maidens."

"They're nothing but a different bunch of clowns in armor, wearing fake beards."

"Who cares what it is, as long as it's not your play? What happens when you leave the stage?"

Silence.

"Some things that are lost are never found again," Bai Du continued. "Don't think it'll grow back if you cut it off. You can't give up a lifetime of happiness over a fleeting thrill."

Silence.

"Make up your mind. Don't wait till the scalpel flashes."

"Did I grow the thing just so I could use it one day?"

"Use it just once or for a lifetime?"

Silence.

"Life may be precious," Bai Du reminded him, "but that thing you've got is priceless."

21

The bunting-draped Capital Sports Arena swelled with the thunderous sounds of singing. Eighteen thousand girls—workers peasants soldiers businesswomen students in every imaginable pose and gorgeous colors, valiant and spirited—filled the bleachers, biding their time by singing loudly and shouting slogans, rubbing their fists and wiping their palms, creating a fervent atmosphere, in anticipation of the opening of the "Oath Ceremony for the Mobilization of Tang Yuanbao for Entry into the Ranks of All-China Female Heroes."

"Basket in hand, go sell your wares, *ai-hai ai-hai ai.* Glean the coal cinders! Carry the water, chop the kindling *en-en-en-en*, it's all up to her . . ."

Girls in the eastern bleachers sang a chorus, and were answered by girls in the western bleachers, even more spiritedly:

"Thunderclaps rock heaven and earth, out on the plains who doesn't know the Worker Peasant girl Zhao Xiaoying . . ."

"Break out the fancy tables . . . guests are coming from all corners, each bringing a lively mouth. They laugh when they meet, they don't care what they've said, and when they leave, the tea is cold *ang-ah ang-ah, ang-ang-ang* . . ."

Girls in the northern bleachers were free and easy, those in the south grim and melancholy:

"My home is in Duckweed Creek in *ai-ai-ai* Anyuan; for three generations we've dug the coal *ai-ai-ai* like beasts *he-he* of burden."

Following a girl in a short skirt holding a wooden sign, Yuanbao, glowing with health and radiating vigor, walked onto the stage, arms swinging gracefully.

He was greeted by thunderous applause and whoops of welcome. The songs rang out crisply, rising and falling, bouncing crazily back and forth.

"At a banquet at Turtledove Mountain we become friends over food and drink, *ao-ao-ao* . . ."

"Listen to Grannie talk of revolution, of heroes and martyrs, but I was born in the wind and grew up in the rain, *ang-ang* . . ."

"Mounting an attack on the Communists, where is your heart, and where is your mind . . ."

". . . circle round, a battle here and a skirmish there, guerrilla warfare is the only way to crush the enemy . . ."

As the song moved throughout the hall, a group of big-bosomed, stern-looking elderly women strode out onto the stage and sat in their assigned seats at the rostrum, where they looked around and whispered to one another.

Yuanbao made a complete turn around the hall, blowing kisses as he went, then joined the others on the stage. One of the elderly women pointed to the spot where he was to stand, in the center of the stage just below the rostrum. He stood there with his arms at his sides and his head down.

"Sisters," announced the emcee, a lovely young man, after tapping the microphone to see if it was on, "elders, aunties, I hereby proclaim that the Oath Ceremony for the Mobilization of Tang Yuanbao for Entry into the Ranks of All-China Female Heroes is hereby opened."

A round of applause accompanied the musical offering of the all-girls military band.

"First on the program is the singing of 'Red Detachment of Women Anthem.'"

The emcee walked over to Yuanbao, pushed him aside, then raised his arms and led the singing.

"Forge ahead, forge ahead, the soldier carries a heavy burden, the woman's hatred is deep. In ancient times, Hua Mulan took her father's place on the battlefield, today the Red Detachment of Women bears arms for the people . . ."

Everyone present raised their voices, foreheads beaded with sweat, faces glowing with pride. Their song drove Yuanbao's soul out of his body as he stood there shaking.

"Sisters, elders, aunties," the emcee announced into the microphone after the song had ended and he had returned to the rostrum, "next on the program will be expressions by women's representatives of what they have learned from their experiences as women. Give them a hearty welcome, please."

A diminutive woman walked bashfully from the spectators' area up to the rostrum, where she shook hands with the emcee, who raised the microphone to her lips as he said, "I'd like to ask you if you are caught up in the excitement."

"Yes, I am. People were turned into monsters in the old

society. In our new society the monsters have been turned into people."

The emcee blinked several times before reacting. "Well said. My sentiments exactly. What do you do? You're so well spoken."

"I work in a restaurant."

"Interesting work."

"Yes. It gives me an opportunity to watch how people eat and to learn how to make conversation."

"Wonderful. Does it take long to become good at it?"

"No, it comes fast."

"Stop pestering her; let her speak. A dog doesn't need help eating shit."

The impatience of those at the rostrum turned vocal.

"I'm sorry, excuse me," the emcee said, turning toward the source of the complaint. He handed the microphone to the young woman. "Go ahead."

The diminutive woman thrust out her chest, held the microphone to her lips, swallowed a couple of times, and rolled her eyes, then spoke rapidly:

"Men suck. They say they come to the restaurant to eat, but they're really there to hassle us. My mother was a waitress in the old society. She was always being pawed by men, and was expected to smile the whole time. My father wound up having her before she could get away from him. Things are better in the new society. The status of women has been raised. We may still be waitresses, but the tables have turned. I've never given one of my customers a pleasant look, not since my first day on the job. If they're hungry, I serve them food. If not, they can get lost. All the waitresses at my restaurant are hard as rocks. Our customers don't dare get fresh with us. If they so much as frown at me, I shove a plate of food in their face."

Applause.

Obviously pleased with herself, she continued, "We're all human, so why should I look on while you eat? Stop treating us women as subhuman. The sisters have stood up. Twenty years of personal experience have shown me that with men it's like squeezing persimmons to see if they're ripe. You pick the soft ones and avoid the hard ones. Treat them with softness, and they're all over you. But come at them like a tigress, and they fall to their knees. One word says it all: 'fight!'"

More applause.

"At first, I was depressed over being a woman. But no longer. After tempering myself over a period of time, I now get a big kick out of being a woman. I'm good at it. I get as much pay every month as the men, actually almost a dollar more. And each year, we not only rest when they do, but we get a half day's more vacation time. I'm perfectly content with my lot, and wouldn't exchange it for anything. It's great being a woman."

Laughter throughout the hall was followed by a round of applause.

After shaking hands with the elderly women at the rostrum and giving them each a hug, she returned to her seat with renewed confidence.

"Who's next?" the emcee asked as his eyes swept the bleacher seats.

"Me, I'm next," came a sweet reply. A gorgeously decked-out young woman in a cluster of equally gorgeously decked-out, giggly young women waltzed up to the rostrum.

The emcee held the microphone out to her.

"Thank you. At this moment I'm almost too choked up to speak." She turned and flashed a seductive gaze toward the emcee, which drew a chorus of laughter.

Blushing bright red, but holding his emotions in check, he said, "Tell us what you do, please."

"I don't do anything. I live by my feminine wiles," she said coquettishly.

Another burst of laughter. The rebuffed emcee slinked over to his seat.

With a glare at the emcee, the young woman held the microphone in both hands after tossing a handful of melon seeds into her mouth and spitting out the husks, then said earnestly:

"I'm a woman who supports herself by her own labor. I'm proud of that; there's nothing to be ashamed of. For too long we've been oppressed by men, who treat us as playthings. They can have several women at the same time, for which they're praised by their own kind as ladies' men. And us? If we have a relationship with more than one man, we're known as tattered shoes—sluts. Is that fair? Our bodies are our own, so what right do they have to philander, but keep us from doing the same? I don't believe this criminal practice has any right to exist. So I've decided to turn this evil tide back. The country's in trouble, with too much floating capital in the freewheeling hands of the masses. If one day they decide to invest it all in the stock market, we could slip into an economic depression. The country cannot provide enough products to take this currency out of circulation, and the consumers are spending their money on household necessities and durable goods. This is a consequence of a disastrous long-term national policy. Everything goes toward symbolic expenditures, such as housing, medical expenses, and sex. It's a government monopoly, an unreasonable structure of consumption that even the developed West would never embrace. But we, a developing country, charge ahead on this path! If we're to have a strong economy, with a controlled flow of currency, it's imperative that we change the current, unreasonable structure of consumption. We must decrease or eliminate subsidies altogether and replace them with a market economy, a policy of selling goods at no less than market value. Everything must be done in accordance with economic principles to complete the transition from Socialism to Communism. We must see reforms in rents, medical treatment, and coverage, even sex. This is the trend of the times. And so in response to the call of the nation, we women must first switch to a commodity economy. Husbands and lovers must be required to pay—a reasonable price, naturally. When we set the price we must take into consideration current national wage standards. We don't want to bankrupt anybody. My research and experience have led me to recommend both a maximum and minimum cap on women's pay, with a fluctuating scale between the two, based upon differences in the subject's ability to pay. Let me state here and now that in my profession I'm counted among the elite. I pay the highest taxes; my labor and value output is in the top bracket. No man, whether he's a scientist or a skilled worker, is my equal in this regard. What's the yardstick for measuring anyone's contributions to society? It's whether or not the person increases the nation's wealth. On this point, we women are abundantly qualified. Whatever a male comrade can do, so can we. Whatever a male comrade can't do, we can!"

Applause, loud cheers.

She whipped out a taxi meter, as if by magic, and held it over her head. "Sisters," she shouted, "we must mobilize.

Everyone run out and sell one of these counters for the greening of the motherland—make all men wear the green hat of the cuckold."

Turning to shake hands with the elderly women at the podium, who were clapping enthusiastically, she poured her heart out in their ears and wished them well. Her face was tear-streaked.

The applause seemed never-ending. Finally the emcee walked up, took the microphone, and tried to speak, but was drowned out by the waves of applause. Lowering his head, he leaned over to Yuanbao and said, "Hey, what do you think of that?"

Yuanbao turned toward the emcee. "Sounds like tinkering with the meter to cheat on electricity."

"As for me, I've been looked upon as just another gourmet food since childhood."

The third speaker was a wrinkled, skinny old woman with droopy eyelids.

"This so-called gourmet food is nothing but stuffed buns from the Chase Away Dogs restaurant. I'm not a pretty woman, for which I've bemoaned my fate in the past and have had an inferiority complex for a long time. When men see me, they either start crying out of fear or run up and try to wrestle me to the ground. You can't imagine how that makes me feel. There were times during my teens when I despaired to the point of suicide. I'd given up on life. All of you, just think what it was like to be a girl with no self-respect. You say the Japanese are sex-crazed? Well, in our county, there were blockhouses in every village, but when the invaders came to my village, one look at me had them turning tail and running off. I'm a human being, just like everyone else. Who among you doesn't have ideals, who among you hasn't been chased by men until you fell all over yourself? Everyone but me, whom no one wanted even as a backup. In the dark of night I jumped over walls, only to have men toss me right back. How could a girl take an insult like that? More than once, I tossed a rope over a rafter to hang myself, but I always changed my mind at the last minute. I couldn't die like that! I asked myself, how come a woman can't go on living without a man? Solutions to problems can only come from the living, and if you have to go to the bathroom, it's stupid to kill yourself holding it in. If I couldn't go to Xi'an, I'd go to Yan'an. If they wouldn't let me go up Mount Lu, I'd climb Jinggang Mountain. The earth had no roads to begin with, but when the first man passed by, a road was made. It only takes one person to start a Cultural Revolution; then everyone else finds it easy to fall in line. Once I'd convinced myself, it was easy to rise up to the challenge and face life with courage and determination. Look at me: Life is good now! I'm sharing that life with a fellow sufferer. With mutual love and respect, we help and learn from one another, and even though sometimes it's hard on us and we get the feeling we're not up to the challenge, that vegetarian noodles can't compare with a real drumstick, we've overcome these challenges, one after the other, and have groped our way onto a new road, with Chinese characteristics, and a new way of dealing with the world. We enjoy a sense of dignity and gratification. We get along just fine without men, a life with unique joys. When we have no leather shoes, we wear straw sandals, when we have no cotton fabric, we wear homespun cloth, but what if we don't give you anything to eat?"

Applause, a seemingly endless burst of applause.

"You dirty dogs!" the woman snarled as she glared at Yuanbao, who was standing with his head bowed. "You're more venomous than scorpions, more hateful than the old landlords! When you have nothing, you shout for us, but when you're given food, you pick and choose. It's because of you that I gave up on life. I ate the food you gave me and plodded through life like a beast of burden. I suffered terribly in the sixties as a refugee and a beggar, when there was only white clay and tree bark to fill my belly. But now, if I didn't cook a little food for myself on the side, I'd starve to death while you looked on. I'm going to tear you to shreds, you ill-begotten bastard. You don't want something, but you won't let anybody else have it either. Give me back my youth . . ."

"Hold on, not so fast. A gentlewoman fights with her mouth, not her hands. Curse him all you want, but keep your hands to yourself." The emcee wrapped his arms around the old maid, who had charged Yuanbao and was about to gouge his eyes out. "You'll have your bread, and you'll have your butter."

"Let go of me! *Now* you're holding me! Where were you last night when I was out searching for somebody to hold me?"

"Let her go," an elderly woman demanded of the emcee. "How dare you obstruct our women's revolution!"

"Look what she's doing. I'm worried she'll kill the guy." The emcee let the old maid go. "I thought we were to focus on remedies," he said with a worried look.

"Who are the ruthless ones?" the old woman demanded with the force of justice. "Over thousands of years, women have shed a river of blood."

"Who does he think he is?" the old maid shouted. "Why is he running our women's gathering? As a man, he should be standing on the denunciation platform."

"Stand up there! Stand up there!" Eighteen thousand women raised their voices in a thunderous roar. "That look, it's neither yin nor yang. Diao Deyi, what are you—up—to . . ." the women sang out as one.

"Women warriors, revolutionary women," the pitiful emcee attempted to explain. "I stand shoulder to shoulder with you. I, too, have suffered bitterly and have a bellyful of hate. I . . . I hereby announce that I am androgynous . . ."

"All revolutionaries stand up and be counted! Everyone else, get the hell out of here! Attack attack attack! Get out get out get out!" The women set up a rhythmic chant directed at the emcee. Then they began to sing: "My mama went out to fight jackals and wolves, and won't leave the battle till they're all *en-en-en* dead . . ."

"Spare me, please," the emcee begged the elderly woman. "I've never taken advantage of women. I fall in love with every one I meet."

"Didn't you hear the revolutionary women's demand?" the old woman asked with a sneer. "Do it on your own initiative; don't wait for us to drag you over."

"Go on, get up there," the old maid said as she shoved the emcee, who staggered up next to Yuanbao and looked around helplessly. They were surrounded by women, each with one hand on her hip and the other pointing at them, hair ruffled, sneering as they sang out:

"Where do you get off *yi-yi* talking like one of us. I don't care if you punish me with the thousand cuts. Sooner or later Shajiabang will be liberated. Then see how you traitors running dogs turncoats—meet *ao-ao* your *he-he* end!"

The emcee's head drooped gloomily. "Where in the hell did this bunch of opera singers come from?"

"Did I hear you talk of your ideals," the elderly woman who took over for the emcee said as she thrust the microphone under the emcee's nose.

"I have no ideals," the frightened emcee blurted out, waving his arms. "I admit everything."

The old woman cast a scornful look at the emcee, shook her head to set her short hair flying, and raised her face, which glowed with health. "Sisters," she said to the audience, "today's revolutionary activity has magnified the power and prestige of women and obliterated the aspirations of a small clique of men! Congratulations! Happiness fills our hearts. We have toppled the fourth great mountain and trampled it with the feet of tens of thousands, so they can never again rise up!"

A broad-shouldered, thick-waisted woman leaped onto the speaker's podium and grabbed the microphone.

"I'll be brief, since the sisters who spoke before me said everything that was in my heart. I say we've shown the utmost tolerance and patience toward Tang Yuanbao. We've reasoned with him, we've shown him the way. Now let's see if he's gotten the message, see if he's willing to break with his past and walk the straight and narrow. On behalf of all women, I await his response."

All the women in the bleachers rubbed their eyes and opened them wide.

"We're waiting," the woman holding the microphone said with a smile.

Yuanbao raised his head slowly, until his eyes met a sea of expectant and fervently encouraging gazes. He walked slowly up to the podium and took the microphone. His lips twitched, but for a while no words came out. Gazing out at a host of women, young and old, he finally said with uncontrolled passion, "I am totally undeserving of the sisters' good wishes and concern."

A loud "ooooh" burst from the speaker's podium, like a clap of thunder.

"You ain't seen nothin' yet," one of the women bellowed. "We have plenty of ways to show our fondness."

"I know," Yuanbao said with a nod. "With all the love and affection I've gotten, I'd have been an ingrate if I hadn't become a woman."

Applause. A thunderstorm of applause.

"You've done it. You're a success." Eighteen thousand women were moved to tears. Holding hands, they gazed up at Yuanbao and showered him with congratulations. "Now we have our own atomic bomb."

"You can't leave me here by myself," the emcee bent at the waist, turned, and said to Yuanbao, "They'll chew me up and spit me out."

Yuanbao looked over at the emcee, then quieted the crowd with a wave of his hands. "I have emerged from the darkness into the light," he said. "But we have in our midst a stubborn holdout." He pointed to the emcee. "Shall we pump ourselves up one more time and help turn him around?"

"Throttle him!" The women screamed as if crazed, fists in the air, laughing hysterically.

The emcee fainted on the spot.

"Kill him! Kill him while you can! Tear him to shreds, then stuff the pieces into a rocket and send them into space!"

The outraged women were in an uncontrollable emotional frenzy. A few of the more agile among them had already rushed up onto the stage, where they grabbed the emcee and began slapping him.

"Stop that, sisters. Don't be hitting him like that." The woman who was running the show pulled the others away. "You're letting him off too easily. Doesn't he look down on women? Then let's give him a taste of his own medicine. Let's throw him into Lion and Tiger Mountain."

"Yay—" The women roared their approval.

They picked up the emcee and carried him off the stage. As he lay across the muscular shoulders of his bearers, he turned to the woman with the microphone, smiled, and said, "I want a guarantee that all the tigers on Lion and Tiger Mountain are females."

"Don't worry," the old woman replied, gnashing her teeth, "you won't die an unfair death."

The emcee was dumped on the floor in the middle of the gymnasium, and all four doors were closed. A worker walked up and tossed a piece of red cloth at him, then backed off. The emcee picked up the cloth, but didn't know what to do with it, so he wrapped it around his shoulders and stood there with a foolish grin on his face. Suddenly, one of the doors flew open to admit an enraged woman, who lowered her head and charged the emcee as if shot out of a cannon. An outpouring of loud cheers rained down on him from all sides, as the women jumped to their feet and raised clenched fists.

At the precise moment the charging woman reached the emcee, in a purely conditioned reflex action, he held out the red cloth and twisted his body just enough for the woman to shoot past, missing him completely.

But he had no time to celebrate, for she spun around and wordlessly launched a second charge at her target.

Holding the red cloth in both hands, the emcee flicked it as the woman bore down on him, causing her to miss her mark once again.

The bleachers seethed with excitement; the shouts of eighteen thousand nearly blew the roof off the gymnasium.

The enraged woman, who was literally seeing red, charged the emcee over and over, tirelessly, unstoppably. The emcee, on the other hand, was slowing down, finding it harder and harder to avoid the onrushing woman, and several times she actually brushed against him, tearing holes in his clothes and scraping chunks from his naked flesh.

Then it happened—he didn't get out of the way in time, and was sent reeling. He struggled a while when she held him over her head; then he was flung onto the railing, where he lay motionless.

"Yay—" Every woman in the gymnasium gasped in alarm. Then they erupted in frenzied applause.

"Scalpel . . . scissors . . . forceps . . . tweezers . . ."

Under a fluorescent lamp, a cluster of doctors in white surgical gowns and gauze masks proceeded methodically with the operation. . . .

22

The doors swung open and a nurse wheeled a gurney out of surgery. The gurney was covered by a spotless white sheet under which Tang Yuanbao lay in slumber.

His face was pale, peaceful, glossy, smooth.

The gurney glided smoothly and noiselessly down the corridor.

Liu Shunming, Sun Guoren, the four women—Zhou, Wu, Zheng, Wang—and the leaders of the women's groups all stood waiting at the far end of the corridor.

When the gurney reached them, they stared down at the sleeping Yuanbao.

"How'd the operation go?" Sun Guoren asked the nurse.

"Without a hitch," the nurse answered. "You have nothing to worry about."

"How long before he can get out of bed and move around?"

"Not long," the nurse said as she pushed the gurney into the room. "What he had removed was nothing but a nuisance, right?"

"That's right," Sun said. "Well, I can breathe easier now."

"There was never any need for you to be nervous," Liu Shunming said. "It's a common procedure. He's certainly not the first person to undergo it."

Sun turned and shook hands with the women. "Thank you all for your support and your help. We couldn't have done it without you."

"It was our pleasure," their spokeswoman said. "Nurturing a new generation of socialists is everyone's responsibility. We were duty-bound to do it, so there's no need to thank us."

"Will Yuanbao move back in with us after he leaves the hospital?" Miss Zheng asked.

"I'm afraid not," Sun said with a broad smile. "You young ladies have fulfilled your duty. Go back and study hard. Once you graduate and enter society, your hands will be full with promising candidates for training."

"We'll miss Yuanbao," Miss Wang said. "But now he has important work, representing all women in the contest. It is a momentous task, far more important than living with us, right?" she said to Sun with undiluted innocence.

"That's right. Once he's regained his strength, he'll be off to the wars."

"We wish him speedy success and total victory," Miss Wang said. She was speaking for them all.

"How can he fail? There isn't another person in the world as well trained as he."

"And it could only have happened in our beloved China," Liu Shunming added.

"How do you feel?"

Yuanbao was sitting up in his hospital bed. There were flowers everywhere. He was being interviewed by a reporter.

"Do you feel strange at all after your surgery?"

"No, I feel great, couldn't be better." Yuanbao looked up to describe how he felt. "It's like walking a hundred miles carrying a trunk on your back. Then you toss it away, and even if it had been filled with gold and precious gems, you feel like you're sitting on top of the world. Sure, there might be losses, but at least you feel like you've gotten your life back, not to mention the fact that you can walk a lot faster."

"Now that you've tossed away your trunk . . ." The bespectacled reporter's question was drowned out by raucous laughter in the room. Clearly embarrassed, he adjusted his glasses and changed the subject. "How did you feel when you agreed to the operation? Not even a trace of . . . um . . . shall we say, indecision? What I mean is . . . um, how shall I put it . . . a momentous decision."

"Of course I was hesitant at first, but I overcame it. Just thinking of the great trust the nation has placed in me, and the dreams and aspirations of my countrymen, all thoughts for myself simply vanished. Besides, as they say, swords are forged from the finest steel; state banquets are where you drink the best wine. In the beginning that thing of mine, even if rid of its odor, could not be served at the dining table. But now it can fulfill a glorious function, putting the whole nation at ease.

It is my honor, for it has now served its real purpose. A war-horse should die on the battlefield; a true hero should die on the sword."

"Okay, enough already, we get your point."

"You do? It looks like I underestimated you."

"Don't think we're a bunch of idiots. In this profession of apple-polishing, I don't think we're inferior to you."

Yuanbao responded with a sinister laugh. "Then let's cut the crap. Do you honestly think this was a momentous decision? Do you really place that much importance on that you-know-what?"

"It's only common sense, isn't it? Everyone should have one, whether traveling or at home, for it can help in the treatment of aches, melancholy, hunger, laziness, back pains . . ."

"Apparently, you folks are very utilitarian-minded. But I can tell you it was one of the easiest decisions I've ever made. No more difficult than agreeing to an appendectomy or tonsillectomy . . ."

Lowering his voice and smiling mysteriously, Yuanbao continued, "And that's because I have no personal life whatsoever."

As if a light had gone on in their heads, the reporters bent over their notebooks to take down Yuanbao's comment.

"In other words," one of them said, with a glance at his notebook, "you've always been one of those warriors who pillows his head on his spear, waiting for day to break, is that it? Standing on both sides of the Taiwan Straits, implementing the 'three-no' policy, right?"

"It never occurred to us that you suffered so," another reporter remarked with genuine feeling.

"There's no need for you guys to pretend anyone's suffered," Yuanbao said with a laugh.

"What are your aspirations for women," a female reporter asked, "now that you've entered our ranks?"

"I admire them greatly, and wish them continued glory. They are a young contingent, and even though they have gotten off to a late start, they can draw on the experience of others and avoid some of the detours. While they are assimilating the essence of men, they must absolutely reject the dross that accompanies it."

"I hear that you attended a public meeting to assess the power of women. Did that experience leave much of an impression on you?"

"Yes, of course. They are imbued with a spirit that can vanquish mountains and rivers; they can sweep away all obstacles; they exhibit extraordinary ferocity."

"Was that one of the major factors in your decision?"

"*Hai!*" Yuanbao replied gravely. "I've always preferred to stand alongside the strong."

"Thank you for spending the time with us. One final question. Is there anything you'd like to say to our readers and viewers?"

Yuanbao sat up, cleared his throat, and spoke into the extended microphones as if he were speaking directly to every citizen of the country:

"Don't feel sorry for me. I have a good life these days, thanks to the concern of the leaders and other comrades, who don't discriminate against me in any way. I perform manual labor every day, and continue my transformation. I'm given meat on Tuesdays and Thursdays, and watch movies twice a month. I'm currently writing a book in which I look back over my life to this point. I plan to act in a movie called *Tears of Remorse,* which will be available on video cassette. I have brought harm to countless individuals during my lifetime, but none of them hold grudges and they continue to treat me like family. If they can be that charitable, why should I complain about a few hardships? I am blessed, and all you people. . . . okay, that's enough. If I say any more I'm afraid it'll come out wrong."

"Is there anything else you'd like to say?"

"Anything I said would be superfluous, except to tell you that I do not accept the charge of betraying my country," muttered old man Tang, who sat with his eyes nearly shut. "I don't belong to the same country as you Han Chinese. I was part of the Great Qing empire, a lost nation, which means it cannot be betrayed. I'm an overseas Chinese. You can call me a foreign agent, if you like, but not a traitor."

"That in itself is superfluous. You are a Chinese citizen."

"But what I did happened during the last days of the Great Qing empire, and ever since the founding of the Republic, I've been a model citizen."

"Apparently, you still haven't come to grips with your problem."

"How can you say that? Of course I have. I shouldn't have participated in the rebellion. I blame Prince Chun for getting me involved. The Great Qing was doomed, so what difference did it make who finished it off? Better to hand it over to a friendly nation than to the local slaves. Take a look at Hong Kong, then at Macao. Are the people there enslaved? As I see it, people who ignore the lessons of history are bound to repeat them. If an old lady is a virgin till death, fight 'em off, no penetration! Otherwise, today we'd all be spending Japanese yen, hard currency, and international foreign reserves, but we'd be eating our own shrimp and using our own hog-bristle brushes. See how things are now? You could get down on your knees and beg every country in the world to invade you, and they wouldn't take you up on it. They're too smart for that. What would they get out of it? Nothing but a quagmire."

"Everything you've said is going into your dossier. The Chinese people would rather be broken than bent, would rather stand and die than live on their knees!"

"Enough, already. As if you never grew a queue. You cried and shouted you didn't want them, so what happened later? You balked when it was time to cut them off. You Han Chinese can't hide anything from me. You pretend you've got backbone, pretend you're tough, try to make people believe you, act like you can take any suffering. In fact, there's no suffering for you and damned few who care to save face."

"Go ahead and be a reactionary. Today I'm giving you a chance to be as big a reactionary as you wish."

"We Manchus are unlucky people. Why couldn't we have been born next to the Americans instead of you people? It sure didn't take much to topple your dynasty. Cheap goods are no damned good. You make all the imperialists in the world lose heart."

"Anything else you want to say? Now's the time."

"Don't you have a confession or something you want me to sign?"

"No!" The interrogator's anger rose. "Don't think you can escape the people's punishment!" he bellowed as he pounded the table and jumped to his feet.

"I'll be happy to place an ad in the paper saying I'm turning over a new leaf."

"Fat chance! I won't rest till I've beaten you to a pulp."

"You mean it isn't enough to admit my mistakes? I can redeem myself by doing good deeds and turning against those I mistakenly sided with. I can take a bite out of some evil backstage manipulators. Tell me who you're having trouble with, and I'll go stand beside them and name them as instigators. I'll take the lead in launching an attack to unmask and denounce them. I'm an old hand at divide-and-conquer putting up propaganda posters floating rumors, and if that doesn't suit your purpose I can eulogize virtues and achievements call a stag a horse lie with my eyes wide open lay my hands on a Gang of Four with my eyes closed and don't worry about me just tell me what you want me to do and I'll do it I'll be your target or your hatchet man I'm a damned good hatchet man and you can put me in the ranks of Rightists if you want do whatever you want with me wherever you see something missing or a shortage I'll fill it up or make it whole and you won't hear a peep out of me!"

"The only thing we have missing is someone to shoulder responsibility for the failure of the glorious Boxer movement."

"The performance is about to begin. Do you know your lines?"

Backstage, Tang Yuanbao was stretching, putting one leg up on the radiator, then the other, limbering up his wrists, stretching his neck with his hands on his hips, and cracking his knuckles.

Liu Shunming was briefing him on what was expected.

"This is the real thing. The audience wants to see the techniques you've mastered since moving into this glorious new stage of development. Make sure nothing goes wrong."

"Don't sweat it, everything's fine."

"I think everything should go smoothly. After our reorganization and research, if Big Dream doesn't emerge as the world's greatest boxing routine, I don't know what to say."

Yuanbao ran a few steps, did some jumps, performing beautiful scissor movements in the air. He landed

on the floor, executed a perfect somersault, and rose to a standing position with his arms outstretched.

"I still have the touch, wouldn't you say?"

"Not bad, very smooth. Except . . ." Liu Shunming walked up
to get a better look at Yuanbao's gymnastic outfit. "I think you'd
look better in baggy pants tied at the ankles, stripped to the waist.
You'd look more uniquely Chinese that way, more spirited."

"If I went out stripped to the waist now," Yuanbao said
with a coquettish laugh, "I might raise a few eyebrows."

"Oh, right," Liu said, throwing his head back and laughing
loudly. "I completely forgot. Okay, this'll do. It's more international."

The emcee, the good-looking youngster who had somehow
managed to cheat death, walked backstage and said to Liu
Shunming, "It's time. Can we start now?"

"Yes, let's get started," Liu said as he turned and strode out
onto the stage.

"You and me, we're not finished, you little prick," the emcee
said softly to Yuanbao as he was walking away.

"Don't be so provincial-minded," Yuanbao replied with a
laugh. "For you it was a one-time thing, but I'm in it for life."

As the curtain slowly parted, the hypnotic strains of music
spread from the stage into every inch of the hall. In their seats
at the foot of the stage, the stockholders and residents of Tanzi
Lane, including Yuanbao's mother and sister, stared wide-eyed
at the stage. Overhead fans turned slowly, their long blades
slicing the air like knives.

"My home is on the Sungari River, where the mountains
and plains are covered with soybeans and sorghum . . ."

Sun Guoren entered from the wing, singing with measured deliberation, then gazed out at the audience with a look of tortured desperation. "September eighteenth, September eighteenth," he sang, stretching his arms out in front of him, "times of misery . . ."

Sobbing so pitifully he couldn't go on, he raised his tear-streaked face and intoned, "Fellow countrymen, who among you has no father and mother? Who has no wife and children? Who is willing to subject himself to humiliation by the enemy? Listen to the tragic song of a woman."

"Wind, don't whistle so. Clouds, don't hide from me." Liu Shunming, hair in disarray, shirt shredded, walked onto the stage. "The waters of the Yellow River . . . my darling, such a tragic death . . ."

Liu swooned into the arms of Sun Guoren as the stage lights dimmed, turning the two figures into a statue of sorrow. The music swelled and worked its mournful magic on the people's hearts and souls.

"And yet," the emcee said softly, "the Chinese people will not be intimidated. At this moment, when Heaven does not answer and Earth turns its back, the light of dawn is reflected on the blue waters of the Mediterranean. The restless movements of an infant in its mother's womb, the first clap of spring thunder over the dry earth . . . listen, listen . . ."

The emcee cupped his hand over his ear to listen.

"I prefer their empty talk to their singing," Yuanbao's mother said to Yuanfeng.

"The wind howls, horses whinny, the Yellow River roars. Ripe sorghum covers the east and west banks of the river, farmers are harvesting their crops north and south of the river, mountains and plains are swarming with heroes of the anti-Japanese resistance . . ."

The stage lights turned bright, and as Sun and Liu sang their manly chorus, Yuanbao mounted the stage as if on a galloping horse.

The applause was deafening. Smiles appeared on the tear-streaked faces of Sun and Liu, who walked to the front of the stage, holding hands like a pair of magicians, and bowed deeply to the audience. Then they stepped to the side, each holding a microphone.

"What are you going to do for the audience today?" Sun asked Liu.

"I'm going to perform 'Big Dream Boxing.' "

"I've heard of that." Sun winked at the audience, then turned back to Liu. "I hear the Boxer warriors used it when they incinerated the foreigners' houses. Do you really know how to do it?"

"Yes, I do. Truth is, Big Dream Boxing was something I dreamed up. So if I can't do it, who can?"

"You're going to box for us?" Sun cupped Liu's chin in his hand and turned his face toward the audience. "Why this skinny face isn't as wide as my foot. I think you're going to be the boxee, not the boxer."

The two men rolled up their sleeves and flexed their muscles. "Shall we?"

"Yes, let's."

Liu began punching the air and dancing around the stage.

"You call that Big Dream Boxing?" Sun said. "Looks more like Big Dream Sleepwalking to me."

Liu Shunming dropped his hands, thrust out his chin, and

laughed a sinister laugh. "That wasn't Big Dream Boxing. Watch *him* if you want to see the real thing." He jumped back and swept his hand in the direction of Yuanbao, who was galloping around the stage.

They waited until the applause died down. The only sound in the hall was a shouted comment from someone in the audience: "Who the hell needs you two up there?" They smiled, they bowed, and they moved to the back of the stage.

"And now, ladies and gentlemen, what you've been waiting for: Big Dream Boxing, performed by Tang Yuanbao."

Yuanbao ran to the front of the stage and, in a loud, crisp voice, said, "I'm a maiden of twenty-seven this year, twenty-seven!"

He ran back to the center of the stage, stretched his arms out to the side, and stood without moving. His bosom was heaving, his lips were closed tight, his eyes narrowed to slits, as he steadied his breathing.

"Is that my brother?" a startled Yuanfeng asked her mother. "All the time I was watching him shimmy around up there, I thought it was some opera diva."

"Those bastards have pulled a fast one on my son," Yuanbao's mother said unhappily. "I could have told you nothing good would come from falling into their clutches."

As the music swelled, Yuanbao ran a few steps, turned an aerial cartwheel and, while in the air, executed a split to form the character 大 [big], with one arm thrust out in front, the other raised high over his head. When he landed, he executed several forward flips and a perfect somersault, coming up with his feet crossed. A crouch called a "reclining fish" led to a handstand and a "black dragon circling a pillar" move that began with a backward flip and ended with a full body twist.

Then came a "Thomas scissor" spin, a second handstand and a "bouncing carp" handspring, a "crag over the sea" horizontal handstand, a series of dizzying pirouettes, a forward handspring, several sideways walkovers—hands never touching the floor—a backward kick to the head, known as the "purple and gold crown kick," and thirty-two face-out pirouettes. . . .

"Big Dream Boxing is one of the true pearls in China's popular treasure box," the emcee announced while Yuanbao flew around the stage. "Its characteristics are strength and vitality and countless permutations. Most remarkable of all is that it requires an absolute minimum of energy, can be adapted to virtually any circumstance, and makes use of the opponent's own movements. What that means is, the boxer waits until his adversary exerts himself, then, by employing the slightest force, turns that exertion back onto his opponent. If the adversary strikes with two hundred pounds of force, he's hit with a two-hundred-pound rice sack. If he strikes out with a thousand pounds of force, a thousand-pound iron lion crashes into his head. The greater his resistance, the more abject his failure. In physics this is called the 'transformation effect.' In more common language it is 'carrying a rock and smashing your own foot.' The winds may blow and waves may crash on the shore, but I hold my ground. You may not think the Chinese are clever, but even Hitler himself never came up with such a stroke of evil."

Yuanbao stood on one leg and flapped his arms—the "golden chicken"—then pointed with an exaggerated motion and sat down in the lotus position, like a rooted tree. With his legs curled inward, he bounced forward and rolled over then blocked the gate and squeezed the chicken's eggs then jammed the stick in the back door then a Minister Su Qin holding the sword behind his back and thrusting forward then an old man pushing a wheelbarrow and then he plucked a feather out of the air then switched to a female impersonator playing the flute then he rode a bike with no hands then he licked the plate then he pushed the candle into the candlestick upside down then he twirled the stick then he pushed and pulled with all his might a good four hundred strokes . . .

"The Big Dream Boxing techniques you are witnessing have been refined by experts," the emcee continued. "They incorporate elements of ballet, gymnastics, acrobatics, bedroom activity, and modern dance. It has made the boxing style of meditating monks more complex and more attractive, more performative and more entertaining. Strong yet supple, rigid yet soft; if it's tired it won't stand up, if it stands up it won't be firm, if it's firm it won't be erect, if it's erect it won't last long, if it lasts long, it won't spurt—all without giving up its original power."

The emcee spun around to face the curtain. "A basin of water, please. Let's give our audience a real eye-opener."

Liu Shunming brought out a basin of water, from which the emcee washed his hands and face. Dripping wet, he turned to the audience.

"It's real water. If you don't believe me, this first basinful is for you."

"We believe you, we believe you," people in the front row said. "Tell us what you're going to do."

"I'm going to dump this basin of water on Tang Yuanbao!" the emcee announced, holding it with one hand and pointing to himself with the other. "If a single drop touches his body, I'm a dickhead."

Holding the basin in both hands, he said, "Watch carefully, now."

Tang Yuanbao raised up on his tiptoes, stretched out his arms, and began opening and closing his hands, a gesture of incredible beauty, as if he'd turned himself into a swan.

The emcee whipped the water into the air, every drop of it. Yuanbao stood there sadly, blinking his eyes nervously, his drenched hair plastered to his scalp, water dripping from him as if he were Donald Duck.

The audience howled with laughter.

"What the hell happened?" Sun Guoren demanded as he ran out from backstage. "Just what the hell happened?"

Sun and Liu had a frantic consultation, while the emcee announced to the audience, "Our star screwed up. Let's try it again."

Liu virtually flew backstage to fetch another basin of water, which he handed to the emcee.

"Jump! Start jumping!" Sun pressed Yuanbao.

Yuanbao's eyelids drooped as he rose up onto his toes again and took a few mincing steps. He stopped as the second basinful of water flew through the air and landed on him like a little waterfall.

"Another basinful!" Sun erupted.

One after another, basins of water rained down on Yuanbao, until he was soaked to the skin, shivering from the cold.

"Hey, there, dickhead, are you watering flowers or taking a bath?" a member of the audience up front yelled as he lifted his pants legs. "It's getting muddy down here."

"It's no good today," Yuanbao said as he hugged himself, his teeth chattering. "You could drown me before I'd ward off a single drop of water."

"I'll get you for this!" Sun Guoren said through clenched teeth. Turning to the audience, he smiled. "I'm so sorry. Because of the heat, our stars body just soaks up the water. Next time, some other day, I'll invite you all back to watch a non-soaking performance."

"I'm sorry, very, very sorry," Liu Shunming added, bowing deeply to the audience. "I'm sure you're all annoyed, so my pal and I will treat you to a bit of comic cross talk, starting out by barking like a dog: Arf! Arf arf!"

"Not so fast!" came a sharp command from the rear.

Everyone in the hall turned to see where it came from.

What they saw was Yuanbao's mother as she stood up, quickly followed by everyone from Tanzi Lane—male, female, young, old—all with dark scowls on their faces.

Yuanbao's mother led the delegation to storm the stage, onto which she leapt like an onion plucked from a dry field. Yuanfeng, Blackie, Auntie Li, Second Sister Wang, and all the others followed her, a whole bunch of onions freed from the parched earth.

In a flash, Sun Guoren, Liu Shunming, and the emcee were surrounded.

"What do you people think you're doing?" Sun demanded, trying to appear calm. "If you've got something to say, out with it. You don't all have to be here, a representative is all you need. . . ."

"Shut up!" The old lady grabbed Sun's wrist. "Tell me what you've done to my son. He's not a man, and he's not a woman. Those movements are nothing like the boxing handed down by our ancestors. They look like something handed down by the ancestors of the harlot Sai Jinhua. You've got him bumping and grinding like some whore!"

"Ma!" Yuanfeng, obviously flustered, forced her way through the crowd. "They've neutered my brother!"

"They've what?" The old lady's eyes were bulging. She grabbed Yuanfeng. "Say that again."

"Ma!" Yuanfeng fell to her knees and sobbed, "I wouldn't lie to you. They've neutered my brother." ·

"Take it easy, old lady; don't get carried away. I can explain." Sun Guoren kept backing away, using his hands to keep some distance between him and Yuanbao's mother. "Struggle demands sacrifice. Our dear Chairman Mao lost six family members to the revolution . . ."

"You've neutered one of mine!" the old lady spat out the words. "Now I'm going to make geldings out of every last one of you!"

"Help!"

Sun turned on his heel and took off, almost, but not quite fast enough to avoid being tripped by the old lady. He flew through the air.

"Enough of that!" Liu Shunming bellowed from the midst of the crowd, waving his hands and spreading his shoulders. "You're legally liable for anything that happens!"

"Fuck your old mother!" Blackie cursed as he reached out and thumped Liu on the top of his head—hard. He hit the floor like a felled tree.

The emcee was caught in the grasp of several old women, who pinched and pulled and gouged and screeched, "We're going to ruin you, make it so you talk like a human without actually being one."

"I said I'm a dickhead, isn't that enough?" the emcee implored them. "I was their dupe; I'm young; they turned me into a weapon."

A detachment of policemen burst through the curtain and was immediately caught up in a wrestling match with the local residents.

The stockholders and other members of the audience ran off like frightened rats.

Tables and chairs sailed through the air behind flying fists and feet.

Backstage, Yuanbao sat in his dressing room, oblivious to the fracas that had erupted on the stage. He tested the springiness of a bamboo pole laid out across two stools; then, with a yawn and a lazy stretch, he lay down on the pole, curled up, and went to sleep.

He seemed at peace with the world, his breathing deep and even.

Bruised and battered, their uniforms torn, the quarreling policemen limped down the street, cursing each other along the way. The trio of Sun Guoren, Liu Shunming, and the emcee were part of this gloomy procession. The men behind them were stepping on the backs of their shoes; from time to time, they reached up to wipe blood from their noses or mouths, or whatever was seeping from a variety of open wounds.

The residents of Tanzi Lane were herding them from the rear and both sides. clubs at the ready, like Communist soldiers escorting Nationalist prisoners, or peasants driving camels into the city, or a mob herding captured government officials and aristocrats.

"They're making a movie," said some bystanders who quickly formed a protective wall to ensure the procession's passage. Many of the gawkers craned their necks to spot the hidden camera.

"What movie is it?" a curious bystander shouted out to the Tanzi Lane residents.

24

No response from the guards, who pressed ahead with their prisoners.

So the impromptu audience opted for conjecture:

"It has to be a guerrilla movie. Just look at that line of puppet soldiers, then look at their guards; not an Eighth Route soldier among them."

"The Eighth Route army was off fighting the Japs, so they left the puppet soldiers for the militia to take care of."

"More of the same old anti-Japanese stuff. How about making a movie about the Four Modernizations?"

"Fuck you fuck you fuck you and all your writer friends!" The outburst came from someone who jumped out of the crowd, a guy who was pissed off at something or someone. "Maybe it's time for another fucking Cultural Revolution!"

A towering palace, sort of Greek and sort of Russian and sort of classical Chinese, appeared up ahead. Two sentries, sort of like upright writing brushes and sort of like wax statues and sort of like metal lions, stood alongside a gate fronting something that was sort of a prison and sort of a museum and sort of a mausoleum, holding rifles that sort of resembled bronze lances and sort of resembled staffs and sort of resembled fireplace pokers.

Yuanbao's mother led the column that looked sort of like candied-haws on sticks and sort of like lamb kebobs up steps that sort of resembled a scaling ladder and sort of resembled a washboard and sort of resembled a mountain slope.

A man in attire that was sort of like a Mao jacket and sort of like a business suit and sort of like a military uniform, who looked like a cross between a eunuch and a yamen runner and a door god, blocked their way.

"What do you think you're doing?"

"Bringing these people to you."

"What people?" The man took a good look at the lineup. "You've come to the wrong place. The recycling center is next door."

"They're your people. A protected species, no buying and selling, absolutely no catching and killing. So the recycling center won't have a thing to do with them."

"Our people? You must be mistaken. I'd know my own people, wouldn't I?"

"I'm not surprised. At first glance, one sheep looks like all the others."

"But all sheep in a flock have the same markings. Have you checked their rumps?"

"Yes, they all have red brands there."

"That's strange. Let me see what they smell like." The door god went up to the string of grasshoppers and sniffed each one of them. "The odor's all wrong," he said, scrunching up his nose. "Everyone in this nest of ours smells like pipe-tobacco tar. But this group smells like raw mutton, how come?"

"You've been hoodwinked."

This friendly comment came from a fat old man who looked sort of like a general and sort of like a sculpture and sort of like Santa Claus as he sat behind a huge desk that was sort of like a Ping-Pong table and sort of like a slat bed and sort of like a chopping board in a vast office that was a cross between a blockhouse a restaurant and a workout room.

"You blind, gullible people, why don't you learn how to use your heads? You were easy pickings for those swindlers. All they had to do was take advantage of your trusting nature and sense of loyalty and of our prestige and reputation. Whereas if you'd been more observant and compared things a little more closely, you'd have seen right off how different they are from us. You shouldn't have deduced that just because they're as fat and well dressed as we are and sport the same slick pompadours and are always hemming and hawing the way we do, that they're just like us. The true is never false, the false never true. The more false someone is, the more he assumes an air of truth; the crazier he is, the more insistently he proclaims his sanity; and the greater he is, the louder he shouts 'Long Live the People.' "

The fat man stood up and, with a considerable expenditure of energy, walked around to the front of the desk; to make room for his bulk, the others in the room flattened up against the nearest wall. He walked up to Sun Guoren and looked him up and down impassively, causing the penitent to lower his head in shame.

"Hmph!" A disdainful snort emerged from the fat man's bulbous nose. "You bunch of woodworms have gnawed at our reputation and destroyed our kinship with the masses." He returned to the desk, where he picked up an oversized pipe and began stuffing the bowl with tobacco.

"You understand, comrades," he continued, with a dignity suited to his position, "that we're completely divorced from everything these people have done. They neither belong to this organization, nor were they our emissaries. They're fakes, to be blunt, and you were absolutely correct in exposing them and bringing an end to their activities, for which you can be justifiably proud."

"We want to see them punished," Yuanbao's mother said.

As he tamped the tobacco down with one hand, the fat man paced the room ponderously, his brow creased in a frown. "Should I be forgiving," he mused, "or shouldn't I?"

Muttering to himself indecisively, at last he made up his mind: "Yes!"

"Why?" the uncomprehending and clearly dissatisfied Tanzi Lane residents asked. "We mount suppression campaigns against bandits, tyrants, Nationalists, and secret agents, for crying out loud."

"So we can close up ranks and march forward in unity," the fat man replied gravely as he removed a match from an over-sized matchbox, struck it, and lit his pipe with the elan of an arsonist. Clouds of smoke emerged from the bowl of the pipe. "A man's head isn't the same as a leek. Once you lop it off, it'll never grow back. If the day comes when his crimes are redressed, it'll be too late for him to benefit from it. Regardless of how serious the nature of the crimes, we must strictly adhere to the policy of killing none and arresting few. Better to keep them around as negative examples. Then when the need arises, we can troop them out. If the country finds itself in trouble, the last thing we want is to be stuck for scapegoats. It's easy for someone to look upon death as going home, but hard to resist being reformed, not to mention painful. I say we go ahead and reform them, let them return to the womb and reemerge as new people. That's the best way I know to annihilate an opponent. Doesn't everyone go around saying death before dishonor? I say, dishonor over death. Forcing them to remain on their feet will be harder on them than allowing them to die. We just let them be the slow instruments of their own demise."

"I appreciate everything you're saying," Yuanbao's mother said, "but we common folk love a good execution. We demand satisfaction. Let them be the chickens you kill to scare us monkeys."

"Executing them is out of the question. That lets you vent

your spleen, but makes me the executioner. How's this? If you remain adamant, why don't we unfurl the flags, break out the drums, and select one as the long-necked chicken. We pile all the unsettled accounts, new and old, on his head, weigh him down with the burden of heinous crimes, so we can go into battle with a light pack."

"Me! Take it out on me!"

Sun Guoren, Liu Shunming, the emcee, and the police all shouted at once.

"I was in charge of MobCom, so the long-necked chicken has to be me."

"I was the enforcer, the one who concocted every dirty trick. Fairness demands that you turn your wrath on me."

"It's my face that was out in front, so it's the one you have to blacken."

"Come on, give us the spanking we deserve," the whole gang said as they threw their arms around each other and huddled together. "We'll be world-famous."

"Stop that!" Blackie scolded them. "Fucking disgraceful is what you are."

"Never mind them," the fat man said with assurance. "I've already made my choice." His contemptuous gaze swept past Sun, Liu, and the others. "The best way to deal with this bunch of pricks is to mortify them."

"Aiyo, Great Upright Arbiter, we residents of Tanzi Lane join in expressing our undying gratitude to you for rescuing us from the sea of bitterness the pit of fire the depths of Hell."

At the entrance to Tanzi Lane, Yuanbao's mother led the neighbors in kneeling in the dust before the fat man, who rode up on his horse. The fat man grinned broadly as he dismounted, helped the old lady to her feet, and announced to one and all:

"Get up, please get up. We can't have any of this. I am your brother, your servant. It is my duty to support you, for which no thanks are necessary."

Yuanbao's mother read a proclamation, a tearful incantation: "Revered and wise and beloved pioneer vanguard architect beacon torch demon-revealing mirror dog-beating club father mother grandfather grandmother ancestor primal ape imperial father ancient sage Jade Emperor Guanyin Bodhisattva commander-in-chief, you have been busy with a myriad of daily matters suffering untold hardships old habits die hard overworked to the point of illness addicted to labor shouldering crushing burdens mounting the clouds and riding the mist soaring across the sky helping those in danger and relieving those in distress restoring justice banishing evil and expelling heresies curing rheumatism and cold sweats invigorating the *yang* nourishing the kidneys and the brain building up the liver harmonizing the stomach easing pain suppressing coughs and relieving constipation, and you personally privately precedingly arrived appeared appeased our anxieties to inspect inquire interrogate make an investigation make the rounds make a case make known make inquiries ask about find out about solicit about our lane, which shows tremendous concern tremendous encouragement tremendous motivation tremendous consolation tremendous trust tremendous consideration tremendous glory tremendous favor. We little people decent people common people lowly people sons and grandsons and grass seed and canine whelps and callow felines herd animals ignorant citizens broad masses hundred names are incredibly blessed incredibly excited incredibly restless incredibly remorseful incredibly happy incredibly ecstatic incredibly flattered incredibly thankful incredibly tearful incredibly emotional incredibly at a loss for words, a thousand statements and ten thousand comments a thousand songs and ten thousand tunes a thousand mountains and ten thousands oceans a thousand moans and ten thousand groans a thousand mumbles and ten thousand murmurs a thousand terms and ten thousand words form a single utterance that resounds through the skies hoarse and exhausted a sound to rock the world lingering long in the air shattering the eardrums shaking heaven and earth music to the ears incomparably beautiful enchanting intoxicating inebriating making people forget the taste of meat for three days for it is the song of the ages: long life long life long long life long life long life long long life!"

Yuanbao's mother, hopelessly breathless, fainted dead away. So Mrs. Li rose to pick up where she had left off:

"Without you we'd still be in the dark in the dimness in the dusk in the dust in the ashes in the cinders in the dirt in the pits in the muck in the caves in the abyss in the soup in the barbecue pit boiling in oil drowning in brackish water splashing twisting tumbling plummeting stumbling . . ."

Mrs. Li, hopelessly breathless, fainted dead away. So Yuanfeng rose to pick up where she had left off:

"You are the light the hope the future the ideal the banner the bugle the drum victory success pride self-esteem triumphant return Heaven Buddha's realm the wise sorcerer genius magician guardian angel Redeemer the sun the moon the stars radiance brilliance luster brightness splendor . . ."

Yuanfeng fainted dead away. So Blackie picked up where she'd left off:

"Powerful deity hawk falcon lions tigers brass head gold face steel legs iron wrists thunderbolt fist cannon missile pillar tombstone Great Wall mountain pass. Without you we would have frozen to death starved to death been beaten to death cursed to death bickered to death hounded to death burned to death drowned hung flung to our death bullied to death . . ."

"That's enough," the fat man said with a genial smile. "Stop there or you'll faint, too. I've heard enough fine words and flattery and compliments and adulation and praise to last a lifetime. But if every resident of the lane talked till he was blue in the face, it wouldn't affect me. Please don't belittle yourselves. If you truly want to make me happy, then look after each other. If you can do that, you'll have brought me great comfort."

"You can't refuse to look after us," Blackie said tearfully. "Without you we're nothing. You are the blue sky, we are green grass. Without the sky there can be no grass. And grass needs someone to water it and mow it and trim it, and that's not something we can do. Besides, we're used to having people take care of us. If you make us our own masters, with nobody to huff and puff and shout and kick or beat or drive us, we won't be able to eat or drink or sleep or shit—we'll be outright incontinent."

"You have to take care of us, you just have to." The Tanzi Lane residents fell to their knees and said as one, "You can ride us beat us yell at us whip us, we don't care. If it makes you happy, order us around drive us ahead step all over us. And if we make you unhappy, punish us humiliate us take your anger out on us. If anyone dares utters a single 'no,' you won't have to raise a finger, because we'll fix his wagon for you. Do anything you want to us, but don't ever mention the word 'leave.'"

"Get up." The fat man sighed. "The truth is, I could never abandon you people."

Tang Yuanbao shuffled his feet in soft-soled shoes as he whirled around the ring, flicking jabs right and left, each jab accompanied by a crisp shout. His shoulders swiveled, his waist twisted, his hips rose and fell, all in a coordinated motion called windmill limbs. As his feet grew springier, he began to levitate without interrupting his movements, as if he were soaring on the wind. As he reveled in his state of suspended animation, his jabs grew more harmonious, more methodical, a throwback to those earlier days of courage, valor, hermeticism. He was being manhandled by the fat man, like an itinerant performer with a marionette.

Someone in the crowd of Tanzi Lane residents shouted, "That kid's gone to waste!"

"You can't say it was wrong to nurture him," Mrs. Li said. "The sutra is fine, the monks have botched the reading, that's all."

The fat man flung Yuanbao to the ground; out of habit, Yuanbao continued with his boxing routine, apparently refusing to come to his senses. The look of concern on the fat man's face indicated that he felt sorry for Yuanbao. "Give him whatever he wants to eat," he said to Yuanbao's mother and sister. "Humor him. It breaks my heart to see someone so young insist on taking the wrong path."

"Is it hopeless?" Yuanbao's mother sobbed. "Isn't there something you can do?"

"We might cure the illness, but his fate is sealed. The master can open the door, but it's up to you to go in; the master can teach the basics, but only the individual can perfect them; three years of proper learning can be wasted in three days of improper deeds. I am incapable of turning each and every one of you into a perfect specimen. It's up to you. But don't be dejected, for he alienated himself from the people."

The fat man rode off on his white horse, leaving in his wake a multicolored auspicious flower and what sounded like the strains of celestial music. The residents cocked their ears to listen, but heard nothing.

Yuanbao chose this moment to bring his dance to an end. With an idiotic grin on his face, he gazed out at the people and said, "How about a bravo, eh?"

"Bravo, bravo." Aching noses all around preceded the widespread flow of tears before the "bravos" had even emerged from their mouths.

"Child," Yuanbao's mother sobbed, "no more spreading your wings to fly. It's time to settle down and live your life in peace. Tomorrow we'll fix up the pedicab, so you and your sister can go to the train station and take turns giving people rides."

"He can use mine," Blackie said as he rolled his pedicab up to them. "Elder brother Yuanbao's pedicab was sold off long ago by those people from the museum."

"Try it out, child, climb up and take it a couple of turns," Yuanbao's mother said as she dried her tears. "The thing that frightened people may be gone, but the thing that needs to eat is still around, isn't it?"

With a giggle, Yuanbao climbed onto the pedicab, stepping down awkwardly on the pedals and shifting back and forth on the seat, yet failing to move the vehicle an inch. Still, he hadn't forgotten the tricks of the trade, concerned first and foremost with pedaling style, maintaining the rhythm of a ballet dancer, the effort front and back offsetting each other—he was twirling his pedicab like a baton.

"Don't be sad, Mrs. Tang," said Mrs. Li as she watched the scene in front of her. "Instead of making things hard on him, just treat him like a child."

Like a monkey, Yuanbao frolicked on the pedicab, rubbing and touching, grabbing his ear and massaging his cheeks, and making all kinds of faces.

"The kid's an idiot," the neighbors said. "Let him do what he wants."

"The court will now pronounce judgment. The defendant will rise . . ."

Dawn had already broken outside the interrogation room, and the first rays of sunlight were filtering in, even though the lights were still on. The faces of the prosecutor and the defendant had a green cast, and wore looks of impatience.

The bald, fat man was holding the judgment in his hand; looking directly at old man Tang, who stood before him with his hands at his side, he read the verdict:

"Tang Guotao, male, one hundred eleven years old, who, prior to his arrest, lived at number thirty-five, Tanzi Lane.

"The accused has consistently held reactionary thoughts. His feelings for the Party and the people are apathetic, his speech reckless and wanton. The accused joined the Boxer troops in the year 1899, but during the fighting he cowered before the enemy, his thinking underwent a change, and he began to indulge in fantasies. Forfeiting his chance to fight with honor, he was responsible for the debacle at Beiwa. He later sired a son, but neglected the boy's education, causing the youngster to enter upon a life of violence and crime. In assuming the role of a longtime revolutionary cadre, he created baleful effects on society and inflicted damage on the prestige of the Party in the eyes of the people. His crimes of corrupting youth, disseminating rumors and superstition, humiliating women, harming intellectuals through slander, launching vicious attacks, dealing in dirty innuendo, hurling abuse and insults, to name but a few, far exceed the limits of civilized society. If this can be tolerated, what cannot? Permitting this kind of phenomenon to spread unchecked would in itself be a crime against the people! It would be a dereliction of our duty! One cannot take advantage of our tolerance and magnanimity; one must not take shelter behind our decency and kindness. We support and encourage the good, the healthy, the fragrant flowers; we oppose and show no mercy toward the evil, the ugly, the poisonous weeds. That is the only way to maintain stability and unity, the sole means of preserving freedom of speech, the wise approach to unite the broad masses of the people in working for the Four Modernizations with one heart and one mind! We must tether this evil horse with the rule of law and wake up the masses to distinguish right from wrong. This is a bad man. Forgive ... or not forgive? Not this time!

"Anyone who thinks we are soft and easy to bully is mistaken!

"Anyone who thinks he can brazenly exploit a loophole in our democratic laws is wrong! Terribly wrong, expressly wrong, and will in the end beat his own head bloody!

"The net of heaven has a large mesh, but nothing gets through it!

"People, you must be vigilant!

"The above-stated indictments are indisputable and have been acknowledged by the defendant.

"I proclaim that defendant Tang is incontestably responsible for the crushing of the glorious Boxer Rebellion.

"He was the architect of all the calamities, disasters, and misfortunes! He was the chief obstacle to all good fortune, tranquility, and progress! A stumbling block on the road to progress. He is more dangerous than typhoons earthquakes fires floods airplane crashes train wrecks automobile accidents ship sinkings capital construction back-doorism banquet-izing all rolled together! He is an enemy of the people!

"In order to preserve the dignity of law and discipline, in order to protect the interests of the people, in order to calm the gossip of society, in order to gain an immediate victory in our great reform venture, and in order to bring peace and prosperity to ten thousand generations of sons and grandsons, it is the judgment of this court that:

"Tang Guotao be sentenced to life imprisonment and the forfeiture of all political rights forever.

"This verdict is final and not subject to appeal."

As soon as the verdict was announced, the prosecutor turned to old man Tang and said, "You have one last opportunity to speak. Do you have anything to say to this court?"

"What will you do if the Communist Party ever returns to power?"

25

While yoga music played, Yuanbao made his appearance in the Sapporo Sports Arena.

A ring had been roped off in the middle of the arena. The bleachers were packed with foreigners in a variety of skin tones sitting beneath their national flags. Cheerleading squads made up of girls in a variety of skin tones were jumping and shimmying and shouting from all four sides of the arena. Bugles blared, drums set up a deafening tattoo—the competition was being beamed by satellite to all corners of the earth.

The fat man was watching on TV in his office.

Zhao Hangyu was watching on TV at home.

Bai Du was watching on TV in an airplane.

Liu Shunming and Sun Guoren were watching on TV on a train.

The prosecutor and the bald, fat man were sucking on candy as they watched on TV.

Old man Tang was watching on TV in his prison cell.

The college girls were watching on TV in their lecture hall.

The residents of Tanzi Lane were crowded into the Tang compound to watch on TV.

Pedestrians were watching on TV sets in appliance-store display windows.

The stockholders and emcee were watching on TV on the stage.

The whole country was glued to its TV sets. Tens of thousands of TV screens were showing the same image: a wrestling ring formed by glistening white ropes in the Sapporo Sports Arena, in color, in black and white, on twenty-inch sets and twenty-four-inch sets.

Tang Yuanbao, clad in a weight lifter's outfit, stood shoulder to shoulder with foreign contestants in a variety of skin tones, a variety of head shapes, and a variety of facial expressions, waving to the cheering crowd, smiling, blowing kisses. Floral bouquets rained down on them from the bleachers.

The judge, all in white, entered the arena. Everyone took their seats.

The enormous quartz digital timer clock showed a row of dark green zeros. Then the seconds began to tick off.

The opening bell sounded.

Several brawny men stepped into the ring, each holding a length of rope. They knocked the competitors to the mat, jumped on their backs, and hog-tied them.

Yuanbao was the first to be hog-tied and lifted into the air. Then the other competitors.

Yuanbao was tied into the smallest, tightest ball, using the least amount of rope; the smile on his face was the most serene, the most content.

Needless to say, he gained the highest score: 9.95.

The second event was an optional exercise, in which each contestant carried a brawny man on his neck and performed any stunt ordered by his rider.

Once again, Yuanbao stole the show. Not only was he able to carry a rider twice his weight and run like a horse, crawl like a dog, and bleat like a goat, he even pranced around on his toes and never stopped smiling, no matter how his rider jolted him or whipped him or pounded him or yanked his face, his smile serene and content yet showing a hint of excitement.

During the exercise, the other contestants had trouble keeping up with Yuanbao. When his rider relieved himself, he drank the man's piss with gusto and, to show his appreciation, gave a big thumbs-up.

Again he gained the highest score: 9.96.

Next, the brawny men entered the ring with long, shiny needles, with which they punctured all ten of the contestants' fingers, one after the other. Some of the contestants withdrew from the competition, screaming in pain. Those who didn't gritted their teeth and stared straight ahead to bear up under the torture, backs bathed in sweat, muscles twitching. Yuanbao's radiant smile was the only one in evidence; gazing tenderly at his tormentor, he seemed to be simultaneously encouraging and consoling the man, as if worried that he, and not Yuanbao, might not be able to hold out.

By the time the brawny men had inserted their needles into the contestants' chests and attached them to electric current, the men were wracked by spasms, their eyes were popping, blood oozed from their pores, their faces were hideously contorted, their hair was standing on end. Except for Yuanbao, on whose nose a few tiny beads of sweat appeared above a smile that never faltered; his closed eyes gave him a rapturous look, as if he were savoring exquisite pleasure.

For a third time, he gained the highest score: 9.97.

A red-hot steel bar was carried into the ring. As each bare-foot contestant stepped onto it, green smoke rose with a sizzle into the air, like a barbecue.

Two more contestants, finding the pain unbearable, shrieked and stumbled from the ring. But even escaping the steel bar lessened neither their shrieks nor their tearful wails.

The remaining contestants either stood motionless, utilizing their body temperature to lower the heat under their feet, or hopped around like shrimp in a fishing net to lessen the contact time of each foot.

Like a man out for a leisurely stroll, Yuanbao walked from one end of the bar to the other, his hands raised in the air, taking care to step down wherever the bar was still red, and moving from dark red to bright red as much as possible. His feet were black, but his face was red, the ruddy glow of a man in his cups.

Once again, his style and endurance gained him the highest score: 9.98

Next to be carried into the ring were gigantic water-filled fish tanks, into which each contestant jumped, sinking to the bottom before swimming around like fish, causing waves on the surface and sending air bubbles to the top, which burst and disappeared.

The seconds turned into minutes. The first competitor shot to the surface, opened his mouth like a fish and gasped for air, then crawled out of his tank, sopping wet and very gloomy.

Another competitor climbed out of his tank, smashing the

glass with his foot on his way out, spilling heavy, glistening water all over the floor. When he was shown a red card, he charged the judge with a roar, fists flying. His glum teammates restrained him, dragging him kicking and screaming out of the sports arena, a towel draped over his shoulders.

Another competitor shot to the surface . . .

And another . . .

The competitors still submerged in their tanks studied one another, holding on for dear life.

As the temperature in the tanks dropped, the water became increasingly translucent, harder and more brittle . . .

Just as the water was about to freeze, the other men broke through the surface; their red bodies turned purple and they fell unconscious. They were carried out of the arena.

That left only Yuanbao and one other competitor in the now-frozen fish tanks, like flies caught in hardening amber, totally immobilized.

The ice masses began to melt, and Yuanbao's rival sank limply to the bottom. Aides ran up to fish him out and perform CPR. Meanwhile, Yuanbao started swimming, head and tail swishing happily in the water. The scaly ice crystals on his body shimmered.

A score of 9.99—on every electronic scorecard.

Yuanbao was slapping his own face—left right left right. Fast and hard. The other competitors were also slapping themselves the best they could, but in terms of technique and force, they weren't in his league. Some could hardly make contact with their faces, no matter how big they were. They either missed altogether or their faces didn't even turn pink.

By then, Yuanbao's face was the purple color of an eggplant.

His thick skin was now as thin and transparent as a sheet of onionskin paper.

A 10!

There was electricity in the air as the spectators erupted in applause. People who had been rooting with banners and shouts and whistles for their own national heroes suddenly began cheering Yuanbao on, led by cheerleaders in all languages and every imaginable manner, shouting screaming dancing singing.

Armed with the confidence of victory, Yuanbao turned to the final, optional, event.

The other competitors took their best shot: One put a live cat down the front of his pants; one pulled a truck with his teeth; one carried a TV set in the palm of each hand; one brought out a tiger and stuck his head inside the bloodcurdling mouth, then scratched the animal with both hands.

When it was Yuanbao's turn, the crowd grew silent, the cheerleaders stopped shouting and singing and dancing and bugling and drumming, as tens of thousands of eyes were riveted on him.

He smiled and calmly, somewhat mischievously, held up a shiny, razor-sharp boning knife. Raising his head and stretching his neck taut, he slowly cut his own throat from ear to ear; blood oozed from the gash. Then, putting down his knife, he reached up with both hands, grabbed the skin between his chin and his ears, and began tugging upward.

The peeled-back skin looked like a perfect cicada slough.

Inch by inch he peeled upward, to the mouth, to the nose; at spots where the skin was attached to muscle and would not give, he picked up his knife and cut it away, then peeled some more.

You could have heard a pin drop. Even the other competitors halted the energetic parading of their own skills and stood with their mouths agape as they watched Yuanbao.

When Yuanbao reached his eyes, the judge said, "You can stop now, you're the victor. The gold medal is yours, no question about it."

Yuanbao looked out at the crowd through eyes that were still covered with skin, an unmistakable smile in evidence, then ripped upward, leaving a bloody mess behind and a perfect face dangling from his hand.

The applause was deafening; the cries of astonishment ear-splitting

Yuanbao raised the dead, expressionless face, a human mask, high in the air to show the spectators, then tossed it away and—a hideous, bloody mess all that remained above his neck—stepped to one side.

Owing to difficulties with the communications satellite, the sound transmission went dead, although the TV image on sets around the world remained. All any viewers anywhere saw was a sports arena packed with people silently shouting, jumping, going crazy, waving their arms and stamping their feet, as Yuanbao shook hands with the other competitors and judges and spoke to each of them softly. Just what the spectators were shouting and the men on the mat were saying, no one could tell.

Yuanbao stood on the top of the award platform, flanked by the silver and bronze medalists. A high-ranking gentleman, accompanied by two young Japanese women, walked up to present them with their medals. He placed the gold medal around Yuanbao's neck and handed him a trophy, then shook his hand and bowed low in a display of enormous respect.

While the gentleman was presenting the two runners-up with their medals, Yuanbao raised his trophy in the air to show his gratitude to the spectators. No sound, no expression. The lasting image was of a man with no face displaying his trophy for all to see.

The man with no face then stood motionless, holding the trophy he had won.

Then the camera trained on the slow raising of three national flags, different colors, different designs.

The highest of the flags was ours.

The camera returned to the man without a face and zoomed in on his featureless visage, as if trying to find a glimmer of light in the two black holes where his eyes had been.

Beneath the image a running text informed the viewers:

SPECIAL REPORT FROM SAPPORO: CHINA'S ENTRANT TO THE INTERNATIONAL ENDURANCE COMPETITION, TANG YUANBAO, HAS WON THE GOLD MEDAL. . . . SPECIAL REPORT FROM SAPPORO: CHINA'S ENTRANT TO THE INTERNATIONAL ENDURANCE COMPETITION, TANG YUANBAO, HAS WON THE GOLD MEDAL. . . . SPECIAL REPORT FROM SAPPORO: CHINA'S ENTRANT TO THE INTERNATIONAL ENDURANCE COMPETITION, TANG YUANBAO, HAS WON THE GOLD MEDAL. . . .

Not a single vehicle moved in the hot, dry city, not a sign of humanity. The doors of shops and offices were closed and secured with aluminum alloy locks. The sun blazed overhead; the streets and lanes were deserted. Off in the distance a dust funnel rose in the blindingly clear sky; it swirled mightily as it reached to the heavens, the top swelling outward, until it was so large it seemed to fill the sky like a mushroom cloud, blocking out the sun, thick and murky, expanding mercilessly and splitting, then turning inward to form rolling layers, like water around red-hot steel, like an exploding air bubble.

The city fell dark, as the enormous shadow of the mushroom cloud spread across high-rise buildings, streets and boulevards, parks and grassy lawns, rivers and lakes.

About the Author

Wang Shuo was born in Nanjing in 1958 and moved with his family to Beijing a year later. After his parents were sent to the countryside during Mao's Cultural Revolution, he and his brother, a pair of protected military brats, had the run of Beijing. It proved to be a good training for Wang's adolescent years, when he skipped school, was involved in petty crimes, street fights, and girl chasing, even landing in jail on at least one occasion. Forced into the navy by his father, he apparently honed his skills as a grifter, living by his wits until, in 1984, he published a story entitled "Stewardess," which launched his phenomenal career as a writer. By the late 1980s he was easily the most popular novelist among China's urban youth, and the most frequent target of official vilification. In 1991, he stopped writing books (he's back at it these days) and turned to writing for TV and the movies. Five years later, at the height of China's "spiritual civilization campaign," his four-volume collected works were pulled from the shelves and two film adaptations of his works were scrapped. It's too early to tell whether this unwelcome attention has slowed down or accelerated his quest to become "famous 'til I'm dizzy, without worrying about the consequences."

—H.G.